DRUMBEATS

can you ever escape your past?

The first novel of the Drumbeats Trilogy

Julia Ibbotson

Award-winning acclaimed author of
The Old Rectory: Escape to a Country Kitchen
(a memoir with recipes to feed the soul, from the rectory kitchen)
S.C.A.R.S, a children's medieval fantasy novel

Front cover design by www.BerniStevensdesign.com

The characters and events depicted in this book, other than those in the public domain, are fictitious.
Copyright © Julia Helene Ibbotson 2015
All rights reserved.

ISBN: 1511553316
ISBN 13: 9781511553315

PRAISE FOR DRUMBEATS

Drumbeats gained Honourable Mention at the Hollywood Book Festival, USA 2014 and New England and London Book Festivals 2014 and was shortlisted for the Readers' Awards at the Festival of Romance Fiction 2014

Media praise for Drumbeats:

"Drumbeats is about confronting challenges and looking beyond what we know" *Janice Ross*

"A truly heart-warming story and one that will stay in my mind" *Hannah Wood*

"Wonderful quality of writing ... a brilliantly crafted book ... sights, sounds and even smells of the Ghanaian way of life are conjured up vividly ... a brilliant read" *Jo Lambert*

"A thought-provoking story" *Kindle review*

"I loved how swoon-worthy Jim was, but also mysterious and possibly dangerous. I'm totally invested in (Jess's) life now!" *Chicklitchickadees*

"One could often feel the searing heat of the country burning right off the pages ...a writing style that for me flowed seamlessly and drew the reader into a fascinating story ...really looking forward to the sequel!" *JB Johnston*

You may also like to look at The Old Rectory: Escape to a Country Kitchen (a memoir)

The Old Rectory won the Biography category in the London Book Festival 2013 and Honourable Mention in three other international Book Festivals 2013

Media praise for The Old Rectory:

"**Destined to become a classic ... I adored this book and think you will too ...**" *Rebecca Johnson, book reviewer, USA*

"**The book is a wonderful blend of personal story (one so many of us can identify with), enchantingly told, with recipes ... It all spreads happiness. Lovely!**" *Bel Mooney, UK, author and journalist, Daily Mail*

"**What a jewel this book is ... truly a delight ... a great writer ... a delightful read, all the way to the end ... loved it!**" *Peggy Fellouris, Massachusetts, USA, author of Dancing in the Rain*

"**A most talented writer...a charming story written by a writer with a wonderful voice**" *Nancy Mills, California, USA, travel writer and founder of thespiritedwoman.com*

"**A beautiful tale ... delightful**" *Vicky DeCoster, Nebraska, USA, author of From Diapers to Dorkville*

"**An inspirational tale that offers many surprises ...**" *Carol Hoenig, USA*

"**A delight for those who love to cook and those who love to read about old English villages ... 5 out of 5!**" *DizzyC's Little Book Blog review*

"A fascinating and absorbing book ..." *Today I'm Reading review*

"Julia's writing style is so warm and engaging ... I could hardly peel myself away from the pages ... I'm a huge fan of Julia's writing!" *Cosmochicklitan review*

"It is a fascinating and absorbing book ..." *Today I'm Reading*

"It will warm your heart ... Lovely book. To be cherished ... 5 stars!" *Bemiown Book Reviews*

"A very charming book..." *True Book Addict*

And for the children, loved by adults too!

S.C.A.R.S (a children's medieval fantasy story)

S.C.A.R.S gained Honourable Mention at the London and New England Book Festivals 2014

Media praise for S.C.A.R.S:

"This is a tale of friendship and strength when the world about you is full of evil." *Hannah Ward*

"If you are feeling a little lost and in need of a fantastical escape, this is the book for you, regardless of your age!" *Bestchicklit.com*

"... captures the imagination and awakens a sense of adventure in the reader." *Bestchicklit.com*

"I like Julia's writing style; it is so easy to read and just flows so well you just get caught up in this wonderful fantasy story." *AJ Book Review Club*

"Julia's descriptions just instantly transport you into this world and you can see it all in your mind. You are there with them all." *AJ Book Review Club*

"A magical story that had me turning page after page, dying to know what happens next ..." *Cometbabesbooks*

"This book has everything: adventure, magic, heart-stopping moments – a lovely story, beautifully woven." *Jo Lambert*

"I really hope that S.C.A.R.S is going to be the first book in a series as I'd love to see our hero and his friends on more exciting adventures. Highly recommended! Just brilliant!" *JB Johnston Brook Cottage Books*

"This tale is destined to become a classic and to be read and re-read many, many times until it bears its well-thumbed pages like the scars left by the monsters in Unor." *Sterna Kruger*

"A must read ... a journey of emotions, laughs and magic that will not easily be forgotten, tickling that spot of belief in magic, tucked into a corner somewhere, that all children harbour, it is true, there is still magic in the world." *Sterna Kruger*

CONTENTS

Acknowledgements		ix
The Year Before: England 1964		xi
Chapter 1:	August 1965, Ghana	1
Chapter 2:	September 1965	37
Chapter 3:	October 1965	68
Chapter 4:	November 1965	112
Chapter 5:	December 1965	158
Chapter 6:	January 1966	202
Chapter 7:	February 1966	224
Chapter 8:	March 1966	241
Chapter 9:	April 1966	258
Chapter 10:	May 1966, England	285
Author's note		299
About the author		305

ACKNOWLEDGEMENTS

With grateful thanks to all those who made this book possible:

For my dear husband, Clive, for all the cups of sustaining coffee, dinners and household tasks while I slave over a hot keyboard – thank you, and all my love x

For my lovely family who provide quiet (sometimes!) support in the background and keep me grounded: Tam, Mel, Neil, Sally, Charlie, Zoe, Grace and Jacob, not forgetting Maria, Rob and David. Thank you for being there x

For my editor, publisher, consultant, beta readers, and all my lovely friends in the Romantic Novelists' Association who are so supportive and generous: you have all made my journey so much easier, more informed, and certainly more entertaining!

For Berni Stevens (www.BerniStevensdesign.com) who created such a beautiful cover image that portrayed exactly the feeling I was looking for - stunning!

For JB Johnston (www.brookcottage books.blogspot.com) for her unstinting and efficient organisation of book tours and advertising.

For Gary Walker (www.look4books.com) for his advertising, ingenious posters and social media expertise.

For the many reviewers, bloggers, facebookers and tweeters who have said so many lovely words about my writing. It means a lot!

And finally to the ever-endearing, wonderful country of Ghana, her people, and all those who made my work there such an amazing experience that will always be in my heart and that gave this novel its inspiration … and especially to "Jim".

THE YEAR BEFORE
ENGLAND 1964

Sundays were for being still. It was the Quaker way. But not for Jess, not today. She squirmed self-consciously in the armchair, tugging her mini skirt down over her slim thighs under her mother's disapproving scrutiny.

"But I really want to do this, Mother," she said. She frowned and bit her lip nervously as her mother shook her head with exasperation. "And it's just about having a year off before I go to university."

"I *have* thought carefully about this ... this "plan" of yours, Jessamy, and I sat in Meeting for Worship this morning seeking the Lord's guidance." Her mother settled her lips firmly in the severe way of Quaker ladies in their tight circle of family friends. *Honestly! Was she really so very frivolous and silly in their eyes? So very different from her older brother David?* "But I have to say that I am most unhappy about it all. Why on earth do you want to go to the other side of the world from us? You're only seventeen. David never wanted to do anything like this. I cannot understand it."

"But Mother," Jess began, trying hard to keep her voice calm, "West Africa isn't the other side of the world. And I'm talking about next year, after A' levels." *Why did she have to keep defending herself? It was the 1960s after all. Wasn't it supposed to be a time of freedom and discovery? Everyone else did it. And she just had to get away, from her mother and her suffocating home. And from her father.*

"I do not know what your father makes of it all. He is keeping his own counsel …"

"Well, I don't expect he thinks anything. He'll just agree with you." Jess thought of her father's detached wordlessness and silent knowing looks. But she heard her mother's sharp intake of breath.

"Your father is a saint, Jessamy." *No, he's not actually.* "And how do you think you will cope? Being so far away from your family, from Friends, from Meeting. How will you be guided without us there to direct you? Taking it into your head to go gallivanting around the world like some flower girl from San Francisco!"

"Flower child," Jess corrected, catching her mother's sharp stare. "But Mother, lots of young people do it now." Her mother frowned.

"We are not like 'lots of people', Jessamy. We are different, and proud of it. *We* have principles to live by." One of her mother's items from her Rulebook: it's "common" to be like other people.

"I'd be helping poor under-privileged people in Africa …" *Actually she had no idea what the gap year entailed. But the very name "Africa" conjured up images of a different world from her own: mud huts, palm trees, heat, dust: exotic, exciting, dangerous … She'd read The Flame Trees of Thika and fallen in love with the whole idea.* She added reassuringly, "It's all properly organised and funded between the church and the government. It's sort of a government project. A challenge."

"Your challenge, Jessamy, is to be grounded in the faith and practice of the church. You need to meet a nice boy from a good religious family." She sighed. "And be settled and safe."

"Oh, *honestly*, Mother! *Please*, before all that, I want to travel, get my degree, and get established in my career. What else was all this expensive education for?"

"You have a full scholarship and bursary for your Quaker boarding school. We could not possibly have afforded it ourselves, as you well know, Jessamy."

"I know, but it doesn't matter who pays the fees, it's still expensive. You don't just leave and marry some convenient Quaker boy who happens to be around."

"You could do worse than Maurie, for one. He is solid, reliable, *and temperate*. Like your father. What else could you want? Believe me ..." *Here we go, she's going to say, I am your mother, I know best.* "... I am your mother and I know best what is good for you. I know what you need in a life partner."

"But I'm *me*, Mother. I'm not like you."

Her mind fluttered away to last summer. *She remembered the oh-so-embarrassing way Maurie had unexpectedly appeared on the platform at Euston station as she returned from France, over-eager to take her suitcase and grab her arm – oh my god, in front of everyone as well – saying in that loud pompous voice of his that he had come down to London to accompany ('accompany', for god's sake?) her back to New*

Street station, and see her home safely. Good grief! He was so middle-aged. He must be all of twenty five!

As if she hadn't been travelling around Doubs, Pontarlier, Besancon, for a few weeks of the school holiday, on her own, or at least with her penfriend, Genevieve, and her glamorous friend Sylvie, and ... hmm ... unbeknownst to her mother, Gerard. The proverbial tall, dark, and extremely good-looking chap in that sensitive Gallic style: sophisticated, knowledgeable ... and dangerous!

But she remembered how Maurie ignored all her protestations tightened his grip on her arm and thrust her into the dining coach. *And oh, the terrible way she had to face him across the table of the dining car on the Birmingham train. He insisted on buying dinner, pompously ordering the wine as if he were a connoisseur of good- living, a bon-viveur. He was portly enough, certainly, red-faced and greasy-haired enough to look the part of a sozzled scoffer. Not exactly "temperate".* Clearly, her mother was unaware of that bit, another item from her Rulebook being "no drinking".

Her mind returned to the claustrophobia of that carriage; *she, trapped, the dark night outside the dusty window, wet shiny walls and platforms of deserted stations skimming by, harsh lights within, making Maurie's face look even more ruddy and sweaty. Him, pushing at his hair which was falling in damp greasy clumps over his glasses, twitching his thick lips and dark obscene moustache.* Jess shuddered.

"You always were recalcitrant," her mother said, her frown deepening over her spectacles. "However, if you are determined ... I suppose we have little choice but to allow you to go. I only hope you can cope."

"Oh. Right. Good." Jess took a deep breath. "Well of course, there's my upper sixth year and A' levels first. I just have to plan my deferred entry date for university applications this autumn. If I'm having a year out it'll be for October '66, not '65. I don't want to be doing UCAS forms while I'm away."

"Hmmm ... And can you do that, Jessamy?"

"Yes, absolutely! I just apply this year, saying that I'm doing a voluntary service year, and have interviews this academic year for a place in '66. Then I'll know which university I've got lined up after Africa."

"I see. You certainly seem to have it all worked out. Most carefully."

"Look, it won't cost you anything, you know, if that's what you're worried about. The letter says that all the travel is paid for, and you get a small living allowance while you're working there. I expect I'd be teaching in a village or helping to build schools in the jungle or nursing, actually."

"Yes, yes. Well, I just hope you get home unscathed ... show me that letter then, Jessamy."

# 1

AUGUST 1965, GHANA

It was hotter than Jess had ever imagined in her eighteen years. Flying in from the UK bound for Accra, she had left the late August skies of the dull wet dreariness of an English summer. But as she stepped off the Ghana Airways VC10, she felt the heavy all-encompassing heat which shocked her system. Although it was only six o'clock in the evening, it was already dark and close.

The flight from London Heathrow had been a long and tiresome six hours and she had felt drained as she pulled down her cabin bag from the overhead and shuffled along the aisle behind the other travellers, nodding and swaying to the strains of the Beatles' "Ticket to Ride" on the VC10's tannoy system. Her mother would have a fit: her Rulebook said no pop music; it's the work of the devil, and no dancing: *Jessamy, anyone would think you were a slut.* So in the holidays, when she was home from boarding school, she'd listened to *Pick of the Pops* furtively in her bedroom, ear pressed to the radio.

Now, as she climbed down the steps in the heat-stifling darkness to take her first stride on African soil, she was recharged with excitement.

She was aware of the male flight attendant standing at the foot of the aircraft's steps, watching her with undisguised admiration as she climbed down. She navigated the steps as gracefully as she could in her tan wedge-heeled sandals. In the heat, she was glad that she had thought to scoop up her auburn-gold hair loosely into a ponytail. She let go of the rail with her left hand for a moment to smooth her pale pink cotton mini dress over her slim figure. At least she wasn't irritable and demanding like the other passengers who pushed behind her as if they were in a great hurry.

The flight attendant watched her all the way down the steps and then wiped his palm on his trousers, and held it out courteously to steady her from the last step. She took it in her own cool soft hand for a brief moment.

"Thank you so much, John. Bye now," she smiled as she passed him and headed for the small wooden shack that served as an airport building.

"No problem, miss. Welcome to Ghana."

"How did you know his name?" hissed Sandra, from behind her. Jess turned. She noticed that John did not take Sandra's hand. His eyes and grin were still focussed on her.

"It's on his name label," whispered Jess. They walked together across to the arrivals building. "OK?"

"OK. Long flight. Tired," answered Sandra curtly. She had been unusually quiet during the flight and, it seemed, almost close to tears on occasion. Jess put her free hand on Sandra's arm.

"It'll be fine. Honestly. I know you're missing Colin." In the short time Jess had with Sandra after they were teamed up to travel to the same school in Ghana for their gap years, she had learned all about the chap Sandra was leaving behind for a year. Sandra showed her a photograph. *Oh dear, he looked a lot like Maurie. Not fanciable. AT. ALL!* She herself had said little about her own personal life, and the guy she had left behind. She wanted to keep him to herself. Her first real grown-up relationship. Simon. His name still tasted so new on her lips and in her head. *Had she done the right thing in dutifully fulfilling the contract to come out here, even though they had only just got together? Would he wait for her? They were an item, weren't they?* She frowned and bit her lip.

They walked across the tarmac in a too-tired-to-speak silence. Even in the darkness of the early evening, the smells of the hot tarmac and engine fumes were overlaid with an unfamiliar aroma of sweetness, frying, fruit, and tree sap. Even through her exhaustion, Jess was so excited, she could hardly think straight. Africa; she was actually in Africa! It was like the scent of freedom, of adventure, of mystery. But she had no idea of what she had taken on: what if it didn't work out, what if she messed up? What if the sadness of leaving Simon behind was all for nothing?

She recalled her eighteenth birthday party in March, just five months ago; the rush of excitement as Simon had finally asked her out. Tall, slim-hipped, attractive, confident Simon. Was he really hers? Smiling blue eyes that crinkled at the corners, thick fair hair that curled just a little into his temples and the nape of his neck.

Her heart stirred as she thought of how wonderful that spring and summer had been, although both of them knew that she was about to leave for Africa, that a year of her life was already mapped out for her, contract signed months before, university chosen and already deferred for a year. Yet neither of them was able to resist those new breathless feelings. She said goodbye to him but assured him that she would be back in his arms again. It was only a year ... *But what if he forgot her and moved on without her?*

Now, on this first night in West Africa, Jess fought to push her memories of Simon, the love of her life, to the back of her mind as she entered the wooden building and gasped at the heat. Ceiling fans struggled to generate some airflow, but the breeze was still hot. It was oppressive and Jess felt herself wriggling to try to free the fabric of her dress from her damp skin.

The dim lights flickered alarmingly as though they were about to extinguish altogether. Disorientated and a little nauseous, she glanced quickly around.

"Stick with us, dear," called a kindly cheerful voice behind her. It was Betty, her Quaker mentor who was somehow in her mother's network, and behind her, Glenda and Chrissie, all three of them permanent teaching staff of the school outside the town of Cape Coast, to which Jess and Sandra were assigned. "Sorry we weren't seated together on the flight. Hope you were OK. At least you two were together." Absent-mindedly, Betty pulled her greying hair more severely back into the nape of her neck with what looked to Jess like a plain elastic band like the ones the postman wrapped around a handful of letters. She looked exactly like the stereotype of the assistant head teacher that she was.

"Awful flight," said the one Jess remembered as Glenda from their quick introductions at Heathrow. She clumsily brushed her short cropped dark hair back from her forehead and pushed her old-fashioned glasses further up her nose. "That food was disgusting, wasn't it, chaps?"

"Oh, it was OK," said Chrissie softly. "It must be so difficult doing meals on a plane." Jess immediately liked the slim willowy young woman who was very attractive: elegant and stylish, with long fair hair swept up prettily into a gold clip. She had quite an aristocratic bearing and a slightly detached manner, as though she had an interesting life elsewhere. *How intriguing.*

Two others, Harriet and Sarah, were also in the party of seven. Jess noticed them, joking together a little way off, and waved. They ignored her and linked arms, heads close together as they whispered. They were also on their gap year but had been assigned to a different school from Jess and Sandra. Although they were staying at the airport hotel with them overnight, they were to be met in the morning by the head of their school and taken off to the northern area of the capital city of Accra.

"Passports! Entry permits! Currency forms!" cried out the airport customs official. Jess fumbled with her papers, blowing her errant strands of hair from her eyes.

Two officials peered at her suitcase with deep frowns and much muttering. *What was wrong?* Jess fidgeted, but tried to appear unconcerned. After much discussion, the customs officers decided it was harmless and waved Jess through. *Honestly! Travelling was certainly wearing on the nerves.*

Finally they were outside in the darkness again and hailing a taxi from the rank of cars, bright yellow in the moonlight. A crowd of small ragged boys surrounded them, calling out, "Your tax!" and "Dash me penny!" They jostled Jess, holding out their little grubby hands to her.

"Take no notice, dear," advised Betty coolly but gently. "We don't want to encourage begging."

"But they look so thin and poor," frowned Jess. "It's so hard to pass them by."

"You'll have to get used to that," snorted Glenda. "Otherwise you're going to get pestered all the time."

"Jess – mind the open drain!" called out Chrissie, reaching for her arm protectively.

A taxi-van pulled up alongside them, and Jess stepped over the drain, foul-smelling and dangerous in the dark. They piled in the van and the taxi driver stacked their cases on the roof, binding them with a length of strong rope. They swerved haphazardly across the tarmac and out to the airport hotel, where he unloaded and assured them that he would be there at eight o' clock the next morning to take them down to Cape Coast.

Across the sandy yard Jess could hear the strains of unfamiliar music: lively, rhythmical, harmonised, magical music, such as she had never heard before. The words were unclear but Jess thought she could hear something like *moba-moba-wuma*. She had read that the popular dance music of Ghana was the highlife, so maybe this was it. The rhythms were stressed and patterned tantalisingly with a kind of hollow drumbeat, making Jess want to dance. She thought that it sounded like hand drumming, not music made with a drumstick or brush. What a pity it was that she had never been encouraged to play an instrument. But of course they couldn't afford the lessons. Anyway, at least she sang in the school choir.

They trekked across to the hotel entrance and checked in. Jess and Sandra had only their small suitcases for overnight. Jess hoped that their large trunks, which were being transported by ship, would be safe until they could collect them from Takoradi port in a day or two.

Jess wondered about Harriet and Sarah who were bringing up the rear of the little English party, heads together deep in conversation. From time to time, shrieks of laughter came from their direction. Harriet had been at the same Quaker boarding school with Jess in York although they were never in the same "clique", and Jess didn't know much about her, except that she came from an old and upstanding wealthy family and seemed to be a favourite amongst the teachers and especially the headmistress of the school. She was made "head girl" in their final year. Jess had already applied the year before to do voluntary service overseas, and been accepted to come out to Ghana, when, at the last minute, Harriet had suddenly decided that it would be a "jolly good idea" too. She hadn't discussed it with Jess at all, so that Jess was startled when Harriet's "noble service" had been duly announced and applauded in school leavers' assembly. Jess's own plans had not been mentioned.

Now, in the bedroom of the Accra Airport Hotel, Jess studied herself in the full length mirror which was propped up against the wall. Did she look any different, now that she was in Africa? She peered at her face. She felt and looked sticky in the heat. She hated having her hair up, brushed off her forehead. Normally she liked to hide her uneven hairline behind a deep fringe and side bangs that gently fell across her cheeks. But anticipating the heat she had swept it up this morning before the flight. And staring critically at herself now, she saw that it exposed her high forehead, her small slanting eyes and big nose. *None of her features were in coordination. And, oh gosh, there was another spot coming, and she only had a small supply of Clearasil cover-up ...*

She knew that if she styled her hair as she normally did, it would be lank and greasy in no time in this sticky heat. Simon said she was beautiful. *Why didn't she ever believe him – or the other boys who said the same to her?* Now she looked down at her figure reflected in the mirror. Legs slim enough, maybe her best feature. But just now they looked so white; she hoped that she might go home with a little tan at least, like a proper traveller. An adventurer.

Sandra slipped in carrying two beakers of water from the ice machine and glanced briefly over to Jess.

"Admiring yourself?" she said. Jess had discovered on the plane that Sandra had quite a sharp tongue.

"Oh gosh, no!" Jess crossed the room to sit on one of the two single beds in the spartan room. She wished she had the confidence to say "yes, absolutely!" and play along, making a joke of it. She pushed aside the mosquito net that hung from a hook above the bed.

Jess kicked off her sandals and swung her legs up onto the thin coverlet, as Sandra placed the beakers on the bedside cabinet between the beds. Jess nodded her thanks.

"Phew!" She raised her arms and locked her hands behind her head, enjoying the cooling breeze from the ceiling fan. "I really need a shower. There's a basic bathroom with a hand-held shower head that you can attach to the bath tap. Hope it works OK."

Ten minutes later when Jess had revived herself with the iced water, she found that the shower didn't work OK at all. There was no hook to hang it up on, so she held it above her head with one hand and struggled to shampoo her long hair with the other. It involved a lot of ledging the shower head in the bath and stooping to pick it up again. Maybe it would just be better to wash her hair in the bath, as she used to do at her boarding school, where there were no luxuries like showers. Finally she was satisfied that she felt clean, scrubbed pink, and refreshed. She slipped on her clean set of white cotton underwear and a fresh white cotton broderie anglaise dress, and sprayed herself with her 4711 cologne.

"You won't keep that clean for long," laughed Sandra, "not in this heat and humidity. I've got bright coloured togs – won't show the dirt and sweat!"

"Yes, well." Jess hid her grimace. "Probably very sensible."

By the time Jess had dried her hair and pulled the top half back in to a large brown plastic clip, leaving the rest to fall onto her shoulders, Sandra was finished in the bathroom and appeared, rubbing her short clipped hair on her towel and thrusting her feet into her flat sandals. Her sleeveless bright floral peter pan-collared blouse and knee-length red A-line skirt looked plain and old fashioned to Jess, and she moved awkwardly across the room, almost knock-kneed. Jess noticed the ghost of a moustache on Sandra's thick upper lip. She flopped onto the edge of her bed and said, "Ready for food?"

"Definitely. The others are meeting us across on the veranda in front of the dining room. Here!" Jess slid her bottle of insect repellent across to Sandra. "Do you want to put some of this on? You don't want to get eaten alive! After dark, mosquitoes are out in force."

"Ha! So, searching for pure virgin blood! How come you think of everything? I'll just have to get stuff here."

Jess hoped that Sandra had thought to have all her injections before she came out here and to take the daily quinine tablets against malaria. Well, she wasn't Sandra's keeper, but still she wouldn't like her to succumb to any awful tropical diseases.

They met Betty, Glenda and Chrissie on the open veranda. They all sat on cane chairs upholstered with huge thick soft cushions and sipped fresh mango juice while they waited for Harriet and Sarah to arrive. At last, Jess could feel herself relaxing and looking forward to the meal. She smoothed her hair, leaned back and crossed her slim legs neatly. Glenda and Chrissie were deep in conversation.

"So what sort of food can we expect here?" Jess asked Betty.

"Actually, dear, here in the Airport Hotel, it's usually quite European. Meat and veg. But there's always a Ghanaian option. We have a lot of rice or fufu, with stew. The favourite is groundnut stew which has a bit of meat in it. The groundnuts are quite tasty actually. Or chicken and rice, ubiquitous here in Ghana, I'm afraid – but it's usually the safest bet! Puddings are mostly made with fresh fruits – there are a lot of exotic fruit salads. There's also mango or passion fruit cream purees, rather like our fruit fools."

"Ugh!" said Sandra, pulling a face.

"Oh, well, *I* think that sounds very nice," said Jess. She recalled another of her mother's Rules: never offend anyone or say what you really think, outside of the family.

"What sounds nice?" called Harriet as she and Sarah crossed the veranda towards them. "Oh," she flopped herself down into an armchair. "I was *exhausted* when we got here ... But now ...Wow, am I ready for partying!" She turned to Jess, "Any decent talent around?" She winked towards Sarah, "Or maybe you wouldn't recognise it if you saw it!"

"Well, not really what you'd call talent." Jess looked around the veranda at the one or two rather large middle-aged men, and added quickly, "But I'm sure they're absolutely lovely."

"Oh, *Jess!*"

꧁

Jess awoke early the next morning, but the sun was already high and hot. It felt to Jess as though the day was already well underway. Over breakfast, Betty told her that the rainy monsoon season would be ending over the next month and that this was the coolest time of year, although it was over eighty degrees Fahrenheit at seven o clock. Jess wondered what it was going to be like in the hot dry season.

Harriet and Sarah were nowhere to be seen but the others were anxious to make the journey to Cape Coast before the noon time heat. They loaded their cases on to the taxi-van again and drove into Accra for Betty, Glenda and Chrissie to buy a couple of necessities. Betty had brought some local Ghanaian currency for Jess and Sandra, an advance on their volunteers' allowance, to tide them over until they could get to the bank in Cape Coast. Jess took the opportunity to start to work out the local currency: cedis and pesewas. She calculated that one cedi was the equivalent of about eight shillings and four pence in British sterling.

The big supermarket in Accra had a giant sign spelling out "Kingsway" above the door, in big 50s style lettering, and underneath it, "Don't mind your wife!" Jess was surprised to see that most of the shelves and refrigerators were empty. There was little in the way of tea or coffee even, some bottles of Camp coffee, no butter, but there was a little margarine, some tins of powdered milk, bottles of sterilised milk, and tinned "Ideal" milk. The prices of even these were high, and Jess noticed that cosmetics, sparse as they were, were ridiculously costly. How was she going to manage when her English supplies ran out? Well, her mother would be pleased; she hated Jess wearing make-up (*"slutty"*, another Rule).

Jess and Sandra bought some bread, margarine, jam, coffee and milk powder. Then Jess spotted some fresh fruit, and added a pineapple and bananas but hesitated over the green oranges, although they were labelled "sweet sweet". There were some other more exotic fruits labelled mango, pawpaw and passion fruit, but Jess had no idea how to prepare or eat them, so she decided to leave those until she had become more familiar with them.

Sandra wandered around the shop some more, and Jess meandered outside and stood gazing around her in wonder; it was so exotic.

The streets were incredibly noisy, smelly, and bustling with people calling out to each other across the streets, jostling Jess. Swarms of little boys were again surrounding her, pushing at her for attention. The hot thick air stank of rotting vegetables, spices, melting tarmac.

Jess pressed herself against the safety of the wall as plump women swathed in bright Ghanaian cloth swept haughtily past her. Their babies swaddled on their backs blinked passively at her with glassy eyes and long black eyelashes. Shallow platters piled high with tomatoes and mangoes were balanced on turban-bound heads, as the women made their way gracefully up and down the dusty streets, taking no notice of the foul open drains and the begging children around their feet. Jess noticed that the women were bedecked in gold jewellery: little delicate gold filigree earrings trembling at their lobes, fat gold chains around their necks, arms and ankles. The younger women, tall and slim, unencumbered by babies, glanced with interest at Jess as they moved by with easy grace; backs ballet-dancer straight and small steps smooth and gliding.

Jess watched them, fascinated. If only she could be that proud and confident. She suddenly felt a hand thump her shoulder and jumped. She swung round to see Sandra holding a shopping bag.

"C'mon," she said loudly and flicked her head to indicate the direction to the right, "Buck up. Stop dreaming. Taxi's waiting." There were the others each with a shopping bag and together they made their way to the taxi park.

They gingerly wove their way across the crowded street as large battered cars roared by, narrowly avoiding pedestrians. Horns blared and drivers shouted across the hubbub. A traffic jam suddenly built up as lorries backed up, and angry yelling filled the stifling air.

Jess had to weave through a group of women who suddenly seemed to appear from nowhere, balancing heavy flat baskets of fruit on their heads, threading their way between the vehicles, leaning into the cabins, exchanging pineapples and bananas for coins. Jess noticed some of the women proffering green oranges, nodding, pulling out sharp knives from the folds of their skirts and expertly slicing off the top of the orange. A hand reaching out from the car, a head poking out and a mouth sucking the juice from the fruit.

Their taxi was awaiting them in an area packed with vehicles Jess recognised from her pre-travel research: "tro-tros", "mammy-lorries", the country buses. Women with their platters and baskets on their heads, young men with crates aloft, young children in tattered tops and shorts and daubed with chalky streaks were climbing up onto the lorries, along with scrawny chickens and bony goats, tethered with string, all piling onto the benches that bordered the vehicles, boys hanging off the sides, shouting to each other and laughing uproariously.

Jess noticed that the tro-tros bore intriguing slogans, painted roughly across the sides and back: 'Never Trust Pretty Woman', 'Sea Never Dry', 'Fear Women and Grow Old', 'God Is My Shepherd – And I Don't Know Why'. She laughed out loud and a group of men lounging nearby laughed and clapped appreciatively.

"Pretty lady!" shouted one. "Too much pretty!"

"Never trust!" shouted his companion, laughing uproariously at his own joke and shaking his head.

Jess smiled at them and slid into the taxi van for the journey out to Cape Coast. The driver helped Sandra, Betty, Glenda and Chrissie to fix their bulging bags to the back and top of the van and they all clambered in, Betty in the front with the driver, Glenda and Sandra behind, and at the back Chrissie and Jess.

Jess had to cling to the hand bar as the taxi swerved frighteningly through the streets with their large, white colonnaded government buildings and drab dirty concrete houses and shops, pitted and crumbling.

Eventually the crowds thinned and the taxi found smooth tarmacked roads through to the outskirts of town. But out of town it bumped and bounced disconcertingly over increasingly rough dirt roads. Jess held on tight as Chrissie pointed out the sights. Town buildings gave way to the huts of the villages that surrounded Accra. The lush green vegetation of palm, plantain and crimson flamboyant trees gave way to scrub land and heat-baked red dust tracks beside the road. Dust clouds flew up from the taxi's wheels as it swerved along the road. Jess watched eagerly as telegraph poles and electricity pylons gave way to straggling trees alongside. Paths between mud huts disappeared into dense scrub.

Yet there was a sense of vast space around Jess. Gone was the suffocating airlessness of the city and the suburbs, here was true space and air to breathe. Women and children carrying heavily loaded platters on their heads, one arm raised to steady their burdens, stopped their work and watched them silently as they passed. Jess saw few men in the villages, but one or two sat in the dirt, lounging against the mud walls of their huts, whittling sticks or grouped together laughing and gesturing over their beer cans.

They stopped a couple of times at wayside village stalls where women squatted splay-legged in front of platters of fruits grown in their small plots or stood beside tables covered with makeshift "roofs" of rough-hewn poles holding up large palm leaves. Jess bought a few more bananas and another pineapple from a woman nursing a bone-thin baby, even though she had already bought some at the Accra supermarket.

Another of the women held out a green orange to her encouragingly. Jess hesitated.

"They may be green but they are actually very sweet," Chrissie assured Jess.

The woman cut off the top as Jess had seen in the streets of Accra, in the traffic jam, and held it out to her. Jess sucked the juice; it certainly was gloriously sweet.

She had not realised that these tropical fruits were so abundant in the little villages nor that they would be sold at the roadside by villagers. She thought that she really should support local enterprise, especially as the women, and their children clustering around them, looked so poor. She felt somewhat embarrassed by the fact that the fruits were so much cheaper than at the Accra supermarket. She gestured that she would buy six green oranges.

"How much?" Jess reached in her purse.

"Don't give her what she asks," snorted Glenda, coming up suddenly behind her, "Halve the price."

"But it's only a few pence," Jess argued. *Surely these ragged villagers needed the money more than she did?*

"Oh for goodness sake!" Glenda stomped away back to the taxi. Jess bit her lip and glanced at Chrissie who shrugged. Glenda drummed her fingers on the door impatiently, until Jess and the others climbed back into the van.

Eventually, they bordered Cape Coast town and took a right turn along a wide red dirt road towards the school.

"It's about five miles out of town," explained Chrissie, her low voice only just audible above Glenda and Sandra's loud laughter in front of them. "Near Kakomdo. In the bush. You'll see it's a large compound. I don't know how much you know about it, but it's a Methodist secondary school. All the girls are boarders and most of them are the daughters of professionals. Many are politicians in Nkrumah's government."

"Yes, I was told about it. I'd hoped for a bush school, teaching village children, nursing and so on."

"Making a difference," nodded Chrissie. "Yes, I know. That's where everyone wants to go. The irony is, that's not where they send you."

"They've said that I can maybe go out to the nearby villages to teach literacy and do basic nursing care, though, so that's something, at least."

"Ah, right," said Chrissie, her words left hanging in the air.

"So what are the other staff like?"

"Oh, we come from all over. Canada, the USA, Ireland, Ceylon. And there are some Ghanaian graduate women teachers, most of them former pupils. There were also assistant teachers from VSO, and from the new American Peace Corps. So it's a mixed bunch. I'm sure you'll like them."

As the taxi drew in through the school gates, between high white concrete walls, Chrissie pointed out the staff bungalows for the married staff and those for the senior staff, little villas surrounded by patches of neatly kept garden, mature shrubberies, with well-spaced with sandy dirt tracks in between. She indicated the shared staff apartments for the mainly Ghanaian unmarried staff at the end of the pupils' dormitory blocks.

"I think you'll be up there with Sandra," Chrissie pointed, "but you'll have lovely views from your veranda. I wish I did. My bungalow's at the back on the edge of the bush."

The taxi drew to a halt and Jess saw the neat geometric design of the low hedging and borders of jewel-bright flowers leading up to the low white school buildings and the chapel, three sides of a square, with an external roofed walkway in front, edged with white columns. The driver jumped out of the taxi and opened the doors, as Jess looked around.

"Wow, it looks beautiful."

Betty turned in her front seat and smiled proudly, "Yes, it is, dear. I think so." Jess hoped that she too would be able to be successful and proud. She wanted to go back to England feeling that she had achieved something here. She knew her heart was full of 'youthful altruism' as one of her teachers had, rather scornfully, commented as she planned her trip. But she really did feel she wanted to make a difference. Somehow.

Glenda stared out of the window, as if reluctant to step out, "Hmph, you just wait till you see how hard it is to keep clean. Rats, bats and their mess. Termites. Great." *So why had Glenda chosen to teach in Ghana, and to stay there year after year, if she hated it so much?*

The school porter, thin, little and rangy, and, Jess thought, quite elderly, came scurrying out to greet them with much respectful bowing. "Miss, miss. I help you fine." He grabbed Jess's bag and Sandra's, then bounded away up a concrete staircase.

"Off you go and see to your bags," instructed Betty. "Joseph will show you your apartment and then leave you to get settled. I'll send him back again in an hour or so to bring you over to our bungalow for late lunch."

The third floor apartment, "flat four", Joseph informed them, was rudimentary, to say the least. The first impression that Jess had was of concrete, bareness, a sparsely furnished space. Glazed double doors from the large balcony or *veranda*, as Chrissie had called it, led into a living room containing two chairs upholstered with bulky cushions with loud floral patterns, and a large dining table.

Joseph ushered them with great pride and flourish into the bathroom – a shower, hand basin and loo, white, basic, a little cracked – and the kitchen – a sink, one small floor cupboard and a fridge which seemed to have a potato peeler as a handle – and two bedrooms, one off the other. The beds, a single one in each bedroom, were draped with mosquito nets, yellowing with age and hanging from a rail attached to the ceiling.

Joseph beamed at them both and waited expectantly. *Mother's Rulebook: always be kind.*

"Oh, it's absolutely lovely," Jess responded and Joseph nodded, but she felt Sandra look sidelong at her. "Thank you."

She smiled at Joseph and, again with much bowing, he scuttled off.

"Good grief!" exclaimed Sandra. "This is certainly primitive. Not what we're used to, hey?"

Jess unpacked her bag and arranged her pretty perfume bottles, tissues and toiletry bag on the small chest of drawers. She had only one, now rather creased, cotton dress to hang in the single wardrobe, apart from the clothes she had worn on the flight, now in her laundry bag, and those she was wearing that day. She fervently hoped that it would not be too long before her trunk arrived at Takoradi port.

She took the photo of Simon from her bag and carefully placed it on her bedside table and thought that this afternoon she must write a letter to him. The photo showed him leaning nonchalantly against a doorway at college. Looking at his beloved sensitive face, with his fresh faced artistic looks, his fair hair flopping over his high forehead, his soft full lips smiling knowingly, his endearing little gap in his front teeth, his crinkly blue eyes, looking not at the camera but off to the right, wistfully, she thought, she felt suddenly empty inside. There had been so much happening on the journey here, and so many new and amazing things to take in, that she had not really stopped to think about anything much. Except new experiences and the anticipation of this adventure that she had planned for so long, even before she had started going out with Simon. *Had she been dating him first, would she have arranged this gap year? Probably not.*

She sank onto her bed and thought – *what have I done?* She was torn: part of her wanted to be home again, clean and comfortable, with Simon, but yet part of her was excited and overwhelmed by the very knowledge of being here in Africa. She was tired, after the journey and all the emotions, the newness of things, the unfamiliar pressing in on her, both exhilarating and horrifying. Her eyes swept the drab room. Even with the little personal details she had brought to it, the copy of Margaret Drabble's *A Summer Birdcage* on the bedside table along with her precious copy of Yeats's poems, the light lacy shawl she had draped on the solitary chair, the photos, it still had the look of a prison cell.

She inspected the bathroom. Basically clean although uninviting. A couple of huge spiders in the shower. Carefully she turned on the water to wash them down the plughole. Nothing. The rusty stain on the tub indicated that there had been water at some time. Jess went to the kitchen and tried the tap in the sink. A burp of water, then nothing. She fiddled with the tap; it was loose and wobbled as she spun it. She tightened it up and then tried again. This time the water gushed and hiccupped sporadically.

Back in the bathroom, she tried the shower again and this time something slightly more than a trickle fell pathetically into the tray. She looked around for a container and eventually found in the kitchen cupboard a plastic dish which she used to collect water from the sink to wash the spiders down the bathroom plughole. A sigh of satisfaction. Clean again. By this time she felt so sweaty she should be wrung out and hung up to dry.

A movement caught the corner of her eye. She stooped down. Oh my god – a cockroach. An enormous giant of a cockroach, crusty and shiny black, scuttling across the floor.

"I think," said a strangled voice from the doorway, "that we've got rats." Jess looked up. Sandra's face was contorted with disgust. "Droppings on my bedroom floor."

"Oh no. And cockroaches too." Jess turned back to the bathroom floor but the creature had disappeared. "What do we do?"

"Dunno. Heaven knows. Well, Betty, at any rate!" Sandra laughed, clasping her hands together as if in prayer and looking heaven-wards. Jess smiled "We'll ask Betty what's to be done. Ugh, what have we come to?"

"I know ... well, I'm sure we'll get used to it." Jess stood up. "In time. I need some air. I'm going to look at the view."

She wandered out onto the veranda, and leaned on the patterned concrete walling that surrounded the three sides. She gasped. The view was amazing, as Chrissie had said. She looked out over the rich green wilderness of the bush and the forest towards the sea. There was nothing but lush vegetation between her and the ocean. The expanse of Atlantic that separated her from Simon. She knew that she looked towards the south west, (not north towards England) and towards, she supposed, eventually, what – South America? – but she could imagine that she was looking out across the water to him. In her mind she reached out and touched his hand. *I have to do this, Simon. I need to breathe. I need to experience these amazing things. But although it seems a long, long time till I'm back with you, it won't really be – what's a year in a lifetime, after all? We have the rest of our lives together. Love you. Hug you.*

"C'mon," called Sandra, "You ready? Joseph's just coming up to get us."

Jess liked Betty's bungalow, which she shared with Clara, the head teacher of the school; it was simple but comfortable, clean and attractively furnished. She liked the wooden and wicker armchairs and sofas upholstered in muted pinks and greens, a lovely carved coffee table, a dining table and matching chairs in polished mahogany, and lots of Ghanaian artefacts: masks, drums, kente cloths pinned up as wall hangings and photographs of village life.

Jess looked around and registered ideas for their own apartment. Betty had explained that kente cloth was the Ghanaian traditional, and very expensive, material for special occasion wear, made by weaving strips of cloth and then sewing them together to form patterns. Each pattern had a meaning, rather like American traditional patchwork quilting.

Clara, a small, thin middle-aged lady, was smoothing a large piece of kente cloth as a throw over one of the sofas. She peered over her wire-rimmed glasses and spoke gently and quietly but with an authority that Jess knew would strike fear into the hearts of young teenage girls. Clara was very interested in their backgrounds and homes, and asked Sandra and Jess many questions as they ate lunch. Sandra's father turned out to be some kind of engineer and her mother a housewife, who "didn't need to work."

"And your parents Jess? What do they do, my dear?" asked Clara with a kindly and encouraging smile.

"Well, my mother's a secretary at the Quaker headquarters and my father's a – well, he works at a … a sanitation firm." Jess bit her lip.

Sandra sniggered, "What? A labourer? In a sewage works? Ugh! Does he muck out the …?" But Clara shook her head firmly at Sandra and changed the subject, as Joseph shuffled into the room.

Joseph, who, as well as being the school porter, was also Betty and Clara's cook and houseboy, served them all with groundnut stew, earthy, rich and thick, with pieces of chicken in it, and boiled rice with fried plantain, rather like banana, and kenkey, a dough wrapped in corn leaves. He beamed as Jess, recovered from her embarrassment, asked him to explain to her what the various dishes were.

"So where did you learn to cook like this?" asked Jess, still licking her lips from the delicious flavours. He looked puzzled, so Jess gestured at the dishes and at Joseph, raising her eyebrows.

"Ah, Mother teach me," he said, grinning proudly as he collected the plates and took them to the little kitchen at the back.

"Actually," explained Clara, "the name Mother could be his mother or just as easily his grandmother or an aunt. Just as the same name is used for father or uncle in Fante. But the females are the cement that keeps the family together. It's a matriarchal society. The women rule the roost. The fathers often tend to be less permanent figures in most of the households, unless he's a "big chieftain", and so the mother's male relatives, the uncles, tend to act as the father figure. Hence the same word is used for them and you don't know whether it's a real biological father or another male relative. The women all work together for the family, caring for the children and so on, so although different words are used for them, often they just say "mother". It's quite confusing!"

Joseph returned, carrying a large serving dish to the table. It contained a light peachy coloured pudding, like a mousse or a puree. "Mango, paw-paw," he announced with a broad grin.

Jess savoured the delicious, light and flavoursome desert, smooth and thick, and she showed her appreciation to Joseph who smiled at her delightedly.

"You must teach me how to make it!" She meant it; her mother had taught her to cook and she really enjoyed it on the rare occasions she was entrusted with the ownership of the kitchen. She would love to be able to use the exotic ingredients she was discovering here, although she couldn't imagine her mother being too keen. Plain, simple and cheap was her mother's motto.

After lunch, they moved from the table to the comfortably upholstered wicker chairs on the shaded veranda and Joseph served them coffee. Jess lifted her cup to her lips: it tasted like bottled Camp coffee essence with a lot of frothy sterilised milk. There was no way she would have drunk it at home, but somehow it tasted so good to Jess, here in the suffocating heat and glaring midday sunshine, surrounded by the smells of wood fires, spices and other strange unrecognisable scents of the bush.

Jess noticed that Sandra was trying to catch her eye and was making odd gestures, nodding sideways towards Betty and crawling her hand in the shape of a scuttling crab over her lap. "Rats!" she whispered, her mouth skewed.

"Oh, yes," said Jess, "Um, we were wondering ... well, we seem to have some ... what look like ... rat droppings in the apartment. We ... er ... don't know what to do."

"Oh, bless your dear souls," cried Betty, "yes, we do get them here. At times there are infestations!" she laughed delightedly. "It's probably because the apartment was empty for a while over the vacation. But I'll get Joseph to come and deal with them. Not to worry!"

Joseph grinned happily.

"And Joseph will also pop over later with some suggestions for shopping he will get you, and please add anything to the list that you might need. He will estimate the cost and you can pay him. He will bring the change and return the list to you with the cost of each item so that you know for next time," Betty instructed, "Is that OK?"

"Absolutely," agreed Jess, "That's very kind."

"Go back to your apartment and get some rest while it's so hot," said Clara.

"Oh yes," laughed Sandra, "You bet! Siesta time! That's the bit I like!"

Later, Jess lay on her bed, fanning herself with a folded sheet of paper. The heat in the apartment was almost unbearable. She had doused herself with cold water from the gurgling tap in the bathroom but it had made little difference. She couldn't sleep; it was much too hot and sticky, but she could doze and think. She longed to see Simon again, to hear him talk softly to her, to feel him holding her tenderly and murmuring sweet loving things.

He was so upset that she had decided to go away. But he thoughtfully told her that she must go if that was what she wanted and that she must think of him all the time. He said that not a day would go by that he himself would not think of her and long for her to return to him. He said that they had the rest of their lives together. How she savoured those words. To have someone (and someone as gorgeous as him, already at university, planning a career in politics or law like his wealthy family), to have him say that to her, actually wanting to be with her, wanting to spend time with her, wanting her forever. *What on earth did he see in her?* It was so miraculous and so wonderful that she could hardly believe it was true. She would have so much to tell him about when she returned to England next summer.

Later that day, as she walked around the school grounds, admiring the neat bungalows and the well-kept gardens, the abundant jewel bright pink bougainvillea, flame red flamboyant trees, and the sweet clipped hibiscus hedges, the night fell abruptly.

Taken by surprise, Jess only just managed to run back to the apartment before the thick darkness descended swiftly, obliterating the colour and vivacity around her. Jess heard the unfamiliar cacophony of insect noises in the air and smelt the exotic scents of nightfall.

Jess and Sandra took supper with Betty and Clara, where Joseph served them with a thick soup, this time made of fish, he said. There were side dishes of spicy red beans and fufu, as he called it, which Betty told them was a dumpling made of pounded yam and plantain. She said that usually Ghanaians dropped the fufu into the middle of the soup like an island and ate it all with their fingers. Jess was glad they had been equipped with spoons. For dessert Joseph had made coconut yogurts, poured into the scooped out halves of fresh coconuts, which was delicious. Jess was quickly becoming accustomed to the tastes of Ghanaian cuisine, the flavours and consistencies. They somehow characterised this hot, stifling, strange country which so fascinated her. She noticed that Sandra picked at the food.

After supper, Betty and Clara had said that they would do some school preparation ready for the pupils' return in a couple of days' time, and then get an early night, so the girls returned to their apartment, carrying borrowed torches, almost running as the nipping insects attacked their bare legs. Although Jess had covered herself in insect repellent, the nasty little things still seemed to have developed a liking for the smell and taste of her flesh. She swatted them off as she ran, and once back indoors she applied more repellent. This time it seemed to work better and she felt more comfortable.

Back in the apartment, Jess duly did her washing by hand in the soap flakes her mother had insisted she brought, grudgingly thanking her for her forethought. She boiled a kettle of water for the washing and did her laundry in the small bathroom sink. She rinsed out her dresses, bra and pants in the sparse spurts of water from the tap, and wrung out the wet clothes as much as she could. Then she draped them on a wooden chair which she carried out to the veranda. Happily, they would still be there with the next morning's heat, dry and fresh, but she did not know, then, that this would be the first and last time she would need to wash clothes by hand herself, as they would have a "houseboy" to be their laundry man.

That first evening, though, she stood on the veranda for a long while, as Sandra lay sprawled on her bed inside, writing her letters home and to Colin, Jess looked in wonder at the vast expanse of dark space before her, the shapes of the huge trees in the bush way out to the sea. She could almost, if she concentrated hard enough, hear the crashing of the waves. Although she couldn't see anything, she couldn't even make out the shapes of houses, she could feel the presence of people out there in the bush, hidden in the trees, and it seemed to her like the whispering of souls. The wind had arisen and on it she could make out the gentle beating of drums, gradually becoming louder and more insistent with their rhythmic rising and falling pitch. The village drums of Kakumdo, the dondo, the atumpan, the talking drums that Betty had told them about just now over supper. It was hypnotic.

Jess could make out bats flying; maybe fruit bats, much bigger than pipistrelles, swooping overhead. But as she turned to retreat inside, she looked with horror at the doorway where the windows were flung wide open. A thick column of termites barred her entry, solid and impenetrable between the ceiling light bulb and the floor. She took a deep breath, covered her head with her arms, and ran through. She had brought an umbrella from England and she fetched it from her bedroom, using it to barge through the termites again to close the veranda doors tight. She secured the wire grid shutters across the windows and switched off the light in the living room. She dived under her mosquito net that draped over her bed, then carefully reached under the net to click on her bedside lamp. Safe.

She propped herself up with her pillow and pulled up her large bag that she would keep on her bed under the net. From it, she took out her pale blue pre-paid airmail fold-up and her pen. The first of many such letters that would travel, painstakingly slowly, between Ghana and England. She smoothed her hair and looked over at the photo on her bedside table.

My dear darling Simon (she wrote),
I can hardly believe I am actually here, in Africa! Africa! I've only just had a moment to sit down and

write to you. The flight was great. VC10 is really a 'super' jet – very smooth (most of the way!). I felt a bit off when we went through a minor storm, but don't worry, I was OK. It was just the bumpiness that attacked my stomach (like going over hump-back bridges in a certain boyfriend's little grey mini!). Oh and I had a ginger ale, for Old Times' Sake! It was a very good one, although as you know I'm no connoisseur! We stayed the night in Accra (airport hotel) as it was late when we arrived (gain an hour because of British summer Time). Didn't take off till about 11 (BST) – about 6 hours. It was all terribly confusing at the airport – lots of little African boys dashing around wanting to carry cases and get "tax" (one of the first English words they learn). Road to Cape Coast is relatively good, though bumpy; would have taken about 2 or 3 hours had we not stopped. Little villages, thick vegetation, most beautiful plants and flowers even at this time of year – rainy season is just ending. It's supposed to be the coolest time of year – temp in Accra yesterday was 90F. Windy on our veranda outside the flat that S and I are sharing.

All very spacious and bare at the moment. Forever fixing our mosquito nets over our beds and spraying insect repellent onto ourselves and DDT onto everything in sight. Every day at 6pm it gets dark apparently, wham, just like that, so we will be having a little ritual nightly spraying I think. I'm beginning to get used to the wildlife – cockroaches, geckos, ants, flies, enormous rhino beetles flying overhead, lizards of every size, shape and colour, scurrying everywhere. You'd absolutely hate it! But I was really nauseated by a large economy sized rat-thing that bounced across my path in the dark. Ugh. Pukey. Honestly, I nearly threw up with horror. Rather scary at night. Especially the sound of the native drums resounding across the bush. Talking drums, they call them – dondo. Apparently they send messages with them – with different sounds and rhythms.

Please thank the parents again for the lovely Yeats book and message inside, which I read all the time - well, I don't really think I'm 'brave', but still ... Can't wait to hear from you. Feels like yonks since I saw you. But I do understand you not wanting to come to the airport to see me off – it would have been so sad! Good luck with the university term and with the resit exams. I wish you were here to be with me and see it all and understand what it's like. Love you, love you, J xxx

Then she wrote a brief card to her parents and her brother David, the first of the dutiful weekly mailings. As she finally lay her exhausted head on her pillow, Jess could still hear the dondo drumbeats of Kakomdo gently but insistently pounding a rhythm on the soft tropical breeze. As she closed her eyes and allowed herself to fall sweetly into sleep, she embraced the whispering souls and spirits calling quietly to her from the village in the bush.

2

SEPTEMBER 1965

School started in early September, and girls arrived excitedly, the younger ones in their green and yellow uniforms. Dormitories filled up and the school compound reverberated with the laughs, shouts and screeches of a couple of hundred pupils.

Jess watched the older girls arrive in trucks and taxis, unloading their metal trunks and boxes for the term, all dressed in their brightly patterned Ghanaian cloth: long straight wrap-around skirts, with short sleeved tops, closely fitted with a gathered peplum at the waist and hips. She noticed that their hair was plaited tightly close to their scalp in different designs, some like corn rows, and some in swirling patterns. All seemed to have the little gold earrings she had noticed in Accra, but no other gold chains or decoration at all, just simple clearly expensive solid gold drops.

Well, she would go into the bush villages and nurse and teach the poor; that was, after all what she had set out to do. She herself had been so lucky, privileged. She'd been able to go to a very good school. Many of these children, the village children, had *no* school. She so much wanted to be able to go back to England feeling that she had done something significant. To *be* someone, in her own right. Her heart went out to those ragged little children she saw in town, their slack mouths and wide bewildered eyes.

With the arrival of the girls for the new school year, the peace and quiet of the concrete dormitory block, where Jess and Sandra's apartment was located on the third floor, was shattered by the noise and commotion.

Jess liked to stand on the veranda in the evening listening to the old record player the older girls were playing across the schoolyard in the school hall, its Heath Robinson sound system flinging the melodies across the compound and out to the villages of Kakomdo and Ebubonku. Belting strains of "*She loves you, yeah, yeah, yeah*" often rang out and sometimes the more gentle, wistful and fluid tunes of "*Yesterday*" or "*You gotta hide your love a-way ...*" Jess loved to hear the tunes that reminded her of the school commonroom and sang along to "*Under the boardwalk, down by the sea ...*" Her mother would have had a fit if she had realised that Jess actually knew the words to a pop song – "a *pop song*! The work of the devil!" It was one of her mother's many Rules: no pop songs ("we don't have any of *that* in this house!"); no make-up, no kissing, no smoking, no drinking, no pop dancing ("wild, disgraceful, leads to goodness knows what"), no sex ... all "dirty", disgusting and damned. Jess counted that she had already broken five of them.

Then suddenly one night, she heard the familiar echoing riff of the mouth organ and the plaintive cry across the compound of Bruce Chanel's *"Hey, hey, hey, baby, I wanna know-ow-ow, if you'll be my girl ..."*

She was startled.

A memory ... *caught singing as she came out of the bathroom, her mother and her brother – what, four, five years before. Her mother horrified, "Stop that dreadful pop singing!" Her brother smirking, "Have you got a boyfriend, Jess? Is that what he says to you, eh?" affecting a daft voice as she shuddered, "Will you be my girl, Je-e-esss?" Her mother's disgusted face. And she had cringed and curled up inside. She was only thirteen then but she had felt dirty, slutty. And then she remembered something else ... she must have been about six when it happened first ...*

But it was so long ago; she must focus on that. Another world. Not her world, not her life, not now. But still, in the hot Ghanaian night, as the strains of "*hey baby*" died away, she felt disturbed and confused. She did not want to remember that time. Everything was different, "all utterly changed" as Yeats had written in the book Simon's parents had given her as a leaving gift. Her own parents had not thought to give her anything to take with her. Her mother had hugged her too tightly and shaken her head sadly; her father had smirked silently in the background.

Now Jess shuddered off the memories, and looked out over the bush to the sea, listened to the girls' giggles and calls until all was quiet again by 9.30 and the dormitory lights were dimmed. She could see the palm trees, their shapes emerging from the half-light shed from the school lamps. She listened to the hollow sounds of the bush, the low animal cries mingled with the deep pounding of the village drums.

Jess thought of Simon, her soul-mate. He always made her feel so good, made her feel that everything was so *right*. They shared so much: a Quaker background, although his family was very different from her own, a whole social stratosphere different. Her mother was satisfied, but that was not what mattered to Jess. She and Simon shared music, books, poetry. They laughed at the same jokes, angered at the same inequalities, aspired to the same goals; they had the same view of life.

Secretly, she yearned guiltily for them to get closer. For the hugs and kisses to become something more. There was a bit of desperate fondling just before she came out to Africa when Jess thought maybe Simon felt he might never see her again. But he had said very clearly that he respected her and that anything more could wait until they were properly together again, together for life.

OK, she could wait. She leaned on the balustrade of the veranda balcony and sighed into the darkness.

She thought of the way her life had changed here in Ghana. It was all so very different from life at home in England.

Jess amazed herself at the early nights she kept; she was in bed not long after the girls' lights out. Of course, here she had to set her alarm clock for 5.30 in the mornings; even at her boarding school in England she had not needed to crawl out of bed until at least an hour and a half after that.

But here in the heat and sunshine of the early mornings, her body had attuned quickly to the new routine. Her body clock seemed content to go along with the light and dark, sunrise and sunset. It felt right, somehow, like a basic primitive response to nature. She found herself enjoying rising early and going out onto the veranda for five minutes with a mug of creamy coffee, to breathe in the African air and look out for a few moments over the wildness of the bush.

She loved having an afternoon rest after lunch, a *siesta* when the heat was greatest and it was most humid. She could settle her mind, read or write a letter on her bed under her mosquito net, before showering again and reviving herself for the rest of the afternoon.

Jess taught her very first lesson in the second week of September. The lesson had to be forty minutes long. *How would she be able to keep going for forty minutes? What about if she dried up? What was she going to say? What if she forgot something important?* She wished she'd had some teacher training. What had she enjoyed at school? That was all she could go on, really.

That first morning after school assembly, Jess collected the register from the staff room for her first year class, and made her way to the classroom. The blue exercise books and the set of old scruffy texts, she had piled up in the room the evening before. It was an abridged children's version of Dickens's *A Christmas Carol. Ah, good, at least she knew this text already.*

The girls arrived, excitedly chattering, but when they saw Jess standing by her desk, they fell silent and settled themselves in their desks. Jess looked around the group. There were twenty five faces of differing shades of light copper to black and with very different features, staring at her, waiting expectantly. The class seemed to include girls of all shapes and sizes, not surprisingly, except that Jess found it difficult to imagine that they were all the same age, supposedly about eleven years old. There were several who seemed much older, much more mature, well set, confident, big-breasted amongst the other child-like pupils with small features, flat boyish chests, and a wide-eyed look of innocence.

Jess took a deep breath and bent over the register of names.

"Charity. That's a lovely name," she smiled. "And where do you come from?"

"Koforidua, miss."

She chatted to each girl about her name, handing out the books and marking off each text number as Betty had instructed. The girls began to smile, hesitantly at first, then more broadly.

"Do you come from England, miss?" one asked.

"Yes, I do."

"Do you know my cousin? She's a nurse in London." The girls seemed to have a lot of cousins, sisters, aunts who lived in London.

"I'm sorry, I'm afraid I don't," replied Jess seriously to each request.

Jess glanced at her watch: she'd taken up about fifteen minutes already. She only had fifteen more minutes to read the first chapter to them and then ten minutes for the activity she'd planned. She did a quick mental adjustment, deciding to set and begin the activity in the lesson, and then they could finish it for homework. She hoped that would be OK.

She perched herself on the edge of the large wooden teacher's desk and started to read the book out loud to the girls. She glanced at their faces, concentrating patiently.

"Marley was dead. Dead as a doornail," she began, trying to sound dramatic.

At first she asked simple comprehension questions to assess that they understood what she was reading to them. They answered politely. Then she became aware of a certain fidgeting in the room. She looked up from her text and saw that Mercy, a beautiful little girl with big eyes, high cheekbones and close cropped hair, was waving her hand in the air, egged on by the other girls.

"Yes, Mercy?"

"Miss, miss. What is this *'snow'*?"

Jess gasped. How could they possibly understand freezing weather, ice, snow? All she had thought about was that she herself already knew the text. These Ghanaian girls would have no concept of snow, of England, especially of Victorian England. The context was totally strange to them.

Why was she reading Dickens to them? Why not African stories? Who were the Ghanaian writers? Surely there was something set in a familiar context and with recognisable issues that they could study?

Finally the bell sounded and the girls filed out of the room. Jess sighed with relief. *Not too bad.* But at break time she asked Betty if there were any other sets of books she could read with the class.

"The next text in the syllabus that they read is Pippi Longstocking," answered Betty, "It's a charming story. But *Carol* goes well this term as a prelude to Christmas."

"Pippi Longstocking? I don't know that. Where is it set?"

"Sweden."

"Sweden? Oh. I was thinking that a Ghanaian or Nigerian text would be better for them to grasp, and might be more significant to their lives?"

"We've always done mainly English texts. Sometimes European. They need to understand the culture."

"Why?"

"Well, England is the mother country!"

"But not anymore," Jess observed, "Ghana won independence in – what? – 1957, was it? Eight years ago. The old Gold Coast became Ghana then, so it's a different context." Then she noticed Betty's surprised expression and added quickly, "Oh dear, I'm sorry – I – I didn't mean to be criticising or rushing in to change things …"

"No, no, bless your dear soul …" mused Betty, thoughtfully, "maybe we haven't changed with the new ways. But we are a Methodist school with a missionary background, so this is engrained in our systems. English literature has always been a symbol of the best in literature. Dickens defines this. I don't think there are many Ghanaian authors. They look to ours."

"I don't want to interfere with the system but would you mind if I explore the idea, and research more local literature?"

"You can do the research, dear, but I don't think you'll find anything. Anyway, come back to me. I will need to monitor any different text, especially an African one – it may contain unsuitable ideas. And obviously we would have to buy a set of books, so it would be a question of whether we have the budget."

It looked to Jess as though no new texts had been bought for the first form for a long time, they were so battered, pages falling out, spines cracked. She had been embarrassed to hand them out to the class, although the girls didn't seem to mind; probably they were used to hand-me-downs, however privileged a group they were.

"Do the Dickens this term, then, and we will discuss the text for the spring term."

"Spring term", thought Jess, was odd, considering that Ghana doesn't have a spring season.

But she determined to scour the bookstores for more accessible texts.

The next time she went into Cape Coast town was two days later. Chrissie was driving in to call at the post office, so Jess went with her and tried to find a bookstore. There was only a Methodist Church bookstore, which didn't contain anything but missionary religious texts. She was told that she would need to try Accra for books. So that would have to wait until she could get a lift the sixty mile trip to the capital.

While they were in town, Chrissie showed her the box at the post office, where they collected the mail. She unlocked the box with her key and pulled out a whole pile of letters, many of them the blue airmail forms.

"Gosh," breathed Jess, "I didn't realise that "Box 61" was actually a box outside that you unlock!"

"What on earth did you think it was, then?" laughed Chrissie.

"I don't know! Maybe just the name of some safe inside the post office vaults, like a bank!"

Jess wandered around with Chrissie, watching the people, buying a stash of airmail letter forms from the post office, visiting the market. She took photographs of the market "stalls" many of which were simply stations where the market mammies had positioned themselves on the ground, with their large flat baskets of produce. A few were raised stalls made of upturned crates and wooden boxes, with produce stacked up high on the little platform.

Chrissie explained that the mammies grew most of the food for the family, raised chickens and goats, sometimes the odd cow, and always grew an excess for selling at the market for money to buy other necessities, meat, cooking and eating equipment, cloth and a few toiletries. She pointed out the baskets piled high with herbs and spices, some of which, she told Jess, they grew in their little patches of land and some they bought from the harbour straight off the container ships and sold at a profit to those who couldn't get to the harbour.

Jess smiled at the mammies with babies wrapped into the back of their traditional cloth, sleepy little heads flopping and bouncing with their mothers' movements. She watched them cooking chicken and fish to sell, pots over open fires at their side, exuding exotic scents of spices, oil and heat, ready for customers with their wooden calabashes to fill with the food.

Jess looked around her and marvelled at the jagged lumps of soap, the pots, and the cloths, the little mountains of plantain, fufu, and rice. She looked around the market and Chrissie pointed out eggplant, okra, chillies, ginger, tomatoes, dried fish, thyme and bay leaves. *So many new things!* Jess saw that the chickens that clucked around the baskets were sold "on the leg" and handed over to the purchaser who wrung the neck on the spot or swung it over her shoulder on a string.

But Jess also noticed that the children ran and splashed in the open drains beside the road, where the water ran with the blood of the chickens, and where the unwanted pieces of fish and vegetables were thrown. She saw that many of the children had appalling sores, open and oozing, on their legs and arms. Yet they splashed with the other children in the fetid water of the drains.

"Oh gosh," she murmured to Chrissie, "do you see that?"

"Yes," grimaced Chrissie. "It's awful. No wonder the kids get sick. And the tropical sores are a real problem. They spread all over their bodies and spread to other kids, of course. The poor, poor little things."

"What can be done?"

"Well, when I first came here, I set up a clinic at the two nearest villages, Ebubonku and Kakomdo. Just to treat the sores. But after a year or so, they stopped it."

"Who stopped it?"

"The school? The church? Who knows? Someone wasn't happy. Apparently I should have been focused on teaching Sunday School. Religion, bible stories, and so on. Safe things."

 ❧

"Would you like to help Glenda to organise the Village Sunday Schools, Jess dear, with a group of the older girls?" Betty asked. "You need to ask her about it, but I think she holds preparation classes a couple of afternoons a week in Activity Time after siesta, then goes out to the villages every Sunday."

Glenda seemed surprised when Jess approached her. "Right, well, if you think you can do it. I've got Guides to organise and Sandra's going to help me out, so you can take over Sunday School from me. But you've got to be firm with them."

She told Jess to organise a meeting with volunteers from the sixth form to go out to the villages on Sundays and to lead the first preparation meeting. She was quite happy to do that on her own and in her own way. So Jess gave out a notice at school assembly one morning that there was to be a meeting of interested senior girls in her flat at four o' clock that afternoon.

Jess wondered how Glenda usually ran the prep meetings but daren't ask her for fear of the usual sarcastic comments. She would offer the girls tea and cake as they talked. She had asked Chrissie if she could borrow a teapot and cups, with the intention of buying some as soon as she could get to Cape Coast again. Joseph, bless him, had offered to show her how to make a typical Ghanaian cake. The sweet rich aroma of banana and cinnamon still lingered in the tiny kitchen.

Jess waited for the girls to arrive at four. As her watch hand crept to nearly half past she began to think that nobody was coming. She paced the flat, frowning. Had she asked in the wrong way, maybe, or chosen the wrong time?

Then, six girls duly peered round the flat door at four thirty, and she breathed a sigh of relief. Clearly, they were on what she'd heard of as "Ghanaian time".

"Come in, come in," she ushered them in, as she infused the black leaves for a fresh pot of tea, and they clustered on the two chairs and the floor cushions which Jess had also borrowed from Chrissie, patient as ever.

"You all look lovely," Jess declared. The girls wore their sophisticated dress, all of them in their best cloth, hair neatly plaited and perfume liberally splashed. Obviously they had taken their time getting ready for the occasion. The girls reserved faces broke into shy smiles. "You must tell me about the traditional plaiting; it's fascinating."

"It's symbolic," nodded one, clearly the leader of the little group.

"It's Agnes, isn't it?" asked Jess, "the new head girl?"

Agnes nodded graciously, trying to hide her delighted smile.

"Well, you can give me a lesson in it some time," added Jess, pouring out the tea through the strainer into Chrissie's delicate gold-rimmed china cups. "Come on, help yourself to cake." The girls giggled shyly and filled their plates with cake. Jess took a bite of hers and closed her eyes at the rich buttery taste of the banana and the sweet spiciness of the cinnamon.

"Now, firstly please tell me what you normally do at the village Sundays?"

"Oh, miss, we tell them about Jesus," came the swift reply from Agnes wearing her best pious smile, and folding her hands primly in her lap. "They are very ignorant."

"I see," said Jess, "and what about first aid and practical help? What's needed?"

"Well, we tell the mothers to take them to the hospital at Cape Coast."

"Hmm ... and do they go there? Do you think that they might have difficulty in travelling to the hospital ... or in going to a big place like that at all?"

"Well, miss, they usually go to the village man instead."

"What village man?"

"The – the witch doctor, miss." The words were whispered and Jess realised that despite their apparent sophistication, these girls were afraid of the old customs, unsure whether maybe they should be respected.

"And what does the village man, the witch doctor do?"

"He gives them leaves to put on the sores and infusions and says things."

"Well, maybe we could try some first aid. It's no worse or less likely to work than leaves, infusions and incantations." She paused. "So shall we try?" The girls nodded hesitantly. "And what else could we do? Apart from telling them about Jesus. Something helpful. Could we teach them to read and write, perhaps?"

Agnes considered this carefully. "And we could teach them to count." The other girls following her lead murmured "yes, yes."

"OK, that's good. Now, what does Glenda – er, Miss Butterworth, do at preparation meetings?"

The girls glanced at each other. The Agnes said, "Miss Butterworth doesn't usually attend. She … she has other more important matters to deal with. Guides."

"So what do you do two afternoons a week, then?"

"Miss Butterworth says we must run meetings ourselves. We have a scripture book we read together. And we have to do prayers and … and then we do it again at the village school on Sunday."

"I see," said Jess. "OK. Well, you know things are going to be different this year. I aim to support you in the afternoon prep sessions and I'll be coming out with you to the villages on Sundays, too."

"Oh, miss!"

"So let's get on with preparing what we're going to do this Sunday. Now I can get hold of some simple texts, starter books, alphabet books or some such," Jess declared confidently although she had no idea at that time where she might acquire anything of the sort. "Or ... I – *we* – might have to make some."

The girls nodded. Jess had hoped that they might be a little more enthused about helping to paint pictures and write simple words, create posters of picture books for the village children. "I'll see what I can find for next time. Now ..."

Jess pulled out a box and opened it in front of the girls. She had begged and borrowed the box and its contents from various members of staff. She brought out a roll of bandage, a box of lint, some cotton wool and Germolene antiseptic cream.

"So, let's see what we can do with these."

※

Jess wondered and worried whether she had done the right thing. What would the folks in the villages think of her first aid, her attempts at care? These were people who really needed proper medical attention, and basic teaching, not just missionary bible teaching. Would they think she was some kind of patronising English girl with no idea of their customs, their beliefs, their practices? *Would they be right?*

Indeed she was aware of their suspicion when she first visited Kakomdo. She walked with the girls the short distance along the dry dusty dirt path through the bush from the school to the village. Along the way the girls swatted away the insects with their cloth and from time to time shrieked when one or other of them decided that they had spotted a snake in the undergrowth. Jess loved the walk, with mango and pawpaw trees overhead, the deep rich earthy smell of the bush and, as they approached the village, the smell of cooking pervading the hot air.

The village was a large group of mud-built huts in a clearing of the bush. Women paused in their pounding of fufu to stare at the visitors. Jess was aware of the children looking at her with puzzlement, intently watching from behind their mothers' skirts as the girls led her through to the centre of the village where there was a wide open area with a central building, a thatched roof borne upon wooden stilts. Benches were arranged in rows inside it under the shade of the thatch. Big dark eyes followed Jess as she entered the roofed area with her girls and settled on a bench at the front under the roofing. She smiled at her vigilant wary audience as she unpacked her tote bag. Little hands fingered mouths and from time to time swatted away flies from shiny faces. Thin little bodies with enlarged malnourished bellies hid shyly behind mothers who hesitantly gathered around the central thatch.

A tall plump man in Ghanaian cloth approached the thatch and said something in a grave voice. It sounded very serious and disapproving. Jess waited and smiled nervously. *Was he going to order them out of his village?*

"This is the village chief," said Agnes. "He welcomes you to his village of Kakomdo and will bring his children to you for teaching and healing."

"Oh, thank you," Jess nodded at the chief, "I am most honoured to be welcomed to your village and hope that we can help you in any way we can." The girls translated for the chief. "Girls, please tell him that I would be honoured to meet and help his children. Perhaps they could start by sitting at the front and the other children will follow their lead?"

The chief's serious face broke into a wide grin and he spread his arms wide as if to welcome Jess to the whole village. Whereupon all the children and the women crowded into the thatched area and settled on the benches with broad smiles. The chief ushered seven children of varying ages, probably, it seemed to Jess, from about three to about sixteen years old and they filed past Jess, nodding and shaking hands as they did so. They sat down on the front benches. The chief sat beside his children in the make-shift school.

Jess led the singing of some very simple songs in English then asked the group to sing in Fante. They happily sang a beautifully harmonious tune for her and she clapped delightedly. The villagers beamed. She taught some simple English: what is your name? My name is ... and so on. Then she asked them to teach her some Fante. That morning she learned *md-waase* (thank you) and *ete-sen* (hello). She asked them about the song she had heard as she arrived at the airport hotel.

"Oh, *'Mo'bo moden ny'adwuma'*," suggested one with a smirking sideways grin at his neighbour.

"And what does it mean?" asked Jess. But the group just giggled. Jess grimaced; perhaps it was something rude!

When the time came for the first aid session, and she and the girls brought out their nurses' boxes, an excited buzz arose. The chief and his children were the first ones in the queue, and women and children followed. At the end of the line one or two grown men presented themselves. Jess and the girls were kept busy for nearly two hours attending to tropical sores and chesty coughs, taking temperatures and advising about care. Many were not so sick but simply wanted to see and respectfully touch the "English lady" and her girls. The chief ordered the women to bring out cold fruit drinks and sweet sticky "pastries".

Finally everyone was spoken to, babies cuddled and children patted. Jess and the girls said their goodbyes and departed to the resounding cries of "bye bye, bye bye" until they disappeared into the bush.

Within a few weeks, they were greeted like old friends when they arrived on Sunday mornings, a group of children always coming out to meet them and lead them into the village. Jess began to notice details she'd missed before – like the fact that most of the huts were simple mud structures with earthen floors with kerosene lamps hanging outside. When she peered cautiously inside she saw pitchers and calabashes of water.

"There's no running water or electricity," Agnes explained, "The village folk can't afford such luxuries. They fetch all their water from the village pump, if there is one, or the river if not."

Jess indicated a woman cooking meat over an open fire outside her hut. "What's that?" she asked Agnes.

"Rat, I think," replied Agnes, peering at the skewer with her nose screwed up in distaste. "It'll be cane rat."

"*What!* Rat? They eat *rats*?"

"Oh yes, of course! It's meat and they're everywhere!"

Jess grimaced and watched the women bent double sweeping the earth floors and the dusty areas of dried mud around their huts with palm leaf brushes, the children following their mothers to the river with bowls on their heads to fetch water for the day's washing, and she thought of the baths, the taps, and the twin-tub washing machines at home. Even here she had a shower in the flat. Yet they were so keen to greet her and to learn when she came with her well-fed body and clean clothes on Sunday mornings.

The chief himself and his children, of which there seemed to be more and more each week, had already learned a number of basic English phrases, counting and days of the week, which they chanted in unison with beaming faces. Tropical surface sores had started to heal. And Jess had learned several Fante words and also how to prepare a groundnut stew.

But every week more and more children appeared at the thatch "to be healed" and Jess began to wonder whether they actually thought that the ointments were some kind of western magic. Some very sick children in dirty rags were carried from the dark interiors of the huts and laid gently on mats in the shade under the thatch. It stirred Jess's heart.

Sometimes, even out in the open air, the smell from the little bodies was nauseating and Jess had to cover her retching. Sweat, vomit, suppurating sores and diarrhoea, dilated stomachs of malnutrition, *kwashiorkor*, yellow-streaming eyes and noses. Small children too sick with vomiting and diarrhoea to swat away the swarms of flies that settled on their faces and skeletal bodies.

What could she do? She only had ointment and bandages. These children were in need of antibiotics, of vaccinations against disease. And of clean water to rehydrate them. It was the same story in both

Ebubonku and Kakomdo; both villages were in desperate need.

On the last Sunday of September, in Ebubonku village, a young mother approached Jess hesitantly. She was slim and elegant but clothed in a torn and faded cloth. In her arms lay her little girl. The mother did not lay her child on the mat on the ground as all the other mothers did, but instead presented her shyly to Jess, her eyes downcast, and placed her on Jess's lap. The girls translated for Jess and told her that the child's name was Amah. The mother's beautiful face streamed with tears. And her eyes as she raised them briefly to Jess were full of agony.

"How old is she?" Jess asked the mother gently.

"Five, six," the girls translated the mother's monotonous despairing words. The child looked about two at the most.

The child lay patiently on Jess's lap, too sick to resist, her stomach swollen with kwashiorkor, and she smelt of diarrhoea. Jess could only sigh powerlessly.

"How long has she been like this?"

"Since the last rains."

The young mother dropped to the dusty ground. "Please, please, what can you do?" she begged. "She is my only daughter." Slowly the story emerged, hesitantly, from the mother's lips. She came from a different village, fleeing her family. Jess wondered why. On the journey here with her baby, she had been raped by a stranger and left damaged, so hurt that she would never bear another child. The women of the village had not been kind to her and she lived alone in a hut on the edge of the compound.

In her awkwardness and embarrassment, Jess began to croon a soft song to the child. Not a nursery rhyme or a child's lullaby that she remembered her own mother singing to her when she was very little, but "Ain't Misbehavin'". What brought that to her mind, she had no idea. How silly she should think of that. She faltered.

The child's eyes glanced up at her. Slowly, slowly, her mouth spread into the sweetest smile Jess had ever seen.

But Jess had no idea what to do. "She needs to go to the hospital," she murmured to the girls, "or she will die." Hesitantly they translated this assessment to the mother.

"I cannot," said the mother, shaking her head, "I have no money for the journey or for the doctors or the medicines."

The mother, whom the girls told Jess was called Adwa, gently shook her head as if accepting that there was nothing that Jess could do for her child. She looked up at Jess from her crouched position at her feet and murmured.

"I will see what I can do," Jess promised, unsure whether she could even keep that simple promise. Who could she turn to, who could help this woman?

In Kakomdo, there was also a boy child, Kwame, weak and laid on the mat before her, disabled from polio. Jess knew that he could have been vaccinated as a baby, but there had been no doctors and no vaccinations. Immunisation from measles, polio and tetanus could save these children: these were preventable diseases back in England, but here they were still deadly to these little ones.

But the polio was not the immediate cause of concern to the thin, gaunt mother who brought little Kwame to Jess. He reeked of vomit and diarrhoea. He was feverish and dehydrated. Jess reached out and touched his forehead. He was burning up and was quite unable to raise his head or even a limb. Jess pulled a flask of clean water from her bag and poured out a cupful. She held it to the boy's mouth but he seemed too weak to swallow. When he gulped a little, what followed was terrifying to Jess. The little boy began to shake violently and judder, his whole body wracked with convulsions.

"Oh, my god," breathed Jess. "I'm afraid he's very ill. He needs proper medical help. The doctor, the hospital."

"He has the malaria sickness," droned the mother in flat tones, as the girls translated for Jess.

Please God, what could she do in the face of this huge need? She prayed that somehow something would turn up. All she could do for the moment was to give them some hope with her first aid and bandaging. But she knew that it was not enough. Not nearly enough to cope with malaria, malnutrition, disease.

An old woman, a cloth wrapped around her middle, her breasts drooping and flat, shuffled up to the little Kwame. She rattled off something sharp. Jess turned to the girls.

"She says that your god cannot cure him. They will bring him into the hut and they will watch him die."

The young thin mother and the old woman gently lifted the boy and carried him away, shaking their heads. Jess turned to the girls.

"How are they catching malaria?" she asked them. The girls stared at her.

"They don't have quinine tablets here. They don't have mosquito nets. Miss, they can't buy them, they have no money."

Jess knew that she wasn't qualified to provide medical help of the kind needed here. First aid was all she had to offer, and clearly this was not enough. She could not treat kwashiorkor or malaria. She could not provide medical drugs or vaccinate the children, and that's what they needed.

She asked around at the school but nobody could give her any help, any possible route to assist these people. Mostly there was a sense of inevitability that these children would not receive the treatment or preventative medicine that they needed. That they would die. That it was a matter for the Ghanaian government to deal with. And all the time Jess knew that even her meagre efforts might be stopped at any moment, as Chrissie's had been.

If only she could get vaccines brought into the villages, anti-malarial drugs like the quinine tablets she took every day, food supplements to combat lack of nutrition. How could people in this same world die for lack of basic needs? Basic food, medicines. Mosquito nets.

But she also knew that at least the first aid was something, albeit little, rather than doing nothing at all.

So far, by the end of September, nobody had said anything detrimental about her Village Sundays, and she kept going every week. She dispensed basic ointments and as much clean water as she and the girls could carry each time, just enough for the youngest and weakest of the sick children to wet their throats for a moment.

She watched Amah and Kwame grow weaker and their mothers more resigned. She kept her fingers crossed and waited, hoping for some kind of help to come to her. Someone to offer her something. Despite her enquiries, nothing had been forthcoming. Betty had told her that, with the best will in the world, it was not her job. That she could not solve the poverty and the sickness. It was too widespread a situation, and needed government intervention. It was not just Kakomdo and Ebubonku. It was all the villages all over the country. What could she, a teenage girl, do? No, she was a great help just taking first aid to the villages. She must focus on what she could do – first aid and teaching in the school.

And so life crept on: there were girls to teach, books to research. She knew that her Village Sundays had come to be regarded with some amused tolerance by the rest of the staff at the school. She also knew that few of them, apart from Chrissie who had given up, had ever ventured into the bush villages.

By the last week of the month, Jess managed to get into Accra to look for West African books. She and Sandra had hitch-hiked their way into the city, getting a lift from a Canadian teacher in Cape Coast all the way to Accra. Her mother would have a fit if she knew.

Jess finally, after much searching had found a bookstore in a Christian centre which also sold local items and African texts, in English. But they were adult novels by Chinua Achebe and Ngugi Wa Thiongo. Jess finally found a book of folk tales from West Africa, based on the traditional tales of Ashanti, but written in English. She bought a copy and decided to read some stories aloud to her pupils in class. It was all she could do. She felt disappointed that she couldn't present Betty with a suitable Ghanaian book to read with the first and second forms, as she had hoped, but there was nothing else she could do.

One night, at the end of September, Jess was sitting on her bed under the mosquito net as usual, writing the first of her regular weekly blue airmail letters, always the letter to Simon first, when she heard the drumbeats of Kakomdo swelling across the bush. It seemed louder and more urgent than ever before.

Dear darling Simon (she wrote),

Thank you so much for all your lovely letters. They are my treasures, my contact with you, with love and with our future together, my darling.

But oh dear, feeling very frustrated. No joy with the African books, I'm afraid. Do you remember that I told you in my previous letters I was trying to find something more appropriate for the girls to read in class? Well, I've searched everywhere I can think of with no success. Maybe when I return to England I can find some suitable texts or maybe organise the translation of Ghanaian books to send to Ghana. There must be some way round the problem. Surely someone could undertake a project like this, so that the children could read about their own culture and context? It's all so difficult here to find anything unusual. Although why it's unusual I don't know. One of those occasions when I really do believe I'm living in the back of beyond. I'm trying to help but I feel such a fraud. What could I possibly do to make any kind of difference here?

The teaching and Village Sundays are still going well, but there are many sick kids in both villages. Nobody seems able to do anything about it. There was a wretched-looking little girl in Ebubonku on Sunday, with chalk markings all over her body and strings of beads. They say that it's to ward away evil spirits. I understand that two of her brothers had died in the past few months, so they think that evil spirits have taken over the family.

Guides not so good – Glenda really cross that I don't prioritise that, but honestly, I'm so busy with everything else. If you want to know the truth (as Holden Caulfield says), I really don't like her that much and she sometimes freaks me out. But Betty is OK, and Clara, and Chrissie is lovely.

Harvest festivities and the procession were amazing although there were soldiers everywhere and someone fired a gun right behind me which was pretty frightening. Everyone laughed! More hysteria in class the other day. A gecko had scuttled through the room and the girls actually screamed and ran outside! I mean, there are geckos EVERYWHERE!

I told you about little Amah and little Kwame in my last letter. I don't know what to do and they are getting so weak. You couldn't even imagine ... I've asked everyone to no avail. I feel such a fraud here. I can only help in such a small way. Insignificant really.

Anyway. Great about the resit exam results. I knew you could do it. Wish you were here with me to see it all for yourself. Love you, love you, J xxx

The drumbeats swelled to a crescendo as the souls and spirits of the villages seemed to be gathering around her, then they softly died away, the barely heard voices retreating into the darkness of the bush. Jess felt disturbed, restless. Sleep, that night, came and went like the surging and dying of the wind.

3

OCTOBER 1965

One Saturday afternoon at the beginning of October, Jess returned from shopping with Chrissie in Cape Coast and walked in to flat 4 to see Sandra and two tall young men sprawled on the armchairs. One, thin and gangly, ginger hair and large round glasses sprang to his feet. He stared at her for a moment.

"Good God! Is she for real?" he drawled.

"Pardon?" was all she could squeak out.

"English! Gee ... A sweet pure little English girl in a prim white dress and hair all tied up neatly. Gorg-e-ous."

"Enough now!" came the deep rich voice of the second chap. "You're an idiot and an embarrassment, Hank!"

Hank shrugged his shoulders, laughed and said, "OK, I'll leave her to you then, lover-boy Jim!" Then he sauntered outside through the open doors onto the veranda, and Jess could hear him, still laughing, as he stomped down the dirt path. Sandra glanced at Jess, smirked, then quickly rose and followed him out.

"I have to apologise for my fellow countryman," said the one called Jim. He spoke with an easy assurance, stretching his arms above his head and linking his hands behind his neck, sprawling in the chair, long legs wide apart, "Although actually I don't really regard anyone from Utah as a fellow countryman!" He grinned. Jess noticed that he had a nice lopsided smile and that his teeth were amazingly white and level.

"It's OK." Jess sat down awkwardly on the other armchair opposite Jim, and smoothed her hair. "I just didn't understand what he meant. Anyway, I'm Jess – Jessamy Philips, by the way, from the UK, well, England, I should say. You get used to saying 'the UK' as everyone seems to say here. I came over at the start of September with Sandra ..." she petered out, knowing that, with his eyes on her, she was gabbling.

"Yes, I know, Jess," he smiled, "and again, I'm sorry if he startled or upset you. He can be a little ... abrupt." He leaned forward towards her and extended his hand. "Jim. James Kennedy." His handshake was firm.

She studied the man for a moment, taking in his dark crisp curly hair and smiling deep brown eyes, his strong lean body and tanned muscular legs in closely fitting khaki shorts. "So where do you come from, then, Jim? From what you said, clearly not Utah!"

"Washington DC," he grinned, "Greatest city in the US. Well, I think so, anyway. And you? Whereabouts in England do you hail from?"

"Oh, Birmingham. Have you heard of it?"

"Yeah, I guess so. City of cars like Chicago and bull markets like – like Spain?"

"Ah, well, I think you mean the Bull Ring. It's just a big shopping area now."

"A mall?" She nodded and smiled back at him. He had a deep gentle voice.

"So what brings you here to Ghana?"

"US Peace Corps," he said, "Hank and me – oh and a few others. We do a two year tour of duty. This is my second year. Then it's back home to med school again, following my dad. He's a surgeon at the local hospital. Brilliant guy."

How lovely to be so admiring of his father. How lovely to be able to be so.

"Have you liked it here?"

"Yeah, sure. You could say I'm pretty involved with things here. It's worthwhile. But I guess my mom would like me home. And Sherrie, my girl."

"You're a close family?"

"Pretty close. But I like to travel, see the world before I settle down. What about you? Close family back home, Jess?"

"Well," Jess hesitated, thinking of another of her mother's Rules: *"our family is the only thing you've got, Jess, don't ever criticise it or disgrace it"*. "I think my mother would like to believe so. They think I'm crazy, wanting to travel when home's good enough. They didn't understand. To me it was stifling."

"You needed to fly."

"Yes. Exactly!" Jess tried to explain about her Quaker background and how trapped she felt. "I just want to be like everyone else."

Jim smiled. "I don't think you'll ever be like everyone else, Jess."

Jess rather liked the way Jim kept using her name, as if he enjoyed the sound of it on his lips. She smiled at him and went to boil the kettle in the kitchen for some coffee.

As they drank the hot milky Camp coffee and Jess found herself telling Jim about the villages and what she had seen there, the concerns she had.

"Hmm," he murmured, "I don't know, Jess. I may be able to do something. Leave it with me. No harm in asking around anyway."

"Oh, that would be absolutely wonderful if you could."

They talked until the sun went down and Jim said he must go and find Hank for the drive back to Cape Coast. At the veranda door he hesitated and turned back, raking his hand through his thick dark hair.

"Hey, would you like to come over to Cape Coast sometime? Have you been to the castle yet?"

"No I haven't but I'd really like to. I've heard a bit about its history."

"It's very interesting. I thought you might like to see it. It's not pleasant but it's somewhere you just have to go … Hey, how about next Saturday? I've got to come over to the school with some stuff for Jack, the Peace Corps guy here. I can give you a lift in the Cadillac …" Jess raised her eyebrows in surprise.

"Sorry, just my joke. Actually it's an old battered pick-up truck. OK?"

"Well, yes. Absolutely. Thanks," said Jess.

Afterwards, she wondered with horror if he had meant it as a date. Oh gosh, she hoped he didn't mean it like that. She had Simon. No, it didn't sound like that. No, she was sure it was just a kindness. He was a friend, showing her an interesting place, that's all. No involvement like that. And why would he? She had told him about Simon and he had told her about his gorgeous girlfriend called Sherrie, back home in Washington whom he'd known virtually since childhood.

Finally, in the middle of that week, the message came that Jess's steamer trunk had arrived at Takoradi port. Only six weeks late. She was relieved that it wasn't lost at sea. And especially that she would have her personal belongings and some different clothes, having had to rely on wash and wear for such a long time.

When Chrissie heard, she offered to drive Jess the twenty miles to the port, as she needed to pick something up herself. She would borrow the school's truck as her own car would not be spacious enough for the hefty trunk.

"I'll come with you to the port authorities, Jess, but I'll need to make a diversion on the way back to see – er – collect something," explained Chrissie.

"OK, that's great," nodded Jess.

The road south west down the coast to Takoradi was rougher than the section between Cape Coast and Accra to the north east. The bush encroached closer to the highway and much of the road was crumbling and hazardous with potholes. As they neared the town, though, it became smoother and wider. The town seemed to Jess like a bleak sprawl of concrete buildings.

Down at the docks there was chaos, the deafening noise of cranes and machinery, the shouting of labourers and dockers, the crashing of huge metal containers on the concrete dockside. It was dirty, dusty and uncomfortably hot, the sun radiating cruelly off the hard ground. Jess felt rivulets of sweat running down inside her blouse. She had taken to wearing a long Ghanaian type wrap-around skirt and sleeveless top, not quite in local style but easier to feel the little breeze there was around her body. She could feel the sweat pooling under her arms.

Chrissie however looked, as always, cool and controlled. She wore a loose western dress, shift style, which still seemed to show off her shapely figure and slim legs. She moved smoothly and elegantly in her heeled sandals and spoke to the uniformed officials with ease and authority. Jess felt like a wilting sponge beside her.

They were ushered in to a stuffy crowded office to sign countless papers authorising her to collect her trunk. Jess was confused by the shouting labourers and slow lazy officials, who seemed to be shuffling papers around on the counter, peering suspiciously at the pages, then interrupting business with constant relaxed discussions with each other, marked by continual shrugging and shaking of the head. Every so often the officials would stroll outside to speak with the labourers, and then stroll back in again to continue their deliberations. There was much opening and shutting of drawers in the metal filing cabinets and speaking on the old grimy telephone on the desk at the back.

"Is there a problem?" asked Jess of one of the officials. "It's been six weeks, you know."

The man just smiled.

"Do you think there's a problem?" Jess asked Chrissie nervously.

"Shouldn't think so," responded Chrissie, "It's usually like this. A bit of self-importance, I think! Don't worry."

Eventually, one of the officials signed a paper with a flourish and pushed it across the counter towards Jess.

"OK," he said with a triumphant smile as though he had personally navigated difficult international negotiations. "You can now collect your box from hut A."

"Right, thanks," murmured Jess with relief. There was no explanation for the delay, but by this time, Jess just wanted to collect her trunk and get out of this place.

Two men in dark blue uniforms helped Jess to identify her steamer trunk, silver coloured metal with leather corner protectors and a brass plate and lock. They lifted it as though it were a light cardboard box and carried it over to the school's truck for her, hefting it into the back. Jess was aware of their eyes on her as she and Chrissie climbed into the truck and turned out of the dockyard.

Jess was glad to leave Takoradi with its bustle and noise. Chrissie drove back along the coast road to Cape Coast and then turned off into town. She glanced sideways at Jess.

"Do you mind wandering around town for an hour while I ... er ... see to my business?"

"No, not at all," replied Jess. "I like exploring the market."

Chrissie dropped her off at the side of the market. "I'll be back in an hour. Pick you up here again?"

Jess waved and watched her drive off. She frowned, wondering what business Chrissie had that seemed so mysterious. "Odd," she thought.

She whiled away the hour, investigating the stalls of fruit, vegetables, cloth and spices. She hovered by a cloth stall, wondering whether she should be bartering. She watched the other customers, large fat women inspecting the wares and cackling in staccato raw voices, much too quick for Jess to follow. She spotted a lovely printed material, in pinks and greys, with swirling patterns. Maybe she could get it made up into a skirt. She picked up a length of the fabric, fingering it lightly, and looked enquiringly at the mammy who squatted beside the stall.

"How much?"

The woman held up four fingers, pointing at each finger in turn with the forefinger of her other hand. "Four? Four cedi?" asked Jess. Was that expensive? Or very cheap? Her mind went blank, unable to calculate the currency. She was unsure, but she felt caught by then. Other market mammies nearby were sitting staring interestedly at her. How embarrassing. She counted out four cedi carefully and handed them to the woman who solemnly proffered the cloth.

As she turned away from the stall, she heard the muffled cackle of laughter and felt her cheeks flush hot. Clearly she had made some awful *faux pas*. She should have bartered. They had taken her for a fool.

She walked as far away from the stall as possible. Fabric tucked under her arm, she wandered some more, squeezing fruit, sniffing at spices, investigating old 45rpm records in tattered sleeves.

Eventually she began to feel impatient for Chrissie's return. It was well over an hour by now. But she couldn't feel cross, since Chrissie had done her a favour by taking her to Takoradi. She spotted a small dark café with a few old plastic chairs and tables outside, on the edge of the market, where a couple of Europeans sat drinking coffee. She crossed the road, jumping awkwardly over the open drain, and sat at an empty table. She ordered a Fanta and waited for Chrissie.

She saw her before she heard her cry, an unusually flushed and flustered Chrissie, hair mussed up for once, searching the market anxiously. "Jess! Jess!"

"It's OK," called Jess across the road, "I'm here."

"Oh goodness, I'm so sorry," Chrissie cried breathlessly as she ran towards Jess. "I forgot the time. Phew … I thought I'd lost you!"

"It's all fine," Jess reassured her, counting her coins into the little plastic bowl. "Are you alright? Did everything go OK? Did you collect whatever it was?"

Chrissie looked at her, confused, for a moment, and then seemed to gather herself. "Oh … oh, yes, thanks." She smiled, "All fine … Right, let's get back to school."

The following Saturday, Jim arrived to take Jess to Elmina, as he had promised. She was waiting on the veranda, gazing over the bush, counting the pawpaw trees which she now recognised, and wondering whether he would turn up, when she heard the sound of a horn down in the quad.

"Bye," she called to Sandra, who was in the flat reading a magazine her friend had sent her from England.

"Have a good time! Don't do anything I wouldn't do!" shouted Sandra with a laugh. "Ha ha! That gives you a lot of scope, eh? I'm going to Accra with Hank later, so maybe see you tomorrow …"

Jess thought that she herself really should go to Accra again soon and this time maybe catch up with Harriet and Sarah. She'd heard very little from them and often wondered if they were OK. Had they settled into their school at Aburi, as Sandra and she had settled into this place? It'd be nice to see them again, have a gossip. Although when she thought about it, they had never been close friends at school, Harriet and she. So maybe Harriet wanted to distance herself from her and establish a new identity, a new life, away from someone who would inevitably remember incidents from school. She well understood that.

She ran down the stairs and stumbled into Jim's arms as he unexpectedly came up the steps towards her.

"Oh, sorry," she stammered, her hand flying up to her mouth. Jim grinned at her with his lopsided amused smile, taking in her confusion.

"It's fine," he said, "I was coming up to collect you, ma'am!"

He held her at arm's length and looked at her face for a moment – a long moment it seemed to Jess, who felt herself flush. "OK, let's go," and he turned abruptly and took the rest of the stairs two by two, then strode over to his pick-up truck.

As he settled into the driver's seat, he gestured to a basket on the back seat.

"I thought we'd get a bite to eat on the beach afterwards … if that's OK with you, Jess?"

"Yes, absolutely, that's great. But I wish you'd said before – I would have brought something with me."

"Hey, it's only bread and fruit – not a fancy hamper from Bloomingdales."

"Well, even so …"

Jim turned to her as he turned the key in the ignition. "Hey, no big deal. Look, it's not a date, Jess." She bit her lip. He glanced at her again.

"You need to eat," he said sternly, although Jess detected a glint in his eye, "So do I."

"Yes, of course."

They drove in uneasy silence, and then Jim raked his hand through his hair and said, "Sorry, bad mood. I had a letter from Sherrie today."

"Oh. So, how is she?"

Jim glanced sidelong at Jess. She couldn't read his expression. "OK." His voice sounded strange and there was a distancing between them. Then he said with a forced jollity, "So, tell me about your trip to Takoradi."

Elmina castle was hot, crowded and noisy. There was a four piece band outside with guitar, bass drum, flute and goji. But somehow it seemed to Jess that the music was depressing, not the usual lively dance music that had become familiar to her since she had arrived in Ghana. This spoke of suffering and pain, hurt and cruelty.

"For all the colour and music and laughter you'll see and hear out here, this is the real history of West Africa," said Jim. "Slavery."

He guided her through the groups of youths at the entrance begging for money. "Dash, dash!" they demanded, not so pitifully as the little boys in the towns, more menacingly. For the first time, Jess felt frightened. Even in the heat of the burning sun, she shivered. While the music of the band sounded in her ears, she heard too the drumbeats of the night, pounding a rhythm that was unmistakeably ominous. She looked around her; there were no village drums in sight. Yet the low deep pounding was reverberating from the very stone of the castle walls.

Was it the same rhythm she heard at night from the villages around the compound? Or was it something different, strange: it seemed to her like the fearful anguished cries of beings in agony, terror, torment?

Jess felt shaken, dizzy. She looked around her wildly. Jim touched her arm.

"You OK?" he asked gently. She nodded and calmed her breathing.

There were three huge cannonballs in the courtyard within the castle walls.

"What are those for?" she asked Jim, and her voice sounded weird in her ears.

"This is where prisoners – slaves who were resistant – were chained for hours at a time in the full sun, unable to move. There was no respite from the heat. It pounded on their bare heads until they collapsed of exposure. They were left there, even after death, as a warning to the others," Jim explained grimly. "Until their bodies rotted and they were eaten by buzzards."

"Oh my god!" Even horrified, she was glad that Jim was being so blunt with her, talking to her without any concessions to her as a girl.

"See that door over there," he pointed. "The Door of No Return, it was called."

"It's a door?" gasped Jess. "But it's very narrow. How did anyone get through?"

"They were starved," he replied simply. "Inside was the death chamber, a cell about eight by eight. They were kept there in the dark. No window. No air. No food."

"So this," Jess looked around her at the bleakness of the castle, "was where the slaves were kept until they were shipped out to the UK and then on to the US?"

"It was. This was the shame of Africa. And of the western world who supported and sustained the slave trade." Jim grimaced. "Thousands and thousands of people lived and died here during that horrendous time. Can you imagine? Husbands, fathers, sons were rounded up in the villages in the bush, wrenched from their families, beaten with whips, chained together and brought here to be sold. They were marched maybe 150 kilometres down here from the north to the coast in the burning sun. At night they were tied up to trees so that they wouldn't escape."

"That's inhuman," gasped Jess.

"To the men who caught them, the slaves weren't human, they were animals."

"But surely if they were going to be sold, the slave traders or whatever they're called, would want to keep them in – well, let's say – good condition? That sounds horrid, but it's surely only logical?"

"I guess there were so many slaves caught that "wastage" was factored in. It didn't matter if some died, there were enough to sell – and frankly, it was all profit. They hardly spent much on food for them on the journey to the coast. They had the minimum to keep them alive and moving until they reached the castle."

"And I read somewhere that the slave ships were horrendous too. Lots of them died on the voyage."

"Well, I guess there were still enough to sell on again when they reached the UK and then the US, and still make a profit. They were packed in to the slave ships, you know. There must have been enough to supply the demand."

"For cheap labour."

"That's what it was all about. Labour on the farms and plantations. It was a culture of numbers, money, and profit. They weren't seen as human beings, just mechanical labour."

Jess shuddered. "Are you OK?" murmured Jim again, solicitously. Jess felt his hand on her back.

"Yes, just – I don't know – shocked, I suppose. Although I knew about the gist of it already. It just seems so particularly awful being here and seeing that it was – *is* – real."

She stared at the walls around her. What secrets they held within the hardness of the stone. Voices of the terrified, cries of the hurt, prayers of the grief-stricken, embedded in the rock for centuries. She felt nauseous.

"OK?" asked Jim again, bending towards her. She nodded. Jim cupped her elbow and guided her out of the castle. "I'm sorry. I can see you were really affected. I wish I hadn't brought you here."

"No, no. You were right to. It was, well, to say "interesting" is a bit weak. Stunning. But I'm glad I saw it."

"And felt it, I think …?"

"Yes," she whispered. How could she ever tell anyone at home what she had just seen and felt? Then she gathered herself. "OK. Let's get out of here."

The corrugated iron and rusted tin roofs of the living shacks led down from the edge of town to the beach. Litter strewn between them, open drains, some simply dug trenches carried untreated sewage to the sea. The smell was foul.

On the outskirts, these gave way to huts which were clearly shops for the beach-goers, the tourists and leisure-seekers. "Come, come and buy!" called the sellers as they gestured towards their kente cloth draped on the backs of old wooden chairs, masks, drums and dolls on display at the doorways.

Jess pointed at the truncated wooden "dolls", some painted black, some in polished wood, all with beads around the neck. The heads were pointed or squared off, the features of eyes, nose and mouth carved roughly on the blank faces. The torsos were all armless and cut off at the breast.

"What on earth are those?" she whispered to Jim. He laughed.

"They're fertility dolls," he told her. "I don't think you want one of those!"

"Certainly not!" Jess turned away, feeling herself flush.

Jim drove as far as he could beyond the huts to where the palm trees reached, bent by the wind, towards the sea. The sand was golden, the sea turquoise and the view idyllic. Jess stepped down from the cab of the truck onto the hot sand. She kept on her flip-flops otherwise her feet would burn she was sure. There was a slight breeze, and she felt the horrors of the castle starting to blow away. The sand was soft beneath her soles and she wandered a little way from the truck, looking at the waves breaking on the shore to her right, where the castle stood on the headland. She turned away from it and tried to focus on the gently swaying, sloping palms and the long narrow fishing boats pulled up on the beach.

"Hey there, dreamer!"

Jess swung round. Jim was carrying the basket to a perch of level sand under two palm trees. She trod the little hillocks of sand towards him as he spread out a rug and began lifting brown paper packages out of the basket.

"This is lovely," she declared, surveying the fresh baked flatbread, chicken, banana, mango and paw-paw laid on the rug. Jim grinned and, with a flourish, pulled out a couple of cans of lager. Jess mouthed her thanks and took the can gratefully from him. She thought of another of her mother's Rules: drinking was totally forbidden.

"Not quite French chardonnay or German Riesling," he said, "but I guess it'll do."

"Wonderful," Jess smiled, sitting down on the rug and sighing. "You'll make someone a great husband!"

Jim turned away so that she couldn't see his expression, but she knew that she had said the wrong thing. *Oh dear, my big mouth again, she thought, hope I haven't upset him. Maybe something bad has happened with Sherrie. Or maybe he's just missing her, like I'm missing Simon.*

Oh, Simon, I wish you were here to share this, she thought wistfully. *The experience at the castle. And this picnic, you would have loved to picnic on the beach ...* Or would he? He didn't like sand getting in to everything, food, shoes, fingers ... Jess remembered him saying that about holidays with his parents in Italy. *No, he wouldn't have liked it at all.*

"OK", said Jim loudly, interrupting her thoughts, and turning back again. "So, let's tuck in!"

After they had eaten, Jim moved the rug further under the shade of the palms, then went for a walk along the sand while Jess lay back on the rug and stared at the sky. She thought that it was the same sun that they would see in England, just as at night it was the same moon above them. That was somehow an odd thought. In a way it meant that home was not too far away, but yet in another way it reminded her of the vastness of the world and the universe. Her eyes slowly closed on the bright hot cloudless sky and for a few moments she could still see images of the brightness on the back of her eyelids.

She dreamed of Simon. They were in his car; it was dusk and he was driving her back home after a long day when he had taken her around to some of his old haunts, places that meant something special to him: a previous house where he had lived with his parents; the fields where he had built a den and played on his own as an only child ("and what about your friends?" Shrug.) How awful it must have been for him, constantly moving around with his parents, wherever his father wanted to take a new promotion, constantly having to make new friends wherever they fetched up. The loneliness and upheaval of it all.

"Oh, poor you," she had murmured to him, "It must have been awful. But you had good friends at school, didn't you? At boarding school?" and he had agreed, a little hesitantly. She had sensed his discomfort and touched his hand.

And then he had stopped the car abruptly, pulling onto the grass verge. He had turned to her.

"I think," he had said softly, "I think I'm falling in love with you."

She felt the gentle stroking of a hand on her arm. Reluctantly she opened her eyes and smiled up. It was Jim. She started, and shrugged off her dream. "Oh! Sorry, must have dozed off. Siesta time."

"Sadly I need to get back to the PC house."

"PC?" Jess frowned. "What's that?"

"Peace Corps House," explained Jim. "So we need to get on our way."

"OK, that's fine by me," agreed Jess, pushing herself up from the sand and picking up the rug to shake and fold. Jim carried the picnic basket back to the truck and Jess brought the rug. She returned it carefully to the back of the truck and climbed in to the cab alongside Jim.

They had not driven far along the coast road when, on impulse, she turned to Jim and said, "Thank you so much for today, Jim. I loved it!"

Jim turned to look at her quizzically, as if he was caught off guard by her enthusiasm.

"It's been a day of contrasts but wonderful all the same. I learned a lot at the castle and I loved the beach and the picnic and everything!"

"Great!" he smiled at her.

Suddenly he pulled off to the right along an unsurfaced track, as if making an instant decision. He pulled up in front of a large white-washed concrete building with an imposing portico and columns at the front door.

Jim pulled on the handbrake and turned to Jess,

"I thought you might like to see our HQ before I return you to your chaperones at the school!"

Jess looked around her at the hallway and stairs. "Gosh," she gasped, "it looks quite colonial!"

"Yeah, I guess it's the plantation style. I dread to think what went on here."

He led her into a large room with a grand piano in the corner. "Do you mind waiting here while I sort some stuff out? Be back in a moment! And I'll take you back to the nunnery – hey, sorry, the school."

Jess wandered around the room, inspecting the huge portraits on the walls. She thought that this was probably what the government buildings looked like inside. Or the homes of the slave owners. Very grand. And very much in contrast to the living huts and shacks in and around Cape Coast. She felt uneasy. Did Jim think of the privilege of being here when all around was poverty? Did he think of the implications of what they had seen at the castle and of what he had here, the horror of slavery and the wealth of the slave traders and slave owners?

The lid of the grand piano was open and she touched the notes absent-mindedly. She thought of Simon playing the piano for her. He was good. He played jazz and blues piano, pretty well, she thought, although she was no authority. It just sounded great to her ear. And because it was Simon with his long sensitive fingers touching, caressing, the keys. She loved to watch his hands. *What was it about a chap's hands?* Did she imagine him touching and caressing her with those same hands that made that wonderful music? He played blues, sometimes slowly and mournfully, sometimes exuberantly. And he sang those emotional blues numbers about longing for home or for his baby, those pounding beats about his mojo working. She could envisage him here playing this piano for her – *for her or for himself? Looking around for his audience, grinning at her, thrusting his face towards her, intense – hey, look at me ...*

Where did that come from? Jess started.

Then a sound behind her. Jim's voice:

"Do you play?"

"Oh goodness, no. My mother did. When she was a child. But she hated being forced to practise twice a day for an hour at a time, so much that she vowed she'd never inflict that on her own daughter," explained Jess, "so she didn't want me to have lessons."

"What a shame."

"Well, lessons are very expensive too," said Jess defensively. "There wasn't the money. But I sing in the choir. Actually my brother is really the musical one."

Jim was looking hard at her, his expression inscrutable. "Hey, singing in a choir isn't bad! Shall I play something for you?"

He sat down at the piano and spread his fingers over the keys. He was very still for a while. Then he started to play. There was no score on the stand. He played from his mind, and, it seemed to Jess, from his soul. He started with a low sorrowful version of the famous bluesy piece, Memphis Slim's Every Day I Have the Blues. Jess knew it because it was one that Simon used to play. But then he moved almost seamlessly into another, and Jess felt her heart fill with longing.

It was the most wonderful piece she had ever heard. Not jazz or blues this time, but a classical piece. The intricate notes ebbed and flowed over her and around her as she listened. It was literally breath-taking. Jess closed her eyes. The phrases were haunting, yearning. It embodied her longing for – for what? For Simon, for home, for something in her life she couldn't quite grasp?

The music stopped. Jess opened her eyes. Jim was looking down at the keys.

"Sounds much better on the clarinet," he said.

"Oh, gosh, no. I thought it was – absolutely amazing," she murmured, hardly daring to allow her voice to break the spell. "What was it?"

"Mozart's concerto in A, really for the clarinet, but I transcribed that bit for the piano. One of my favourites," he added sheepishly. "Sorry to inflict it on you. Just felt like playing it."

"I'm glad you did. It was lovely. What other pieces do you like to play?"

"Mozart is my favourite, I have to confess. I love the Requiem. And lately I've been playing a piece that's new to me. It's a choral piece but beautiful on the piano too. Faure's *Cantique de Jean Racine.*"

"Oh, I know it! We sang it at choir at school. Please play it for me!"

"You sure?" Jim hesitated. "You're going to be late back."

"Yes. Honestly. You play so beautifully."

The soft, low notes drifted gently through Jess's head, with the pleading melody filling her mind. She imagined herself singing it in the choir and found herself singing with the haunting strains of the piano. She was transported to a time before Simon, when she sang with the sopranos in the combined school choir. The boys' school and the girls' sometimes sang together for concerts. She found herself soaring, as if she was flying free. Her final note was soft and low, and Jim completed the last bars of the piece gently as her heartbeat and her mind slowed and settled.

"You're good," said Jim, "You ought to join the interschool choir in Cape Coast. It's schools' staff plus a few hangers-on, including me – Peace Corps but honorary member of the choir – mainly because I play the piano for them. You sing great."

Jess flushed. "Oh, no, I don't think so, but I enjoy it."

A flicker of amusement passed across Jim's face. "OK, then. You *enjoy* it great. But we're always on the look-out for new members, so think about it."

Then he closed the lid on the keyboard, stared at it for a moment, then looked up at Jess, raking through his hair again. "Jess … I was a bit abrupt earlier today. I told you I had a letter from Sherrie."

"Yes?"

"Bad news. For me. She's met someone else. She's started dating some guy back home." Jim shrugged. "Well, it happens. I've been away a long time."

"Oh, Jim. I'm so sorry."

"Come on. I'd better take you back."

It was the following week that Jess fell ill.

On the Wednesday afternoon she was walking back to the flat from the teaching block when she suddenly felt overcome with weakness and a rush of heat swept over her. She stopped abruptly, holding on to the wooden upright which supported the roof of the walkway at the bottom of the apartment block. She knew that she had to get up to her bathroom, and quickly. She gasped and ran, taking the steps two at a time, the urgency pushing her above the weakness of her legs. She struggled with the lock on the veranda doors, cursing Sandra for not being there to let her in, but thanking god that she wasn't as she staggered into the bathroom.

Afterwards she sat slumped on the bathroom floor, not caring about the cockroaches that she had seen again that morning, not capable of caring about anything at all. The toilet refused to flush any more. The sink was blocked. The smell was appalling.

"Oh god … oh god …" She could barely move her limbs. Everything was swimming before her eyes. The slightest movement of her head made her feel terribly nauseous.

Drained and feeling faint, she knew that she must crawl her way to bed and lie down. The room was swinging round, the walls of the small bathroom pressing in upon her. She pushed herself along the floor, groaning.

Somehow she found a bucket in the kitchen to drag with her. She felt so nauseated she didn't think she would ever stop vomiting. The heat was unbearable and she knew that she was drenched in sweat. Never had she felt so terribly ill. No – wait – she had experienced a fever as a child when she became hallucinatory. *Crying, gasping, swamped with terror, she's seen the bombs falling, shrapnel flying into the bedroom, no, numbers, numbers bombarding her, bricks, killing her… gasping, crying, yelling out save me, save me … and nobody comes …*

She didn't feel safe in bed but she did feel the softness beneath her, cushioning her fevered limbs and fiery brain.

Simon hovering over her, smiling down at her, kissing her forehead. Dance music. Louder now. The room sways and judders. Reaching up, her arms entwining round his neck, pressing him down to her, pressing her body into his. He's running his hands over her arms, her breasts, her stomach, thighs. She is liquid with wanting. Pulling him to her…oh god, she remembers. A bathroom. She feels sick with shame. She pulls back. And it's another girl giggling, hanging on to Simon's arm. Entwining her arms round his neck. Ready to do anything he wants. He's laughing with her. Over her shoulder, he looks at Jess. His eyes dark with scorn. It happens. You've been away a long time. Trembling. Nausea.

Nausea. Running out, away. Wrenching open the door. Footsteps on the stairs, creeping. Hurtling into a solid body. He's standing there. Her father. He's grinning, mocking. Silently.

Silently. A darkened bathroom. He's standing up in the bath. He's naked. Laughing at her shivering little body as she tugs her thin Cinderella cardigan closer around her. Scornful. Soapsuds and water sliding down his body. Downwards. His hands are moving rhythmically.

Bricks falling around her, flung towards her….loud rhythmic music pounding. Bombs. Mortars. Shrapnel. Desperately she looks around for escape. She's chained to a rock.

Drums beating, a rhythmic insistent beat, hammering into her head. Drumbeats retreating…returning. Talking drums. Telling her something. Something awful, horrifying, warning her. It happens.

Then Simon, stroking her face, whispering …

Dark crisp curly hair. It's not Simon.

Gradually, in time, she became foggily aware of someone in the room, whispering to her, touching her cheek. A deep voice. Reassuring and gentle.

"It's OK."

"Jim?" Her voice sounded oddly far away. She was so very tired. She couldn't keep awake.

Then later someone moving around the room. Hands wiping her forehead with a cool damp cloth.

"Oh you poor poor soul," came a soft low voice out of the fog. She struggled to open misty eyes to see Betty, bent over her, brow furrowed.

"Thank you," she murmured in a whisper. Every sound reverberated through her head like a violent loud noise. Her head pounded; she could hardly endure such intense pain.

She turned her head slightly and immediately her body was wracked by a bout of heaving, vomiting up nothing but bile. "Sorry," she whispered.

"Don't worry, dear," said Betty gently. "That's what happens with malaria."

"Malaria?" echoed Jess. She knew that she had taken all her quinine faithfully, and that her net was permanently secured over her bed. She even checked it regularly for any small tears that might let a vicious mosquito through. *But, oh my god, malaria! People died of it! Was she going to die, then – out here, in Africa?*

"Yes, a mild bout." *Mild?* Betty removed the bucket and mopped Jess's brow again. "I know it feels like death but you've been taking your pills. You'll recover. It happens all the time."

Betty was right. It took Jess a week to be able to get up, eat a little and walk again. In the meantime, on the Saturday afternoon, when she was sitting slumped in the armchair, trying to gather enough strength to fetch herself a cup of hot sweet tea (the only thing she could drink), while Sandra was out somewhere, she heard a deep masculine call outside from the corner of the veranda.

"Hi! Anyone at home?"

"Yes, Jim! Me! Come on round."

"And are you decent?" called Jim, "Or can I hope not?"

Jess laughed as he appeared at the veranda doors. He was dressed in his casual khaki shorts and white t-shirt, his thick dark hair rumpled. He carried a large box.

"Well now, that's what I call a pale face – white even." He looked at her and frowned. "Wow."

"You're really making me feel good," she grumbled, as Jim lowered the box to the floor and spread his tanned body on the other armchair.

"Do you need a doctor's opinion?"

"Oh, go on then," Jess demurred.

"Definitely unwell," he declared with a grin. "No seriously, Jess, you look in need of a little TLC. You've succumbed to a spot of malaria."

"Yes, but feeling much better now. I can even open my eyes without collapsing!"

"Poor old Jess," he smiled. "It happens. Even," he added as she opened her mouth to protest, "even when you're taking all the drugs. They're not 100% effective, but they do mean the attack's milder than if you weren't taking them at all – when, of course, the chances are that it'd be fatal."

"Oh, thanks! Well, I'm still here."

"I'm rather glad about that," he smiled. "Now look at what I've brought you." He started to open the box. "I've been working up in Hapa and Hamali on the northern border. I looked in, but I guess you wouldn't have wanted too much scrutiny while the D and V were at their worst. Thinking of a lady's sensitivities and privacy …" he grinned.

She remembered the sound of a deep male voice and the touch of a large strong hand. But maybe she had been dreaming, or it was part of her hallucinations. She didn't know what had been real in that awful time, or what had been part of the long dark nightmare. How sweet of Jim to understand.

"No, I wouldn't have wanted any chap to see me like that – wasn't too happy with Betty and Sandra being around. Although Sandra apparently made herself scarce."

Jess was suddenly all too aware that she hadn't even powdered her shiny nose or applied the little eyeliner she had left. But, then, she hadn't bothered much with make-up since she'd been here; it only slid off in the heat. And Jim had seen her bare-faced like that many times.

Jim lifted a record player out of the box and opened its lid. He unwound the cable and plugged it into the only socket in the room. He released the turntable and stylus from their palm leaf packing and took an LP from the box. Sliding the disc out of the sleeve, he carefully placed it on the turntable, and guided the stylus to the edge of the disc. The sweet joyful strains of Mozart's clarinet concerto, the allegro, this time actually played on the clarinet, drifted around her.

"Oh, Jim, thank you so much," she said. "How on earth did you get hold of all this?"

"The PC HQ is one amazing junk store," he grinned. "On loan for as long as you like."

He reached into the box again and brought out another sleeve she recognised, Faure's Cantique de Jean Racine, then the Requiem, and a Bach which she didn't know.

"And now I'm going to make you a drink." He stood to go into the tiny kitchen. "Hot sweet tea is my guess?"

How did he know?

Jess curled up more comfortably in the armchair and rested her head on the padded upholstery while she listened to the comforting sounds of Mozart and the clinking of china in the kitchen.

※

"Jim ...?" Jess was trying to catch up with her marking and lesson preparation after her enforced absence for a couple of weeks recovering from her bout of illness. Sandra had gone to the beach with Hank. Jess had noticed that her friendship with Hank had become more intense lately and also that she had not been writing so many blue airmail letters. Unlike Jess who wrote faithfully to her family and to her beloved Simon every week and received letters back, although often they were delayed in transit and arrived haphazardly.

Jess still felt weak, but needed to get back into the classroom and take lessons before she forgot how to do it. Her first day back in the classroom was tomorrow. Her classes had all sent her up hand-made cards and some individual pupils had placed small gifts of fruit and yams at her door. "Jim?"

"Yep?" Jim looked up from the papers he had spread all over Jess's living room table. He sat with her quite often through her convalescence, quietly getting on with his own work as she dozed or read her books. John, their new houseboy, who had taken over from Joseph, would frown at him and in sullen silence move around the flat doing his housework, cleaning, washing, taking orders for the shopping. He seemed to be suspicious of Jim, but whether it was a general dislike of white males, or something personal, Jess didn't know. After all, John was glum with her too.

"You know when you acquired the record player and vinyls for me from PC HQ?"

"Uh huh?"

"Well, what else can you *acquire*?

"Like?

"Like anti-malaria pills and mosquito nets ... Vaccines? Food supplements?" suggested Jess tentatively, thinking of Adwa and her little girl Amah – and the many others.

Jim looked over at her and smiled. "Ah, I heard about the kids." He put down his pen and rubbed his temple. "You asked me before and I know I said I'd look into it. I did. But, it's difficult, Jess ... political stuff. Americans have to be careful here. It's not as easy as you might think. And there are many kids, hundreds, thousands. In every village. In every hut. How can you hope to help them all?"

"But if we could help just one village ...? Just a couple of kids ...?"

"Hell, Jess – it'll never be enough. You have no idea of the issues, the problems." He paused, contemplating Jess's eager face. "Look, I may ... *may* ... be able to get hold of some nets, at least for the huts where there are kids. I don't know about anything else. Vaccines, no. You can't just dispense vaccines without proper authority. Quinine, again, I don't think so."

"But you have the medical squad and supplies."

"Yes, but they're all earmarked by the US government agencies for specific projects. That's how we work – on specific government chosen projects. And anyway, you're talking long-term daily supplies." He paused. "Jess, you really can't interfere with political situations; you have to be sensitive. You can't just grab a load of drugs and dispense them all over the place!"

Jess frowned. "Oh!"

"Hey, listen, I'll see about some nets. Can't promise. But I'll investigate."

Less than a week later, Jess was in the middle of a lesson with her second year girls, teaching creative writing, when a figure appeared in the open doorway of the classroom. At first she couldn't make out who it was, as the sun was casting the figure in shadow, then, as he stepped forward in to the classroom, she could see it was Jim holding up a set of car keys.

"Sorry to interrupt," he said without formality, "But when you're ready, there's a truck full of nets in the yard." He tossed the keys across to her, grinned, and retreated through the door into the glaring sunshine again. The class erupted with shrieks and questions. Jess ran to the door and watched Jim walk away to the yard.

"Is that your *apache*, miss?"

"No, that is not my 'apache' – er, boyfriend. Shush. Girls – sit back down!"

"He's very beautiful," called out Charity. "Are you going to marry him, miss?"

"Who is he? Who? Who?" thirty girls shouted.

Jess sighed. "He is a good friend who has been kind enough to find some mosquito nets for the village."

"Then we must go thank him!"

"Not right now," Jess insisted firmly. "Sit down and let's finish the last five minutes of the lesson in peace and quiet."

Afterwards, Jess found Jim bundling mosquito nets into piles in the back of the truck. There looked to be dozens. Her face lit up with joy.

"I knew you'd do it! Thank you so much. You're a marvel."

Jim shook his head, but Jess caught the pleased grin. "OK, you can do me a favour in return."

"What's that?"

"Join the choir."

The following Sunday, Jim was able to help Jess deliver the nets to Kakomdo and Ebubonko. They had divided the supply carefully in half and spent an hour at each village demonstrating how they were to be set up over the mattresses. They showed the chiefs and the most important men of each village how to use the nets and explained how they would work to avoid malaria.

"Ah," nodded the men sagely, and the girls translated the gratitude of the chiefs for such a generous gift to their people.

"Thank you, thank you," repeated the chiefs and the men. The women looked on quietly, staying at a distance.

In Kakomdo, Jess noticed the figure of Kwame's mother amongst the crowd. She turned to Agnes.

"Could you ask her about Kwame. How is he?"

Agnes approached Kwame's mother and Jess watched as Agnes spoke to her. They seemed to be having a heated exchange, and then the mother abruptly turned and walked away.

"What did she say?" asked Jess anxiously as Agnes returned to her side.

"Kwame is dead."

Jess had to fight her tears as she walked back to the school. Jim had to take the truck back to town, but before he drove away, seeing her distress, he had said gently, "I'm sorry about that little boy Kwame." He shook his head. "There are so many like him. But hopefully the nets will help to prevent more deaths. You've done all you could."

But Jess could not erase the image of sick helpless little Kwame from her mind and it was a very long time before she stopped wanting to cry.

In order to ensure that she fulfilled her part of the bargain, Jim came to pick Jess up the following Friday evening at six to take her to the choir rehearsal. She had bitten her mouth into crevices.

"I haven't sung in a choir for yonks," she complained.

"*Yonks*?" He imitated her accent. "What? Is that some quaint English expression?"

"It just means "a long time" – so, watch it, Jim!" she smiled.

"OK, just teasing. You'll enjoy it. There's no pressure, just enjoy."

"And you're sure there's no try-out? No audition?"

"No," he smiled, "Anyway, I already told them your voice was great, so you're in. We really need some good new sopranos."

She was very surprised when she first walked in to the hall, though, as she spotted Chrissie across the room. She was engrossed in deep conversation with a man Jess knew to be another member of staff at her school. He was a science teacher from Scotland, Angus, who lived with his wife in one of the staff bungalows on the school compound. Jess knew that Angus also did some research work at the university college in Cape Coast where he had an office in the science department.

There were no other members of staff of Jess's school at the choir rehearsal, so Jess chatted to a girl Jim introduced her to, who was teaching at another school in Cape Coast. She was also a second soprano so they sat together in the section and Jess felt as though she was amongst friends. Jess was pleased that there was a good sized men's section, a strong tenor and base presence, as she liked to hear the male voices in a choir, providing a deep contrast to the ladies'. Jim sang too, as well as accompanying the choir on the piano: a rich deep tenor voice. *Wow, he was good!*

Choir rehearsal was indeed enjoyable and as Jess already knew several of the pieces they were preparing for the Christmas concert, Handel's And the Glory of the Lord, and three Christmas carols, A Maiden Most Gentle, The First Noel set to Pachelbel's Canon, and Silent Night, she felt quite comfortable and at ease. She remembered how much she loved singing in a choir, voices blending, listening out for the others around you, working together as a team. She hadn't sung since she started going out with Simon. He didn't sing in a choir, the thought horrified him. He sang only when he played blues piano, doing his own thing. But Jess loved losing her individuality to the choir, melding her voice into the whole.

Jim's piano accompaniment was wonderful, of course, and Jess did allow herself to feel a rush of pride that she was acquainted with him, she was his friend. At a couple of points he openly winked his encouragement at her and she flushed hot with pleasure at his contact and his remembering that she was there. That was nice of him.

She noticed how well Jim picked up the phrases that the musical director, Rose, had wanted different choir sections to repeat throughout the evening. He was so confident and competent in his role, Jess envied him his certainties.

The younger female choir members laughed and giggled at every joke he made and every deprecation when he got momentarily lost in the score. They nudged each other and she over-heard one say, "God, he's so hot!" Jess's section was near enough to the piano for her to sneak glances at his hands as he played. His hands were larger and stronger than Simon's but as sensitive and gentle on the keys, and he played with assurance and authority, his eyes fixed on the keys, his brow furrowed as his hands moved briskly, his white shirt open at the neck to reveal dark chest hair. She could understand his appeal to the girls. Actually, he *was* really quite sexy.

By the end of the evening, Jess realised that she had not spoken to Chrissie or Jim at all, even in the brief interval. Chrissie disappeared outside for the ten minute break, and Jim was talking to another girl, who, Jess noticed, giggled most of the time, trying out some phrases and intros with her.

Jess was wandering out of the door at the end when she felt a hand on her shoulder. She glanced round. "Chrissie! I hadn't realised you belonged to this choir," she exclaimed, "Actually I didn't realise there *was* a choir until very recently."

"Oh, well, yes, I come along to ... but I didn't know you sang ..." Chrissie clutched her music to her chest uneasily.

"It's nice that Angus sings in the choir too. I guess you can share lifts?"

"Yes ... er ... listen, I'd offer you a lift – only ..."

"Oh, gosh, no, that's OK, Jim has told me in no uncertain terms that he will pick me up every week. I think he imagines that I will abscond if he doesn't!"

"Oh, right," Chrissie's face relaxed into a smile. Odd. Chrissie was usually so generous with offering lifts into town, into Cape Coast and even Accra. She had even taken her to Takoradi to collect her trunk from the port that time she had business in Cape Coast.

"Are you ready to go?" she heard Jim call across the sea of singers making for the door. An awful lot of eager female faces turned but their expressions dropped into disappointment as Jim approached Jess.

"Ah, your chauffeur awaits," smiled Chrissie, and she waved, disappearing into the darkness.

※

The following Sunday, Jim was not with her when Jess went to the villages for her weekly clinic and class. She visited Ebubonku first, hoping to see little Amah and her mother.

As she walked from the bush path into the village clearing with her girls, Jess sensed a scurrying away into the huts around her. She looked around. Where were the women? The men were there already, standing under the palm roof, and most of the children. The men looked happy. And expectant. There was something odd that Jess couldn't quite place.

There was a rustle of anticipation and heads turned to watch the chief arrive.

"Come, come," he beckoned to Jess. She and Agnes walked with him beyond the huts to the large communal patch of dry earth where the women grew their vegetables and fruit. There the women were standing silently.

The chief gestured to the vegetable patch. Jess could see plainly that the crops were surrounded and covered with mesh.

The chief spoke and Agnes translated, "He says that it will keep away the vermin."

Jess stared at the mosquito nets carefully skewered into the ground.

※

Later that night, back at the flat, sprawled on her bed under her net, she wrote:

Darling Simon,
 Bad day. We managed to get some mosquito nets for the villages, but they destroyed them by tearing holes in them and using them for the crops. No use now.

Yes, thanks, I'm fully recovered from the bout of malaria. Apparently it was very mild although it didn't feel like it! No need to worry. And no, I won't come home – I do want to see it out. So, really, don't worry.

But good to hear all your news about uni and your friends. Glad about you becoming editor of the college newspaper. You seem to be very busy these days.

Yes, I did finally get my steamer trunk from the Elder Dempster shipping line at Takoradi. Six weeks, would you believe? God, how I've managed for all this time, I just don't know. I think they just mislaid it. How lovely to have books and changes of clothes here now. I can now read Catcher in the Rye again and think of you.

Went to Cape Coast castle, Elmina, monument of the days of slavery. But the awfulest thing was the fact that there were families living in cardboard shelters around the walls. The smell was appalling. They have to wash themselves and their clothes in the open drains and the polluted river. They cook on little fires at the side of the drains. Children all over here are malnourished and sick. We went on to the beach outside the town and I never felt so relieved to smell the fresh air and see the sand, the sea and the fishing boats and surf boats all pulled up and lined on the beach, nets spread out to dry. It was just lush after the castle.

We are so rich by comparison. Yet these people are happy and welcoming and would gladly share absolutely anything with you, their last crumb. We could do with some of their generosity in the UK (sorry, getting used to saying that instead of England)

I told you about Amah and Kwame in my last letter. I'm afraid that Kwame has died.

Had another bust up with Glenda. That woman makes me see red. She's so patronising and brusque and unsympathetic and scathing and she clearly does NOT like me. Sandra is spending so much time with her on Guides and such like that I think it's rubbing off on her too. Oh dear, enough of my troubles.

I shouldn't really say this but Sandra's also spending time with an American Peace Corps guy called Hank from Utah and I think there's something going on. She's got her boyfriend Colin at home too, it's not as if she's unattached. I'm making her sound like a femme fatale which if you saw her you'd know she most certainly is not. I think it's awful, don't you? I mean I'd never ever be unfaithful to you – gosh, I don't mean that they're necessarily actually sleeping together (I don't know), but it's still betrayal, isn't it?

Anyway. What's all this about the Moors murderers that you mentioned in your last letter? And what did you mean about your reference to Khrushchev and Yuri Gagarin? Good grief, they'll be walking on the moon next.

Oh there's another Peace Corps guy here besides the awful Hank I told you about last time, called Jim, very helpful and all that. But I wish it was you here. I long for your letters to keep me sane. Lots of love, J xx

She sighed. Her letters were becoming more curt and disjointed, somehow, and she had difficulty giving details as she had before, when she had first arrived in Ghana. She was acutely aware that letters took so long to be delivered that today's news was last month's impressions. Sometimes she received nothing for three weeks and then all three arrived together. Like Birmingham buses. And then they got completely out of sync with each other's feelings. She tried to respond to what he had said in his last letter but she knew that he had moved on since writing it. It was so difficult.

That evening the drums were loud and their insistent beat pounded in Jess's head until late into the night. She tossed and turned, unable to settle to sleep. And when she finally drifted into slumber, her dreams were garish and crowded.

4

NOVEMBER 1965

At the beginning of November, a note from Harriet and Sarah arrived unexpectedly.

Jess tried to correspond since they all arrived in Ghana, but with little success, other than the odd note which was full of Harriet's conquests in the boyfriend department. Through various casual acquaintances, Harriet sent her and Sandra a couple of vague invitations to visit them in Accra and to join in their parties.

But neither Jess nor Sandra really felt the need, nor had the time, as they had plenty of work and things to do in Cape Coast. But Harriet had clearly decided that they were in desperate need of fun.

"Don't be so unsociable!" Harriet wrote this time, *"You miserable pair! Both of you MUST, I INSIST, come to the party at Legon next weekend. I'm not taking no for an answer. For god's sake, Jess, grow up and get a LIFE!"*

Jess frowned. What did she mean? She showed the invitation to Sandra with a sigh.

"I suppose I'll have to go – if just to keep her quiet," remarked Jess, biting her lip as Sandra read the note. "But, don't worry, *you* don't have to go. She's my ex-school-friend, not yours."

"Oh, I'll come too," offered Sandra, although without much enthusiasm. "I've nothing better to do. Hank's away up in the north next weekend so I could do with the company – especially if you're away as well. But why Legon, I thought they were at a school in Aburi?"

Jess explained that, in a rare note a few weeks ago, Harriet had referred to her becoming friends with some of the university students and lecturers at Legon University. She had seemed quite full of it, especially the lecturers who must have been years older than them. She had enthused about one such chap called Rafik, who was a senior lecturer in economics and politics. He sounded very clever and impressive. He was "an older man (wow, 36!!!)" Harriet had written, and apparently very important in the Legon community. Harriet called him "Rafe" and had mentioned him in just about every sentence.

"It'd be interesting to meet him," said Jess. "What sort of chap would Harriet like, I wonder? And what sort of chap would go for Harriet? Quite intriguing!"

"So what was Harriet like at school then?" Sandra looked up from her papers and sucked at the end of her biro.

"Oh, Quaker family, quite a famous family, I think. Well behaved at school, did all the right things, the darling of the teachers. Became head girl. Very popular."

"But what did you *really* think of her? C'mon! Dish the dirt!"

Jess giggled. "Well, actually, she was stern, disapproving, rather – oh what can I say – prissy. Pious."

"God, she's changed a bit, then?" Sandra snorted.

"Yes, looks like it." Jess grimaced. "I don't relish the thought of a party with a load of people I don't even know. But we'll probably never see any of them again."

So it was to be, then, they would hitch-hike lifts up to Accra on the Friday afternoon. They'd done it before and it was perfectly safe for the two of them together, even Betty had confirmed that. The Ghanaians were known to be respectful of English girls, and only too willing to share any free space in their cars if they wanted a lift. They didn't trust each other, but they trusted and honoured the English, rightly or wrongly. So there was never any problem about hitch-hiking here. She'd keep it secret from her mother, though.

The agreed plan was that they would meet Harriet at the apartment at Aburi School where she and Sarah lived.

"Oh, you're here at last," said Harriet as she opened the door.

Jess glanced at her watch. "Um, we did say about four o'clock – didn't we?"

"Oh, whatever," shrugged Harriet, standing aside to let them into the apartment. It was a lovely apartment, so much more luxurious than flat 4. Jess noted the smart comfortable chairs and sofa, the burnished coffee table, the gleaming wooden flooring.

"Gosh, this is lovely!" she said to Harriet.

"It's adequate," she shrugged. "Nothing like as lush as Rafe's at Legon."

"Well, it wouldn't be, would it?" Jess checked herself. "I mean, presumably his is a senior lecturer's apartment? Goes with the job?"

"Mmm. But they could at least give us something decent. I suppose you want a coffee?"

"Where's Sarah?" asked Jess, watching Harriet moved languorously around the kitchen while Sandra settled on the sofa. Harriet brought two mugs of coffee into the living room and placed them carefully on the mats on the table. She turned to the sofa and plumped up the cushions which Sandra had moved, arranging them again with careful deliberation. Jess sat on one of the chairs which didn't sport a cushion.

"Oh, she's gone to the beach with her boyfriend for the weekend." Harriet draped herself decorously over the other chair.

"Ah – so she's not going to this party tomorrow then?"

"No. Her loss." Harriet looked irritable.

"Are you not having a coffee?" Jess asked.

"I had one just now with Rafe," said Harriet, "He's gone back up to Legon. Had to take a class tonight. I'd have gone with him, as I usually do on a Friday night, but I had to wait for you. May as well stay here tonight now, and go up tomorrow."

Jess tried to ask Harriet about Aburi and her work but she seemed oddly uncommunicative, and the conversation was stilted and awkward. Jess felt her stomach grumbling as they had not had the time to eat properly at lunchtime after classes. Sandra was clearly feeling the same as she suddenly cut in,

"Does your houseboy cook dinner?"

"Oh, I'm not bothering with *supper* tonight, "said Harriet, "Rafe and I had lunch late so I'm just going to have some fruit. I'm dieting anyway, Rafe thinks I'm too fat."

Jess looked at the tall slim Harriet, and didn't know whether to feel sorry for her or angry with Rafe.

"Well, I'll have to eat," complained Sandra, "I'm starving."

Harriet shrugged and told them that there might be somewhere in Accra where they could get something. Sandra and Jess had to call a taxi to take them into Accra to find the airport hotel which was the only place they knew they could buy dinner.

That night, Jess and Sandra were assigned the sofa which pulled out as a bed and a chair with a footstool pushed up to it. All night Jess struggled to keep chair and stool together, before giving up in the early hours and settling down on the hard floor instead.

"Don't know why she invited us up here," grumbled Sandra before snuggling up under the quilt Harriet had finally produced.

In the morning, Jess struggled up from the floor feeling bruised and heavy with sleeplessness. She hesitantly went to find coffee in the kitchen, unsure, as there had been no invitation to help themselves. By about eight o' clock, Sandra had roused herself and staggered into the kitchen, grumbling. She accepted Jess's offer of coffee and returned to the sofa with it. Jess noticed that she deliberately squashed the cushions and balanced her mug precariously on the sofa arm. She smiled behind her hand.

Harriet finally emerged from her bedroom by lunchtime.

"There's only bread and jam," she called, "The boy doesn't come on Saturdays."

Harriet was anxious to get to the university campus at Legon, and she went to the school's office to telephone Rafe. He sent a taxi to pick them up and when they arrived he appeared at the door, a surprisingly small but suave eastern European chap with a goatee beard and wearing black from head to toe. He pecked Harriet on the cheek she offered, but ran his hand over her bottom. He courteously shook hands with Jess and Sandra, but Jess noticed that he greedily swept his eyes over her body as he greeted her. Then he ushered them all into his living room. It certainly was beautiful, as Harriet had intimated. All plush white leather L-shaped corner seating, shining glass tables and unusual gleaming gold artefacts.

The room was full of people. Jess glanced around. All men, eastern Europeans like Rafe, lounging comfortably, draped over the sofas. They were all smoking. Jess was used to the smell of Simon smoking sometimes but these cigarettes made an odd acrid woody smell in the room. The loud talk was in a language Jess couldn't identify. Harriet disappeared with Rafe.

Sandra glanced at Jess with distaste. "God!" she muttered under her breath.

Two of the men politely stood to offer the girls room on the sofas. "Come, come," they mumbled but smiled and sat too close.

Jess could not have been more relieved when a couple of women joined them and began to address them in perfect English, asking them about their work in Ghana. By then the men had decided to join the conversation, also in heavily accented but perfect English. The men were dressed in elegant suits and the women looked glamorous and rich, gold jewellery on glossy dark skin, artfully draping silk dresses that rippled over their tall svelte figures. They were all beautifully made-up as though they'd spent the day at a beauty salon. How did they manage to keep it fixed and fresh in this heat? Jess licked and bit her lips to try to make them look a bit better. She wriggled in her strappy cotton top and long skirt. Her outfit had seemed party-ish that morning but now felt dowdy and inappropriate. Harriet had not seemed to "dress up" either so Jess had not thought anything about dress code.

Finally, Harriet and Rafe returned to the living room, each bearing a dish steaming with delicious-smelling food. Harriet had changed into an elegant jade silk gown with an Indian-looking scarf scooped across her shoulders. She had put on mascara and lipstick, although Jess noticed that it was a little smudged. But she looked much more cheerful. They had probably had a good chat in the kitchen.

"Harriet ..." Jess began, wondering what the schedule was.

"Oh call me Harry – I'm Harry now!" laughed Harriet, too gaily and sharp, glancing conspiratorially at the elegant women. "God, you're so ... so ... conventional, *Jessie*!" she added irritably. Jess wondered why she was taking that tone. How odd.

Jess, who had never been called Jessie in her life, winced. It sounded to her like an old woman, and she was sure that Harriet meant it to. Someone old and plain. The glamorous women laughed.

"Now *you*, Harry, you look so beautiful today especially!" drawled one of the women, tossing her long back glossy hair.

"Dear Harry, so ... so *natural*," smiled one of the women graciously. The other woman nodded knowingly, "And glowing."

"Mmmm, thanks to Rafe!" They laughed again. Jess caught a look passing between them.

Rafe ushered in his houseboys, two of them, who brought a further host of dishes to arrange on the large table at one end of the room. They brought round trays of glasses filled with wine and dishes of small sticky pastry bites.

"Oh well, may as well," boomed Sandra, grabbing a wine glass and a handful of pastries. "This is getting a bit more like it!"

"Come and help yourselves," invited Harriet, sweeping her glance round to everyone, graciously gesturing to the table, "As soon as you're ready."

The eating seemed to go on for the rest of the day and evening. Sandra piled up her plate and kept going back for more. She seemed to have an endless capacity. She occasionally spoke to someone but mainly just sat and ate.

Jess enjoyed the meats and sauces, and the fragrant rice dishes, but found it difficult to balance her plate and glass although she tried to remember those lessons at school about how to look elegant at a cocktail party. She tried to talk to as many people as she could, although there were not many she felt comfortable enough with to stick with for any length of time, and found herself moving on after only a few words.

There were a lot of lecturers there, who seemed to want to engage her in heavy debates about subjects she wasn't the least bit interested in and didn't know anything about. There were also economists, engineers and a couple of politicians. She tried to be polite and listen to them but she found it increasingly difficult to follow the drift of the arguments. These people clearly shared their ideas frequently enough to understand the others' subtle asides, and Jess felt an outsider. Often she found herself in the middle of a group of people raising their voices excitedly about engineering projects or driving roads through the bush or the president's latest speech. She thought it best to just stand there and make agreeable noises.

But one topic caught her interest. She heard the name Akosombo and pricked up her ears. Jim had mentioned it to her not long ago, but told her to be wary of discussing it. The engineers were talking about the Akosombo dam project which seemed to be very important and the topic of much speculation. Jess knew that it was a hydro-electric plant which Nkrumah had sponsored. Yet the electricity even on the school compound was unreliable to say the least.

"So why are there kerosene lamps everywhere in the villages then?" asked Jess innocently. The group laughed at her and shook their heads.

"It's not for the Ghanaians!" choked one of Rafe's friends as though she had made a hilarious joke, or else was incredibly stupid. "Well, not for the villagers anyway!

It's for industry and to sell to foreigners. Ghanaians couldn't afford electricity anyway!" The group sniggered again and turned away from her.

She backed into the wall, away from the group, and frowning at her own stupidity. She felt better just watching, listening.

Drink flowed copiously. Wine glasses were filled and refilled. Jess eased up after two glasses, aware that she got headachy and uncomfortable after too much wine. More people arrived as the evening wore on and the apartment was soon a crush of bodies. Someone put vinyl music on the Dancette record player and as the hours passed the loud rock n' roll gave way to smoother dance music. Jess grimaced at the smokiness of the room, the heat and the loudness of the voices. She felt woozy. Her mother's Rule of no alcohol was well and truly broken, but she wished that her mother would recognise that she was actually pretty sensible.

Jess gradually became aware that a low and intense conversation was murmuring behind her.

"… *disappeared … strange circumstances …*"

"… *ah, the 'disparu'…*"

"*First class brain … wife, kids … nothing out of the ordinary at all … no sign …*"

"… *no, nothing at all, no word … well, what can we do?*"

"*Nkrumah's men …*"

The men's tone of voice was fearful, surreptitious, and it was frightening Jess. What were they talking about? The 'disparu'? That was in Chile, wasn't it? Or

Argentina or somewhere like that? Something about people disappearing: political dissidents? So they were referring to – what? – people in Ghana, academics, being abducted? By whom? Why? Her brain felt befuddled and muddied.

The speakers moved out of hearing range. The heat, the press of bodies, the noise, the smoke, the strange acrid woody smell combined to swirl about her mind. She began to feel quite nauseous and wondered whether she could find the bathroom.

People were moving sinuously around her. They had started slow dancing and Jess shrank to the side of the room watching the entwined arms and the closeness of the bodies. She really wanted to escape but just as she was contemplating how to do this without being rude, a well-built, muscular Lebanese guy, one of the engineers she had been listening to earlier on, loomed over her.

"You wanna dance?" he demanded, leaning in to her and breathing alcoholic fumes into her face. She remembered that someone had introduced him as one of the bosses, a very important and wealthy man, they had said, in awed tones. He didn't look very important to Jess at this moment, as he thrust his red sweaty face at her, leering. Granted he was very smart, sporting what was clearly a designer suit, and would have been handsome, had his features not become slobbery with drink. He grabbed her roughly and pulled her to his chest.

She somehow found herself being pushed into the middle of the dancing couples, the man holding her tightly against him. The room was swaying and she could hardly breathe.

"Beautiful, you are so beautiful," the chap was groaning into her neck, staggering slightly, knocking her into other smooching couples. Jess was aware that the music was a strange tipsy song about Christine Keeler. "*I'm a good girl,*" he sang along, suggestively, intoning tunelessly into her hair.

He bumped Jess into Harriet who was swaying drunkenly, closely wrapped around Rafe. Harriet grinned at Jess. "At *last*!" she mouthed at her over Rafe's shoulder, and actually smiled with encouragement. The Lebanese chap pulled Jess even closer and she could feel the hardness he thrust into her pelvis. She felt disgusted. Enough was enough. She struggled to escape, but he held her firm.

"Come to bed with me, sleep with me tonight," he growled into her ear as he swayed to the music.

"Oh my God!" she suddenly shrieked, "I'm going to be sick!" In his surprise he slackened his grip on her and she pulled away enough to put her hand dramatically over her mouth. In an instant he stepped away from her, looking down at his immaculate suit in horror, and she fled the room.

She found Sandra sitting on the steps outside and sank down beside her. The air was close but fresh after the fetid atmosphere inside and she felt much better. Even her brain seemed to clear.

"Awful party," said Sandra, "The food was good but then it all went downhill. I've been mauled by a particularly unpleasant man. Well, he tried it on, but I gave him the old knee in the groin and he ended up on the floor. How about you?"

Jess managed to giggle. "Oh pretty much the same."

"Remind me never to come to a party with you again."

They sat in companionable silence for some time, Jess dozing even on the hard concrete steps.

Eventually people left, staggering past Jess and Sandra on the steps, silky dresses now sticky and creased, hair lanky, suits sweaty, stained and smelly. Sandra kicked them away from her unceremoniously. Jess found herself giggling uncontrollably. "I think this is the most ghastly weekend I've ever experienced!"

"And we've got to stay here overnight," grumbled Sandra, "What's left of it. Too late to travel now. Have they all gone?"

Tentatively they made their way back to the deserted living room Harriet had disappeared into Rafe's bedroom, and, not knowing what else to do, Jess and Sandra curled up on the sofas for the rest of the night, still in their clothes, amidst the lingering stench of sweaty bodies and abandoned food. At first light they would leave quickly and quietly and find a taxi to get back to Cape Coast as hastily as they could.

But, in the event, they fell sound asleep, and didn't awake until late. The sun was high and bright in the sky by the time Jess pulled herself up and peered through the steamy plate glass windows of Rafe's apartment. The room was a total mess, the luxurious beauty now defiled. The white leather was stained with red wine, the wooden floor littered with cigarette butts ground into the boards. There was something very nasty in one of the gold vases, and it looked as though someone had engaged in a food fight across the table. Jess thought that she detected what looked very much like skimpy lace knickers draped over the lampshade, and there was something awfully sticky-looking smearing the floor behind one of the sofas.

She found the bathroom which she vaguely remembered from the night before. It smelled horrid and the sink was blocked with filth. She didn't wish to spend any more time in it than she had to. She would keep her grubby clothes on and forego a shower until she got home. Home to their nice flat 4, however basic, kept clean and fresh by John, their houseboy. She even started to think of John with affection. Here, she felt dirty.

"I think they owe us a coffee after all that last night," groaned Sandra, stretching and yawning. "Ugh, I need a wash and to clean my teeth."

"You don't want to wash in the bathroom," warned Jess. They found the kitchen, washed their hands, splashed cold water on their faces, and brushed their teeth in the sink. They made themselves a coffee with boiled milk to stave off the sharp gassy pains and hunger pangs with which the wine and spicy food of the night before had left them. Jess tried as best she could to tidy herself up, smoothing her crumpled skirt and brushing through her hair with her fingers and pulling it up again into the band that had drooped from the day before. They took the coffee into the living room and Jess drank hers feeling very grubby sitting down in the clothes she had slept in, and longing for a shower.

Sandra looked around her with an undisguised sneer on her face, "Good grief, god-fearing posh family, did you say? Dragged up, more like!"

Before they had finished their coffee, Harriet emerged from Rafe's bedroom looking decidedly dishevelled, sweaty, hair mussed up and hurriedly buttoning her flimsy baby-doll nightie. Well, at least she had been able to change into nightclothes. Presumably she kept them here.

"Phew!" she breathed, "What a night. Great party, wasn't it?"

Jess nodded mutely. She just wanted to get away. The flat seemed to reek of something sour and earthy.

"Well," Harriet stopped, and looked disparagingly at Jess, neat with her hair scooped up into a topknot, and her long white broderie anglaise skirt and gold sandals. "I guess you didn't score in the sack last night! Thought you might have got off with that Lebanese guy, good god, he was trying his best. Opportunity there. But no, I should have known …"

Lost for appropriate words, Jess fiddled with the contents of her bag.

"Hair of the dog?" asked Harriet, snorting as she went into the kitchen. Sandra glared at Jess.

"No, no thanks." But Harriet had already pattered from the kitchen, armed with a glass of evil-looking yellow liquid, to the bathroom. They could hear her in the shower. It seemed to work much better than the one in flat 4. Water actually seemed to flow freely.

Rafe wandered out of his bedroom, naked and glistening, paying the girls no attention. Jess looked away quickly but he opened the bathroom door and went in. Jess could hear the unrestrained splashing, a loud grunt, and then the flushing of the toilet. There were low murmurings, the swish of the plastic shower curtain, and a giggling squeal from Harriet.

Sandra laughed and jerked her head towards the apartment door. "For goodness sake, c'mon!"

"We're off!" she yelled to the bathroom door.

Harriet emerged from the bathroom, towelling her short fair hair. Rafe was whistling tunelessly out of sight.

"Look," started Jess, "we really must go. Thanks for the party…and the weekend, but we must go to … er … get back."

"If you can hold fire till tomorrow morning, you can wander round Accra today and then Rafe will drive you back tomorrow," declared Harriet with ruthless disregard. "He's got to go to Cape Coast college in the morning to give a lecture on the "Ghanaian cultural shift", whatever that means, so he can take you, it won't be putting him out!"

"Oh, thanks so much, er … *Harry,*" (she had remembered) "but we really have to get back today – well, as soon as we can, really. We'll get a taxi or hitch a lift."

"Yeah, right now!" said Sandra, dropping her still half-full coffee mug on the table and standing up.

Harriet shrugged. "Oh well, up to you. Shame you couldn't enjoy yourselves a bit more. I've tried my best." She looked at Jess with a sneer, "And, Jessie, for goodness sake get your face done – your expression is *so* unattractive."

It was well into the afternoon before they managed to get a lift first down into Accra, and then on the road to Cape Coast. For once there were few vehicles going all the way to Cape Coast and they had to settle for a lift half way, where they managed to get a taxi. Jess was only too aware of the smell of her unwashed skin, spices oozing from her pores.

Jess never thought that she would feel so happy to see the concrete of the school buildings and hear the shrieks of the girls across the sultry evening air. She noticed Betty waving to them from her crouched position tending the flowers at the edge of her little garden. As she and Sandra climbed out of the taxi she thought "home at last" with relief.

She could hardly wait to run up the stairs and dive under the cleansing water even though it only dribbled tepidly from the showerhead. She scrubbed her body, her hair, her nails, and doused herself with cologne, as if she were eliminating all traces of the weekend experience, and she emerged, fresh and thankful in clean and sweet smelling clothes an hour later. Back to the gentleness, the calmness, the relief of familiar routine.

꧁

Jess was getting used to the mundanity of daily life at the school: the heat, the hysteria of the girls, the strangeness of the food and traditions, the views over the bush with its tropical plants, the slow pace of life in Ghana; all had become the norm and familiarity had dulled its initial excitement. Not that she exactly took it for granted, but it was just that she no longer thrilled to it in the same way as she had done when she first arrived. She still loved the life here, but there were so many mundane jobs to do, for school, in the apartment, in the villages. Although John, their houseboy, did most of the laundry, apart from Jess's underwear which she still insisted on doing herself out of sheer embarrassment, and most of the food shopping in the markets, the cooking, and the cleaning, she seemed to have to do lots of sewing and mending, home-making and repairs, attending to emergencies, preparing lessons and marking endless exercise books, scrabbling to find supplies and resources for the villages of Kakomdo and Ebubonku.

She rarely saw the beautiful young mother Adwa with her little girl Amah and wondered what had happened to them. She had asked after them in the village but was greeted with an impenetrable wall of silence. She recalled that Adwa had told her that the villagers weren't kind to her and that she lived alone on the outskirts of the compound. She should try to find her. But she knew that it would be difficult to make contact if the villagers or the Chief were not willing. The veil of ignorance still prevailed.

And mosquito nets still found their way to the fields instead of over the beds, children still died of malaria, women still grieved for their lost babies. Jess had come to accept that her work involved only two little steps forwards and then one step back.

As for herself, she still loved the heat, the sunshine, the sitting on the verandas in the afternoons whenever she wasn't marking, the walking through the bush or round the towns, the visits to the colourful noisy markets, the coffees and chats with Chrissie or

Betty, the weekly choir rehearsals in the sultry air of the evening-time.

And she had learned another skill. Although she didn't have to cook, she loved to watch Joseph in Betty's kitchen preparing meals, and sometimes he allowed her to help, like a chef with his assistant. Teaching a white English girl was clearly a novel task for him and one he relished. She had learned to cook cornmeal porridge with the finely ground roasted cornmeal called *ablemamu,* hot milk and brown sugar. She had ground the peanuts in a wooden pestle and mortar, releasing their rich earthy aroma. She had learned how to make *kelewele:* marinating the plantain, with just the right amount of ginger and cinnamon to create the sweet piquant taste. She had mastered the groundnut stew with chicken, using wild mushrooms, crushed tomatoes and smooth peanut butter, learning just how much cayenne pepper, curry seasoning, thyme and bay to add to allow the earthy intense flavours to be released.

But most of all, she realised more and more that she looked forward to Jim's visits to the school, the way he talked about Ghana and explained to her the way of life, the history and the politics of life in West Africa. He was full of surprises and mad spontaneous ideas. One time he had taken her down to the school hall, to the old grand piano there and played Great Balls of Fire so loudly that most of the girls had run, shrieking, down to see his crazy impression of Jerry Lee Lewis.

Jess had laughed until she cried, and then he had settled them all down again with a gentle performance of a Chopin nocturne, and she wondered if that was what he had intended them to hear all along. But other times, they had debated big issues of the world, the Cuba crisis, Kennedy's assassination, racial tensions in America, world poverty, but somehow, however serious their arguments, they always ended up laughing over their coffee mugs about some silly thing she couldn't even remember afterwards.

૨

One afternoon, in mid-November, after teaching and siesta time, Jess was trying valiantly to mark the first year class's latest English compositions. John was brushing the floors in a rather desultory fashion, having done the laundry in the morning and then escaped for a few hours with some garbled excuse which Jess did not understand. She preferred him to get the jobs done in the morning while she and Sandra were teaching, so that they could have the flat to themselves in the afternoon, for marking (Jess), meetings (Sandra), and so on – sometimes actually just chilling out. But he had been insistent and Jess did not feel like another battle with him. He was often surly and, if she was totally honest with herself, Jess was a little afraid of crossing him. Sandra was out in Cape Coast with Hank for the afternoon until Guides' meeting at four o' clock.

Sandra never seemed to have the horrendous piles of marking that Jess accumulated. Maybe that was because she taught maths: Jess knew that much of the time Sandra got the girls to mark their own exercises in class so there was less for her to do in the afternoons. She claimed, supported vehemently by Glenda, that it was "a learning tool". Glenda made no bones about the fact that she considered Jess incompetent, and constantly told her how she should go about teaching English, setting tests and getting the pupils to mark their own..

Jess wished that it were that easy for English. But it couldn't be done, not effectively anyway. She sighed as she ploughed through the pile of exercise books on the table in front of her and took another sip of her mango juice, which she had prepared for sustenance as she worked, along with a plate of pineapple from the market. She always tried to give the girls something different and creative to write, rather than the essay titles which Betty suggested, that tended to be, in Jess's opinion, rather dry and dull.

Jess had asked them to imagine that they were the head teacher of the school and propose changes, justifying each one clearly. She had encouraged them to tackle the task in a humorous way. But most of the girls so far had maintained quite seriously that there was nothing much they would change as the school was already so perfect, although they would enhance the food and the rules for uniform. In their opinion girls should be allowed to wear kente cloth from year one, braid their hair and wear make-up like film stars. Meals should be available whenever they were hungry and include "burgers" which they had read about in their American magazines.

Many of the pieces of work ended with a supplication to her as marker, along the lines of "Miss, please do not give me bad mark. I try so-so hard. I bring you pawpaw from the market. Thank you, miss" or "Sorry, sorry, sorry, miss, I had to wash my hair." Quite what significance this had, Jess couldn't imagine. At first these charming and funny notes had amused her but by now they were beginning to pall. She just wished they'd simply get on with it.

She prodded a chunk of fresh pineapple with her fork and was just lifting it to her mouth when she was startled by a voice,

"Hi! Busy?"

Jim was standing in the doorway. Jess put down her fork and pen and turned to him.

"Hi stranger! Haven't seen you since the last choir rehearsal. Been somewhere good?"

He looked at her for several moments, and then he looked away.

"I was ... called away to the north ... it was difficult ..."

"An emergency?" asked Jess

"Uh, kinda." He crossed the room to her and touched the back of her chair. "Jess ...?" His voice sounded odd, strained.

"Are you OK?" she looked up at him, anxious. He looked at her for a second, and it seemed to her that he was searching her face for something. He touched her head and drew in a breath as though he was about to say something, then he seemed to change his mind.

She didn't know what to make of it. What on earth could have happened? She felt a strong sense of concern for him; she really wanted to hug him, but what would he think? Would he hug her back – as a friend – or something else? That would be awkward. Or would he in fact step back from her; that would be even more awful. She daren't risk it. He was a really good friend and she wanted to keep it that way. Good grief; it was all so complicated. She really liked Jim.

Then a glimmer of a smile, the moment lost, and he turned away. Jess noticed that John was glaring at Jim from the kitchen doorway, leaning belligerently on his broom. She looked sternly at him, and he resumed his brushing.

"Looks like you need to be taken away from all this," Jim said, changing the mood in an instant. "Want to come into CC?"

"Oh, yes, absolutely. I could do with a break from this," Jess smiled. "And actually I was thinking of getting some bits and bobs for the flat."

"Like?"

"Like a drum, kente cloth, paintings. Stuff like that."

"Ah, I know just the place," Jim nodded. "C'mon!"

"I can't be too long, though. I need to do some lesson preparation for tomorrow, a class on how to write a decent letter – for my first years."

"Yeah, I bet you can put them straight on that! I think you have a lot of practice in writing letters. I see piles of blue airmail forms."

"Yes, you're right there."

Jim had borrowed the truck again so Jess climbed aboard and they set off along the bumpy dirt road down to the coast. This time he took her along tortuous tracks behind the town, skidding and bouncing the truck between palms and undergrowth. Finally they bumped into a dusty compound surrounded by red dirt huts, thatched shelters and piles of drums in various stages of completion. Jess saw that there were artisans sitting on the dusty ground outside the huts, working the wood of the drums or stretching skins over the barrels, or pulling on strings and wooden pegs.

"This is the place to get your drum," Jim assured her. "It's not the usual tourist shopping. These are the real musical McCoy." He swung down from the cab and held out his hand to help her jump down onto the dusty ground. He led her, his hand gently on her lower back, towards the drum-makers. She liked that. He hadn't done that before. It was courteous, gentlemanly, caring. *Did he care for her?* Perhaps more than she had realised before. Did blokes usually touch girls' lower backs like that if they didn't care for them? Had

Simon touched her like that? Somehow, she couldn't remember.

But it didn't matter what she could or couldn't remember. She knew Simon loved her. He said so often in his letters. She just liked the way Jim acted with her. It was nice, kind, gentle.

Jim hailed one of the men, old and lined, black leathered skin and white hair. He greeted him with a nod, solemn and formal, "Good afternoon."

Then Jim adeptly asked after his health and that of his children, naming each one in turn. He asked about his house and village. With each query the old man responded with a grunt and a nod. Then the formulaic greeting was done, and Jim said, "So, hiya Joe. How's it going?"

He held out his hand and the drum-maker rose to shake hands with Jim warmly with a grin spreading across his thin wizened face. He looked towards Jess and seemed to be drinking in her features and figure as if he were admiring a painting of the Madonna – or the Mona Lisa.

"Your girl?" he asked Jim beaming broadly with approval.

"A friend," said Jim firmly. *Why did Jess suddenly want him to say yes? Of course she wasn't. What was she thinking? She already had a boyfriend.*

"Uhuh, mmm," nodded the drum-maker, shaking his head with disbelief.

"Anyway," resumed Jim, "I'm showing Jess the real drum-making skill, the real Ghanaian drum – not the bog standard tourist stuff!"

"OK." The old man sat down again to his work, the drum held between his thin brown legs, and Jim began to describe what was being done to craft the instrument.

"This is a kpanlogo djembe, a peg drum" said Jim, "That's the name of this kind of drum. It's not the same as the dondo, the talking drum. It's made with tweneboah wood. Joe's whittling the design all round the body. Here, look." Jess watched as the craftsman chipped delicately, smoothed, and caressed the wood body of the drum he was fashioning. As she watched she marvelled at the deftness of the thin black dusty fingers as he lovingly carved out the patterns, constantly holding the drum back to look critically at his work, smiling with satisfaction or grimacing if a line was not as accurate as he wanted. "All Joe's designs are traditional and they all mean something significant. The history of the country. Religious messages. Every one different. So every person who buys one of Joe's drums is buying something really unique. Joe is the best master drum-maker that I know!"

Joe glanced up and grinned at Jim affectionately.

"Look at these djembe that Joe's working on," instructed Jim as he gestured towards the large drums lined up against the hut wall, in various stages of completion. He picked up some flattened skins, dirty beige in colour. "Goat skins." And another pile: "Cow skins. That guy over there is shaving them ready for the drum."

He indicated a small pile of strings on the ground. "Goat. For the best stringing of the skin."

Jess marvelled at the range of patterns on the drums, the burnished shading of the wood, the rounded shape of the body, the way the strings were fashioned to hold the drum skin taut, woven into a diamond pattern and fixed to the pegs that were driven at an angle in to the body of the drum about two inches down.

Some of the drums were a different shape and design, with a waisted body and with a hoop of string round the top circumference of the skin. Long strings held the hoop and the stretched skin from the top to another hoop half way down the body, without pegs.

"And what about the talking drums? Which are they?"

Jim pointed towards some smaller drums lying on their sides, without pegs, but still with animal skin stretched taut over the top and bottom, held in place with strings crossed between the two ends. They had an even more pronounced waisted shape. Jess peered at the ends. Joe suddenly laughed as though she had done something hilarious.

"Two bottom!" he gasped, then showing her the base of the kpanlogo djembe he was working on, "No bottom!" Indeed the drum was hollow with no base.

"That's because the kpanlogo is used for making music, not talking," explained Jim. "It's larger and stands on the base so that the musician plays it from the top only. With the dondo the drum is held under the arm so it's a lot smaller, and it's played with both hands, or either."

"May I …?" she asked indicating one of the finished drums. Joe the drum-maker nodded. Jess touched the skin carefully and felt its coolness, its roughness, its dustiness.

"Want to hear it?" asked Jim. He picked out a drum that stood a little separately from the rest, sat on a wooden crafted Ashanti stool and began to caress the drum skin of the kpanlogo djembe.

Then he frowned and drummed patterns of sound that Jess recognised from the drumming she had heard in the bush beyond her apartment. Rising and falling, it was haunting and mesmerising, and she couldn't take her eyes off Jim's hands as he drummed, long fingered, muscular but sensitive to the touch and sound of the instrument, *feeling* the music as he had done the piano in the Peace Corps house. She knew that she loved to watch his hands, his fingers drawing out the responses from the drum skin. She thought of Simon's hands as he played the piano for her and how she loved to watch him. How long would it be before she could watch his hands again? Sometimes it seemed that watching Jim was like watching Simon.

And as she watched she felt as though a wind swept about her, and then the voices on the wind filled her mind as they had done with the dondo in the bush. But this was not the dondo, the talking drum, but the kpanlogo whose rhythms she also recognised from the bush sounds at the fall of evening, echoing and reverberating between the huts of the villages. And then she understood: it was the kpanlogo that had swept her mind clear to hear the messages of the dondo.

Jess felt herself transported to her flat, at night, listening to the rise and fall of the drums across the African darkness, speaking to her, calling out to her. Some kind of message that seemed important for her to hear. She heard it. Why couldn't she understand what it was saying to her?

The insistent beat was the same one that pounded on her mind at night as she tried to sleep, that seemed to summon up the spirits of the bush, ancient souls, ancient ghosts, crying out to her. The sounds surging and surrounding her, filling her brain, her body, her soul. Trying to tell her something, but she couldn't make out the words. Her head was spinning, she felt dizzy, drunken. Simon? Simon, where are you? His figure was there at the periphery of her mind. But as the figure turned, she felt fear and she knew that the face was not Simon's. Why couldn't she see his face? Then it seemed to her that the face was Jim's.

She became aware that the drumming had stopped. Joe had halted in his carving and was gazing intently at her face. As she looked around she noted that the other men had stopped their work also. Jim too was looking at her, but quizzically.

"What?"

Jim shook his head. "I don't know. You seemed … Are you OK?" It was like the time at Elmina castle.

Jess pulled herself together, took a deep breath and smiled at him. "Goodness, you're very talented. Piano. Drums. What else?"

He shrugged modestly. "Well, I do my best. Aim to please. You liked it?"

"Wow, yes. Very … evocative." Jess concentrated on inspecting the patterns on the wooden drum bodies stacked against the hut wall. She was aware that Joe was looking intently at her. "So they all have meanings?"

She felt Joe's gaze leading hers back to the drum that Jim had played and that he had replaced a little away from the others. This drum had circular patterns that swirled around the drum, with deeply carved "eye" shapes. "What does this mean?"

Joe smiled at her, a little sadly, she thought, and nodded slowly as if he knew that she would pick out that one. "Ahah. That one just for you, lady. See into the heart. And see into the spirit."

Jess thought that he probably said that to everyone who asked – that one just for you. A sales gimmick.

"Here," he said, pulling himself to his feet and lifting the drum she had indicated. He held it out to her. "For you."

Jess startled. How awkward. "Umm. How much is it?" She pulled out her purse.

The old man shook his head and flapped his had in refusal. "No, miss, no, no. For you." He hesitated then he said quietly. "It calls to you. It speaks to you and you will treat it well. It has to be for you. I give it to you."

Jess shook her head and turned to Jim for guidance. What a difficult situation. She couldn't take something precious, hand crafted, clearly expensive and unique. He could sell this in the shops for a lot of money. No way could she just take it for nothing.

"He really wants you to have it," murmured Jim quietly, looking at Joe and holding his stare. "He sees something in you. Joe is the "wise man" of the village, the spiritual leader." And then he added something Jess found really odd. "He sees into people's souls."

Joe nodded slowly. What was going on here?

"Love," said Joe gently. "I see love." Then he frowned and his face darkened. "I see loss. And I also see fear. Branches of the same tree, growing from the same earth, the same dust. Love and loss, and the fear that binds them. They are together, always ... But for now, what I see is love."

"Take the drum," Jim told her, "And when you're back in England, you'll remember it was the one Joe chose for you. And," he added quietly, "the one I played for you."

"OK. But I must give him this." She pulled some cedi notes from her purse, and held them out to Joe.

"For you, for your village. Whatever you want to do with it. I really can't take this beautiful drum for nothing, whatever you say. Please."

Reluctantly the old man took her money, but he nodded. "Yes. For the village. I will."

"Thank you. It's lovely."

"Keep it with you always."

"This day will be etched in my memory," said Jess, "And every time I look at my drum, I'll think of you."

Joe smiled a small sad smile.

"Right," interrupted Jim brusquely, "we really must be going now, Joe. And thanks." He gave the old man a hug and patted him affectionately on the back. "Look after that old heart."

He carefully lifted the chosen drum into the back of the truck and tucked it up with a woollen rug as if he was caring for a child. He handed Jess up into the cab and as she looked back out of the window she saw him slip something into Joe's protesting hand and again pat the drum-maker on the arm. He waved goodbye and climbed into the cab alongside Jess. She could see Joe waving and smiling at them. The other men raised their hands in goodbye too and carried on with their work.

Jim started the engine and the truck had bumped over the rough track for some yards before he glanced sideways at Jess.

"What was all that about?" asked Jess. "What did he mean?"

"Oh, that's just Joe. Don't mind what he says," he said. "Poor old Joe." He sighed; a long deep sigh and Jess felt the sadness in it.

"What is it, Jim?"

"Old Joe. You see – he's dying. Had a heart attack a couple of months back but won't go into hospital. Thinks if he does he will never go home again to his village." He grimaced. "And of course he's right. That will be the end. So he's better here carrying on working on his drums until one day his heart finally gives out."

"Oh, goodness."

"His wife died last year. He told me he needs to go to her. Children all grown and families of their own, off in Accra. He's actually regarded as a very important spiritual adviser in his village, you know." Jim frowned. "It's strange, but he seems to see things that the rest of us don't."

"What did you give him as we left?" asked Jess.

"Oh, just a little money for the village equipment. They need hoes and spades."

"You're very kind," commented Jess. Jim shrugged. "And thoughtful. You're a really nice man, you know." She turned to him and smiled shyly. "Honestly, I count myself honoured to be your friend."

"Oh god," exclaimed Jim. "Please don't get all flowery on me."

Jess laughed. "OK," she conceded. *Chaps don't like emotions. Most chaps, anyway. Simon was different, she mused. He was very emotional. But for most chaps she knew before Simon, emotion made them embarrassed.* "So where are we going now for my other stuff? You found me a real-life authentic Ghanaian drum-maker in the middle of nowhere. So find me the same for masks and pictures!"

"Oh, I reckon the tourist trail for those!" laughed Jim, "I know nothing whatsoever about masks and art!"

꩜

The apartment was starting to look more homely and lived-in, thanks to the traditional woollen rugs that Jess bought from the tourist shop in Cape Coast and the masks and paintings on the wall which Jess had acquired from a roadside vendor. "Nesting" as Sandra had somewhat sarcastically noted. And Jess had, in her turn, noted silently that Sandra had done nothing at all to make the flat look comfortable. Although she wasn't there that much, and rarely lounged around or spent much time being homely there these days, so why should she?

The paintings, the trader had assured Jess, were real Ghanaian artwork, painted by a local artist, his brother in fact, from Kakomdo, who only sold them on this stall. But later she had seen exactly the same in various other places, roadside stalls and town shops, in Accra and Cape Coast. It didn't matter; she just wanted to brighten up the flat and they were quite cheap. She also acquired a brightly coloured kente cloth which Chrissie had given her as surplus to her own requirements, and Jess pinned it up across the wall of her bedroom like a tapestry.

She also bought an Ashanti stool from the tourist shop and a wooden oware board, a game with dried beans for counters.

"Why are there tourist shops?" Jess had asked Betty one afternoon, after classes, as they had coffee together on the veranda of Betty's bungalow, trying to work on compiling the examination papers which were the traditional end of term tests before Christmas for all the classes. "I mean, there aren't any tourists."

"Oh, well, dear, we call them tourist shops but they're for the various workers who come out for a while and like to take home souvenirs. Mainly masks which aren't even Ghanaian, paintings which are usually Nigerian, and kente cloth, which is of course local. Drums are very popular too but they are not the real thing, just made for tourist artefacts, not musical instruments."

Jess's heart plunged thinking that the paintings weren't even Ghanaian but probably Nigerian. She felt rather stupid, and daren't admit to Betty that she had been duped. Ah well, at least they might hopefully be West African of some sort. She'd bought them now, so too late …

Jess told Betty about her foray with Jim into the bush to the drum-makers' village, and about Joe and the drum he had chosen for her. She didn't tell her about the odd experiences she had there, of course. Those she had voiced to no-one.

"Well, you *are* the favoured one, then, dear," declared Betty with open admiration. "I do know of Joe's compound. It's very special and *hoi polloi* don't get to visit, so you were clearly very specially regarded by someone! Well done! It's where they make the real Ghanaian drums, the ones the true musicians use, the traditional ones for the villages and in the bands. They don't sell them to the tourist shops. And the only Europeans who have them have to be well-respected musicians. Joe – he's said to be quite a character, although in my many years here I've never met him. Something of a figurehead, I think, a headman. Some sort of spiritual leader. Like the Quaker saying of "seeing that of God in every man"; Joe actually sees the Holy Spirit working in every man."

Jess would have liked to speak more about Joe and his special powers, but at that moment, Sandra came bounding up,

"Hey, I've been looking everywhere for you," she shouted to Jess as she flopped herself down on one of Betty's veranda chairs, spreading her legs widely in a very unladylike manner. Jess noticed that Sandra seemed to have put on quite a lot of weight since they arrived in Ghana and seemed even more physically awkward. Jess hoped that she herself was a little more graceful – like Chrissie whose elegance she admired and tried to model herself on. She tried to hang around Chrissie as much as she could, as though some of her grace and sophistication would, in time, rub off on her by association. A memory suddenly flashed into her mind:

"You're so naturally beautiful," Simon's mother had said to Jess that summer when she had spent so much of her time at Simon's house with his parents. *"We're so glad that he has you. Not some painted tarty girl!"*

Jess felt very comfortable with Simon's parents; they didn't try to make her be someone she wasn't. They didn't find fault in her all the time like her own parents did. His mother had even presented her with the lovely hardback copy of Yeats's poetry (her favourite), remembering Jess's comment of sometime before (how on earth had she recalled that?), and said it was for Jess to take with her to Africa to remember them every day! There was a lovely inscription on the inside cover: "to our beautiful "daughter", Jess, you are so brave. Come back safely to us. We'll miss you." If only her own mother could be like that.

"Phew, I'm sweating buckets here!" said Sandra to Betty, who smiled gently, and went indoors to fetch another coffee cup. "Listen, Jess! We've been thinking. What about a Christmas trek to Timbuktu?"

"What? Oh! ... er, well, who is "we"?"

She had the awful feeling it might be Hank and she really didn't want to spend Christmas or any other holiday with that unpleasant chap. He hadn't improved in the weeks he had been seeing Sandra. She had kept out of his way as much as she could, with only a polite greeting when necessary. And he had seemed to be happy with that distance. Jess had asked Jim about Hank but he had claimed that they were not close friends, only that they had worked together on certain projects and he didn't really know him much at all. She got the impression that they didn't share the same interests.

"Well, Glenda, of course!"

Jess's heart beat in double time. Her face must have registered dismay. But Sandra added, "And possibly Chrissie might come too, if she can be persuaded. I know you two get on well."

Jess would not have been keen to trek to Timbuktu, or anywhere else for that matter, alone with just Glenda and Sandra, but Chrissie – well that was different.

Timbuktu! The epitome of adventure. A remote outpost. The sort of place that explorers went to. Goodness, the more she thought about it the more she seemed to revive her early sense of excitement when she had first come out to Ghana.

Oh yes, she certainly would like a Christmas trek to Timbuktu!

"So, what's the plan, then?" she asked Sandra.

"Well. Take the two cars – Glenda's and Chrissie's – always best to have a backup in the desert, just in case. Drive up through Ghana into Upper Volta and Mali, and take the steam boat up the Niger to Timbuktu! We can apparently stay in rest houses on the way. And it seems that Glenda has some contacts where we might cadge a bed for the night too, in central and northern Ghana."

"Oh yes," exclaimed Betty as she came back out on to the veranda with another coffee cup for Sandra and a pot for top-ups. "Clara and I have a lot of contacts up there, too. That *does* sound a good idea! Clara and I did that trek the first holiday I was out here. I think she'd already done it previously with a friend and she wanted to take me when I came out. It's great fun! I'm sure you'll love the trip. You've worked hard, you deserve it."

"Well that sounds wonderful," said Jess, "You could maybe give us some advice on our plans."

Betty set the coffee down on the low table. She also had a map under her arm and she dropped that onto the table too. When she sat down, she unfolded it and spread it out so that Jess could see it was a detailed large scale map of Ghana, which included Upper Volta to the north and the southern part of Mali even further to the north. Her finger travelled up to Timbuktu in the top corner.

"Now, let's see. We have friends here in the Ashanti region, in Dunkwa, oh and in Kumasi – the Robinsons, lovely Quaker family, been over here about ten years, two children born out here," Betty pressed her finger on the map, "oh and here at Koforidua, a lovely couple, Methodist missionaries, then you could go up to

Kwadaso. We visited Wenchi, Bole, Wa, Lowra – oh, there's a Quaker Friend at the boys' school, I'm sure they'd put you up for the night. Hapa – there's a very interesting chief's compound, most hospitable." Betty looked thoughtful. "We took the Bamboi ferry across the Black Volta. The border's at Hamale and then you travel up to Ougadougou, in Upper Volta!"

Jess couldn't help but laugh at her enthusiasm. Betty smiled broadly and looked up at Jess and Sandra. "What am I doing? It's your trip to plan! Here you take the map."

"The place names are just wonderful!" exclaimed Jess. "It sounds fabulous! What about the terrain? Is it very remote? What about organising beds for the night? And food …?"

That night, Jess had so much she longed to tell Simon. Her heart was full. She was more excited than she could possibly imagine about the proposed trek to Timbuktu. She really needed this break to somewhere remote, away from the daily schedule and mundane activities which had become her life as a teacher and as a nurse in Kakomdo and Ebubonku. She was visiting the villages every week but she knew that her passion to do something to help the poverty and ignorance she found was shaken by the events which touched her deeply: the death of Kwame, the destruction of the mosquito nets.

"I need to get away and regroup my thoughts," she mused, "try to get a new perspective."

But what would Simon think of it all? What would he make of her hurtling herself with just three other women into the unknown territories of northern Ghana, Upper Volta and Mali, across the desert and through the Arab townships, up the infested waters of the Volta and Niger rivers, sleeping in rest-houses along the way with maybe just the odd comfort stop in a European home sleeping in a proper bed?

She felt a little guilty that she didn't feel more of a longing for Simon to be there with her right now and on the trip, but somehow she knew that he would hate it. The discomfort, the insects, the vermin, the not knowing what the next overnight stop would be like. He'd love the driving, though: he loved the freedom of the road and the control of the car. But she really didn't think he'd be impressed with the adventure of finding your way over the desert to a watering hole somewhere in the middle of nowhere. He did like his home comforts.

It was odd that he seemed so exciting and adventurous at home, but when she thought about him being out here with her in the bush she couldn't imagine him putting up with the heat, the noise, the daily uncertainty of electricity or water. So, in the end, she made light of the trek and the strangeness of the drum-maker, her odd fits or whatever they were, not wanting to worry him, so far away back in the UK.

My dear Simon,

I've bought a large Ghanaian drum, and some masks and pictures which we've put on the walls in flat 4. It's starting to look homely now – you'd like it.

The teaching continues to be interesting although quite tiring. A group of us are thinking of taking a holiday up to the north at Christmas, and maybe across the border. I'm looking forward to it, having a break from school and nursing in the villages. Still going to the villages in the bush on Sundays, two more cases of malaria but they don't or won't use the nets. What to do?!

Oh – I must tell you about the lovely stories that my first year class wrote for me yesterday. They are really fab. A kind of mixture of Ghanaian reality and some idea of English life – apparently it is always snowing in the UK (they learned about snow some time ago when we started A Christmas Carol) even in July. We all live in London. And we are all teachers, doctors or nurses! Actually sounds like our career adviser at school!

I am trying to get them to do a little play to act on the stage in the school hall for the rest of the school. They're keen but also frightened at the prospect. We're doing Hansel and Gretel which is one in our book of short plays for junior classes, and Mercy has found some music for the song, the one by Humperdinck, so they are all learning it. They were so keen to show me that they burst in to song at the tops of their sweet voices in the middle of morning class, and Glenda, who was teaching maths next door, came bowling in, red faced and furious. She had a go at me, in front of the class which was very embarrassing, but as soon as she had gone, the class started saying to me, "don't mind her, miss, she's always bad tempered! We love you, miss!" So in the end it was really quite sweet.

Sorry to hear about more exams coming up again before the end of term, but I'm sure you'll be fine. And yes, I miss you terribly too. Have a good time at the recording of "University Challenge" – give my love to Bamber Gascoigne – well, not really, as it's all for you. Will write again next week and hoping to get another missive from you in the meantime. Glad that the editorship of the college mag is still going well. Yes, I will write a short piece for it on my experiences here in Ghana. I feel that I've gained and learned far more than I've given. Oh, that sounds a bit prissy. Anyway, I'll send something in the week.

But "if you want to know the truth" (shades of Holden Cauldfield – remember?) I feel really cut off here, though. I haven't a clue what's going on in England – or in the world. No newspapers here. There's a "wireless" (really!) in Betty and Clara's bungalow, but reception's poor and the electricity's very unreliable. We're very much left to our own devices. Oh well, only for a few more months! Then I'll be with you again!

With love, J x

Drums, a furious beating tonight, filled the close night air. Sleep eluded Jess until the early hours of the morning. Her mind kept returning to the drum-makers in the village where Jim had taken her. The echo of the drums rolled and reverberated like waves on a shore, crashing violently onto the rocks and sweeping back again, ready to build and climax once more.

The outside world seemed faded and in her sleep-deprived fevered brain Jess saw it as a sepia photo, familiar, but a part of another life. Simon's face was becoming increasingly hard to detail in her mind. A general impression of his dear features, his loving mouth and clear eyes, his fair hair curled around his ears, his gentle sensitive smile; all seemed to be saying to her, words remembered from his letters, "remember The Lady's Not for Burning, "you have such tiny hands, I knew I should love you." Yes, she remembered that very well, the way he took her hands in his and stroked them tenderly, quoting the words in the university play he had helped to direct.

Only the things he had said to her were clear and ever present. She would always remember the words, "come back to me soon, I miss you so much, I want you back here in my life. I love you. I always will."

5

DECEMBER 1965

Not long afterwards, as Jess returned from Kakomdo on a Sunday morning, weary from the nursing work, hot and dusty from the walk through the bush, sad from the sight of the running sores on the children's legs, she found Sandra and Glenda in flat 4, pouring over a map and making notes in a large spiral bound reporter's notebook.

Glenda hardly ever came up to the flat, so Jess was surprised. She was also a little taken aback as she and Sandra had agreed to look at the map later that day when Jess returned from the villages.

"We're getting the schedule together," said Sandra, briefly looking up from her notebook, "for the trip. We're about done now."

"OK," muttered Glenda, scraping her chair back from the table and stretching in an exaggerated display.

"See you later, Sandra." She pushed past Jess and swept out of the door. How on earth was Jess going to stand weeks away with this woman?

"Here's the list of stops en route," Sandra held out the notebook page to show Jess. "Some are in rest-houses and some are with people that Betty or Glenda know."

"Have they arranged them with the hosts already then?"

"S'pose so," shrugged Sandra.

"OK, so anything I can do?"

"No, it's all done."

Jess went into her bedroom to change her dress which was sticky with sweat from the morning's work. Ah, well it saved her a job. But it would have been nice to have been included. Glenda was a difficult woman. And Sandra was getting very involved with her these days. Jess wondered why she seemed to be drawn to rather difficult people: Glenda, Hank ... it created a bit of a barrier. Jess was aware that they would never be close friends – what a pity as they shared these experiences and were both going back home next summer. How nice it would have been to meet up and keep contact back in the UK.

That afternoon, after Jess had finished her preparation for the next week's lessons and done an hour or two of marking, she left Sandra writing letters and went over to Betty's bungalow to enjoy a peaceful couple of hours talking through the host accommodation on Glenda's list. She liked to have some idea of what to expect.

As it was Sunday, Betty had been to Hill House Quaker Meeting that morning and she looked at peace, her gentle features soft. Jess had gone with her on a couple of occasions but of course she normally had the village work to do. ("Well, that's just as much God's work as sitting in Meeting," Betty said, "although you should come when you can.") Betty held a Meeting at her bungalow every Wednesday evening for anyone who cared to come. Jess always felt she was obliged to go but wished she didn't have to feel guilty if she didn't go. She was used to it from home, of course, but when Sandra had attended one time she had grumbled afterwards about how peculiar it was, with everyone expected to sit in silence for an hour. She never went again and pulled a sneer whenever Jess said she was going. Jim simply declined, very graciously and with an apologetic smile, saying that it was "not his scene!" Jess quite enjoyed having the time to sit and think without interruption, although she was not sure that she actually thought about the godly things she knew she should be meditating upon.

They sat on Betty's veranda and Jess felt her anxieties quietened as she listened to Betty's calm, serene voice. She had grown up with such Quaker women with their self-assurance and dignity. Their quietness radiated confidence as though nothing could shake them; everything would always be alright. Yes, they could be stern and disapproving but there was always the confidence, the security that came from being an insider within the group. She thought about her mother mailing Quaker tracts and pamphlets out to Ghana, as though afraid she might forget her heritage. Jim had looked over her shoulder at the leaflets as she tore open the package eagerly before realising with disappointment that it was the familiar Quaker Advices and Queries, and Christian Faith and Practice. Jim had looked sideways at her face and said, "Ahhh, never mind, the parents are always giving me static, too!"

She smiled. Jim had the gift of being able to make her feel smiley and OK, even about her parents and her home. The warmth of the sun soothed her and she felt happy and content.

As she and Betty talked, or rather Betty talked about the hosts on Glenda's list and Jess listened sleepily, she became aware that clouds had drifted across the sun, blanketing the brightness. The sky turned dark and ominous. The trees began to tremble. The Harmattan had blown in from the desert carrying with it the Saharan sands for the last few weeks but it could also bring tornadoes and sometimes, even in the dry season, torrential rainstorms. Betty looked disconcerted and half rose from her veranda chair.

Joseph scurried out to them, gesturing wildly.

"Come inside, miss, miss," he waved towards the veranda doors, "Angry storm coming!"

They only just managed to dive into the bungalow before the storm broke. The violence of it was so amazing to Jess that she watched its magnificence from the safety of the house window in awesome wonder. The sun had been blotted out completely and it was as dark as nightfall. The hurricane wind blew the trees into horrendous tortured angles, and the rain descended upon the world in one continuous fall so that Jess could see no raindrops at all, just a curtain of water. The noise was terrifying; the rain pounded on the hot concrete, sending billows of steam into the air, and water splashed wildly from the overloaded gutters.

For half an hour, Jess watched in fascination; she had never seen anything comparable even in the worst storms in England, even in the previous storms in Ghana. It was an "angry storm" indeed!

As it eased, Jess said to Betty, "Goodness, there'll be awful floods. I hope nobody's outside caught in it!"

"Oh, they happen quite often at this time of year," replied Betty, going into the kitchen to boil a kettle for a pot of tea. Jess heard Joseph take over the task and usher Betty away. "Hopefully, everyone's at home this afternoon. But you just have to dive into the nearest shelter if you're out. Actually it all dries remarkably quickly."

The storm began to abate, and Jess could see that the paths had become muddy rivers. Nothing was moving out there. But within five minutes the sky cleared, the sun appeared again and the heat returned. The trees rose upright once more, gently easing out of the odd angles the storm had battered them into, shook their branches indignantly, shaking off the disturbance. The veranda steamed. All was quiet once more. People started to emerge from their bungalows to check for damage, but they looked happy and unperturbed.

"That's given the plants a good watering. We needed that!" said Betty. They finished their cups of tea as the sun dried the paths back into their usual dusty state. Then Jess glanced at her watch and decided she must get back to the apartment. Thank goodness she hadn't left any washing out to dry on the veranda of flat 4; it would have been swept away by now!

But as she rounded the corner of the block on the third floor, she saw with horror that the veranda doors were not only wide open and hanging off their hinges, but smashed, glass littering the concrete.

"Sandra! Are you OK? Where are you?" Jess shouted, panic catching her voice as she imagined that Sandra must have been caught in the flat with the onslaught of the storm, beaten by the wind, drowned by the rain, head smashed, unable to close the doors in time …

No answering call came and Jess 's heart thumped wildly as she crunched through the broken shards of glass, sloshed through the rainwater in the living room, gasping at the devastation of drenched papers scattered over the floor in inches of water, took in the sight of the mosquito net in tatters in her bedroom, her bedding saturated … Oh goodness …

Sandra's bedroom door was open and Jess, with great trepidation at what she might find, made her way through. But Sandra wasn't there. And there was little damage in her bedroom. The hurricane and rain had not penetrated that far into the apartment. Sandra had clearly simply gone out, leaving the doors wide open.

Jess waded back through to the veranda and leaned over. With relief she spotted Joseph checking the school hall. She called out to him and he looked up to see her stricken face.

"Please, Joseph! The flat's flooded and there's so much damage!"

"OK. I find Kobina and others. No worry! Stay there!"

Where on earth was Sandra, and why were the doors left open? Jess had left her busy writing letters in the living room earlier that afternoon. Well, at least she wasn't lying there injured in the flat, battered by the storm that had swept through the rooms. But why had she left the flat vulnerable like this? For goodness sake, how difficult was it to close the main doors at least? Even if she had to dash out suddenly. Or she was distracted. How much thought did it take to close a door?

Annoyed with her flat-mate's irresponsibility, she found a bucket and started to collect up as much of the broken glass from the veranda and living room as she could. The water they were lying in was dirty and ridden with insects and bugs. She could see the corpses of what looked like beetles and cockroaches floating in it and she had to gulp back her nausea as she worked. Her feet in their light flip-flops were wet and cold from wading through the rainwater and she couldn't imagine how she was going to get everything dry and straight again. She wished that Sandra had been there to help.

She had just noticed that she must have cut her feet on the glass shards, and that blood was swirling through the rainwater, when Joseph arrived with re-inforcements: Kobina, who Jess recognised from his work occasionally as Joseph's assistant, and two other houseboys from the compound - but not John. They carried buckets and mops. Without a word they set to work, bailing out the water and tipping the full buckets over the veranda wall to the compound below. Young Kobina, who looked about fourteen, had the muscle power and stamina of an ox, bending, scooping, tossing. He picked up the sodden papers from the floor and laid them with such care and respect on the table top that Jess's heart began to pump less violently and she started to feel a relief and comfort from the presence of these capable men.

In her bedroom she found photo frames smashed on the concrete floor and the photos ruined. Simon's handsome face smiled up at her from its watery resting place. Jess pulled down her torn and tattered mosquito net from its frame, dropped it on the wet floor and then inspected her bedding. The bedspread and top sheets were wet through but the mattress was only damp. Jess scooped the net and bedding up in her arms and took them through to the bathroom where she dumped them in the shower tray.

Betty had arrived too and was directing operations from the veranda doorway. A large very dark-skinned Ghanaian was busy replacing the glass panes in the doors. He had already managed to rehang the doors and clear out the broken windows into a bowl. Joseph and his crew had mopped the floor to a drying dampness and were working now on the bedroom floor. All the damaged papers and photos were laid out carefully on tables and chairs. Joseph nimbly swerved around her carrying the bundle of bedding outside, and Kobina followed lifting the mattress as though it was a paper plate.

"Best not to risk a damp mattress. They'll replace everything straight away, so don't worry," Betty reassured her. "But I'm sorry about the papers and photos. Hopefully they'll dry out but I'm afraid they won't be perfect." She sighed. "Always see that your windows and doors are shut before you go out, especially the main veranda doors."

"Yes," said Jess, unwilling to lay the blame on Sandra, although she was mad with her, and longed to say that she herself would never do such a stupid thing. Jess had peered at the papers and found that they were Sandra's marking and her private letters. While Sandra tended to strew her stuff around the place, Jess always kept her own things in a box in the top drawer of her chest so thankfully hers were safe. She felt a flutter of relief and even satisfaction that Sandra's carelessness had only harmed herself and not Jess or anyone else: "Sorry but it serves her right," she thought guiltily to herself, and then felt horrible and in penance went to check that Sandra's bed was dry and warm, and then scurried around tidying up her housemate's belongings neatly.

"What the hell are you doing?" came Sandra's voice. Jess swung around. Sandra looked furious. "And what on earth's happened here?"

"There was a flood. You left the doors open."

"Well, get out of my bedroom for a start," demanded Sandra. "Nothing in here seems wet!"

Jess backed out to find that Kobina and Joseph had replaced her mattress, bedding and mosquito net already and that the floors were almost dry. She could hear Sandra in her room, angrily banging her belongings back to their previous chaos before Jess tidied up. Jess made a mental note never to bother again.

"By the way, your papers and stuff got blown around and very wet. They're drying out on the table!" she called out to Sandra. "Best to see that the doors are shut before you go out. There was a terrible lot of damage."

"Well I didn't know there was going to be a storm, did I, Jess? For goodness sake I'm not the oracle! Hank came for me and we weren't around to shut doors and such. I can't be everywhere doing everything!"

"OK, just saying." Jess silently and privately raised her eyes up to heaven; the helpers had all disappeared so there was nobody to see her – so she reckoned it didn't count.

"Anyway, it looks fine, so I don't know what you're so uptight about."

Later, when Jess had regained her composure, she went down to Betty and Clara's bungalow to thank Betty and the houseboys for all their help. Joseph and Kobina lowered their eyes to the ground shyly but nodded that they would thank the others for her. She wanted to offer the men some money by way of a thank you, but Betty said it was not necessary as it was all part of their job but anyway she would give them an extra tip in their pay packets.

Two days after the hurricane and flash floods, Jess awoke to find that there was no water in the shower or the taps. The girls who did the morning clean in the flat arrived full of excitement to say that the water had been cut off; the authorities were connecting a pipeline to the hospital so there would be no water all day, or maybe even longer. Jess made do with a quick wash in a bowl she half filled with bottled water which she had the foresight to always keep handy in the fridge in case of emergencies. Her hair would have to wait but as she washed it every couple of days it wouldn't matter too much.

She had taken to keeping the kettle full too so she was able to use it to boil water for washing her breakfast dishes. As she cleaned her bowl, plate and mug, she thought of England and smiled at the knowledge that if the water was going to be cut off at home, they would all get letters, leaflets, and announcements from loudspeaker vans to warn them all in advance, so that they could fill baths, kettles, buckets and bottles for the emergency. With the water supplies here in Ghana normally being unpredictable to say the least, let alone being totally cut off, Jess at least kept a bottle and kettle ready. Although of course Sandra often emptied them and forgot to refill. Still – Jess was getting better at coping with the vagaries of life here and, hurricanes and flooded apartments apart, was feeling much more able to "keep calm and carry on".

Sandra appeared out of the bathroom, whistling, and promptly used the rest of the opened bottle and kettle, "Oh thank god, I thought I couldn't wash! You're an angel!" she declared, suddenly uncharacteristically pouncing on Jess to give her a bear-hug.

"From one extreme to another!" smiled Jess, and she didn't just mean the water situation.

It had been decided that Jess and Sandra would have some practice in driving the two cars that they would take on the trek to Timbuktu: Glenda's and Chrissie's. That would mean that they could share the driving and it would also be safer in the wilds of the northern district of the country where roads and conditions were less predictable. Although Jess had never been behind the wheel in her life, Sandra had taken some driving lessons before she came out to Ghana. There were no such things as driving tests and licences in Ghana, so anyone could swerve a vehicle around the potholes and bump along the rough roads of the interior. Jess knew from her experiences of taxis, mammy lorries and hitching rides in other people's cars, that driving here was more like dodgem cars at a fair than speeding down the M1.

She was excited at the prospect of learning to drive. When she returned to England she would brush up her skills with a few lessons and then take her test, get her licence before she went to university – and then she would be all set for real grown-up life. Simon had always said that there were just two things that parents needed to equip their kids with for adulthood: a passport and a driving licence. Wow, she was half way there and this was the opportunity to get the full Monty.

As Sandra had driven a little previously and as she had seemingly become Glenda's assistant in a number of ways, she was to drive with Glenda in her large tough Land Rover. Jess would travel with Chrissie in her more modest VW Beetle. That suited Jess just fine and cemented the friendship grouping. Chrissie had been a little startled when she was asked if she'd like to come on the trek, saying that she wasn't sure what she was doing in the Christmas break, that it depended on – well, something undefined, she'd have to check something – but the next day she had agreed wholeheartedly, and declared that she'd love to come with them.

Chrissie had started to take Jess out for practice drives two or three times a week and whenever they went out to Cape Coast or even Accra together she let Jess drive. Jess felt a mixture of fear and exhilaration. They didn't have a car at home, so it all seemed very new to Jess. She'd driven with her grandfather in his car, knowing that he had owned one of the first cars in the country, and he had pointed out things like gears and steering to her but that was about all. Of course, she'd driven around with Simon whenever he could borrow his mother's little grey mini but he hadn't ever suggested teaching her to drive and she had never thought of it herself. He'd always said that he loved driving – and especially driving her – so she'd just let him drive without any question. It was lovely to watch his strong sensitive hands on the steering wheel and to know that he was in control. He'd be so amazed to find out that she could drive when she returned to England that summer!

As soon as Jim heard what their plans were for the holiday, he volunteered to take Jess out in the car too, so that she would have plenty of practice.

The conversation had taken place at the end of choir rehearsal after an exhilarating couple of hours practising for the Christmas concert which was to be held in the last week of term.

"How kind of you!" declared Jess gratefully when Jim made his offer of driving instruction. Chrissie had smiled and shaken her head in a knowing sort of way, Jess thought, but then she spotted Angus beckoning, and she patted Jess on the arm and left her to stare quizzically after her as she made her way through the crowd to her lift back to the school compound.

"So we'll start straight away," said Jim emphatically, taking Jess's arm and guiding her through the mob of chattering choristers to the door, "Not tonight, obviously. I don't want you driving into a ditch in the dark. But tomorrow afternoon if you're free and up for it?"

"Yes, of course. That's wonderful. But are you sure? I don't want to impose – or for you to feel you have to!"

"*Jess!* I wouldn't have offered if it wasn't OK!" He suddenly stopped in the middle of the crowd and turned to her, looking into her eyes, smiling. "Listen. I'd love to. It'll give me a bit of time with you before you go gallivanting off on your trek." Then before she could even think about what he'd said, he grasped her arm again and led her to the door and out into the dark cool air.

Jim was true to his word and began to call for her regularly to take her driving in the truck. He was a patient teacher and didn't even flinch when she crashed the gears of the truck or muddled up the double de-clutch. What with the practice she had with Chrissie in the VW on a regular basis and with Jim in the larger more ungainly truck, whenever he could, Jess gradually felt that she was becoming more proficient and confident, and began to look forward to driving. In fact she felt grown up and powerful, not like a student but like a professional woman, a teacher.

As she drove with Chrissie they chatted about school and the pupils' foibles, but with Jim she listened as he told her about Ghana, its history, its traditions and lifestyle, and pointed out a whole host of interesting things as they passed. She felt quite in awe of his knowledge and enthusiasm about the country and its people. On one session they found themselves still a mile or so out from the school after darkness fell. Jim told her that it was good practice to try driving in the dark now that she was reasonably confident.

They passed darkened huts at the side of the road, very different from the way they appeared in the daylight and sunshine. They were lit only with kerosene lamps casting an eerie glow over the gloomy mud walls. Jess wondered what went on inside. Men with rasta dreadlocks sat in the dirt in doorways, smoking ("ganja," said Jim, then seeing Jess's incomprehension, "marijuana") and swigging from dark bottles. "Palm wine," Jim told her, "It's very potent and it's the favourite hooch."

"Palm wine? But I thought that the palm trees produced coconut and oil – and palm leaves for building roofs and shade?"

"Oh yes, that too. The different palms are very useful for Ghanaian life. But the wine – ah, that's a problem here. A lot of drunkenness – and so a lot of work for us at the hospitals. But I guess they need some kind of relief from the hardship of poverty." He paused for a moment in deep thought. "You can't blame them. I guess I'd be the same in those circumstances. Scratching out a living. No running water or electricity."

Jess had a sudden flashback to the conversation she had overheard at the party in Legon with Harriet and Rafe. The engineers had been talking about the electricity generation plant. They had sneered at her when she couldn't understand why the villages had no power when there was such a huge hydro-electric project at Akasombo. She recounted the conversation for Jim and said,

"Do you know what happens at the plant?"

"Well ..." Jim looked sideways at her and frowned. "It's President Nkrumah's baby, this plant. Lots of foreign financial backing. Big prestigious project. Like saying "hey, I'm a big guy, a big player in the world – look at me, look at Ghana". But nothing's for the people. It's for internal industry – fair enough, but the excess is sold abroad. Nothing's for the folks that live with no jobs, no money, and little food to feed their kids, no medicines for the hospitals, the clinics." Jim shook his head and grimaced.

"But maybe if it attracts international attention, it'll also attract money for aid?"

"It's my guess – and that of many observers – that even money designed for aid goes into his personal coffers. Look at the lavish lifestyle, the cars he drives, the fancy palace he lives in."

Politics was never an easy subject for Jess, despite her mother's left-wing pronouncements and despite Simon's many attempts to persuade her of his own beliefs – "we're all socialists these days," he used to say, "well, all students at least, so if you're going to university, you'd better get to know the ideas." She also knew that his old Quaker family, although wealthy and titled, had acquired their money, not from some long standing aristocratic inheritance, but from industry like many other Quakers, and had gained their title in exchange for a very generous donation to the Labour party. Jess always thought that somehow contradictory, in spite of her mother's Rulebook: "Quakers are always right."

"Well, I've read about that argument," she said to Jim, "but what about the argument that you have to spend money to get money?"

"That depends what you want the money for. I'm not convinced that Nkrumah's intentions for the country are honourable. For himself and his family and hangers-on, yes, but not for Ghana and the ordinary people. Oh, he's doing pretty well out of it. And of course there are many loyal followers – guess why? Loyalty bonuses, gifts, generous entertaining, a word in the ear of contractors, investors. Hey, here's my man, great guy, give him the contract, the job, the sinecure."

"So you don't think that building up Ghana as an international power will benefit the ordinary people? Won't it make the economy stronger, and then make Ghana able to provide for its own people?"

"You think Nkrumah would spend money on – what? – schools, hospitals, housing? Why should he? He can afford to build the luxurious home for himself, to send his family abroad for medical treatment, education. He and his buddies don't need local services. So why should he provide them for people he probably despises? The ordinary Ghanaian is merely the worker bee, the one who mines the gold, harvests the cocoa, collects the nectar for Nkrumah's honey. He doesn't want them educated so that they question anything. And there are enough of them to be expendable. Just like the slaves herded by the West."

"But isn't it about common decency?"

"You and I may think that, Jess, but I guess there are many folks in the world who don't care to share or to look after others, only themselves. There's an argument that says: I've worked hard, I've risen up the ranks, so why should I have to share what I have with anyone else?"

"So is that why you came here to do what you do?"

"Yeah, I guess so. Just trying to make a bit of difference. I like to think that's what Kennedy intended for the Peace Corps. Putting something back."

"Kennedy. He seemed a good chap," said Jess. She sighed, recalling the American president's tragic death.

"Oh yes," Jim agreed, "He was one of the good guys in American politics. Distant relative, actually. But yep, everyone remembers where they were on Friday November 22nd of '63."

"I was at boarding school," recalled Jess. "We were expected to be aware of current world affairs. We had "news prefects" who wrote the day's headlines on the hall blackboard. We were doing our "prep" and one of the prefects came round to the prep room and told us to go straight away to the dining room. She looked awful, red eyed and white as a sheet."

"Was she American?"

"No. We just all loved him. And America's like, well, like heaven, the promised land. That wonderful country over the sea where the music and the films and the fashion all comes from. So we trooped to the dining room – it was really odd, because we were all in silence, we just knew something earth-shattering had happened. The teachers were ushering us to the seats and they all looked aghast. We knew it was something really bad. Then we realised that the radio was on and there was that terrible announcement." She remembered it so well, word for word: *"President Kennedy has been shot today by an unknown assassin. He sustained a fatal bullet wound in the motor cavalcade through Dallas, Texas, and was pronounced dead at Parkland hospital at one o'clock Central Standard Time."* She sighed. First the drama of the Cuba missile crisis, the edge of the abyss her mother had said, and then Kennedy's assassination.

"Yeah, I was at college. Similar thing. How strange to think it was the same from one side of the Atlantic to the other."

Jess drove on in silence for a while, knowing that beside her Jim was deep in thought. Then she said gently, breaking the spell,

"So you really don't like Nkrumah, then?" she smiled, staring intently straight ahead through the windscreen as she tried to anticipate potholes. "I mean, I don't know him personally, obviously. I wouldn't like to say what his intentions are!"

Jim did not speak for several minutes, but raked his hand through his hair. Jess didn't break the silence; she knew he was mulling something over that was important to him.

"Well, just between us, I guess I know quite a lot," he murmured at last. "But keep that quiet, hey?"

Jess wondered what he meant but as she glanced sideways at his profile beside her, the shuttered look on his face deterred her from taking it any further.

She worried about what else the chaps at the party had said – about people disappearing, political dissidents, the "disparu". Presumably those opposed to the President and his ways. She bit her lip hard and frowned deep creases into her brow. She hoped to goodness that Jim wasn't in any danger, with his anti-Nkrumah ideas. Her mind was in a whirl: what on earth was Jim involved in? She felt her face flush, her pulse quicken. What if he was doing something stupid? What if he came to harm? She felt her grip on the steering wheel tighten and her eyes blur.

"Watch out!" Jim shouted, reaching over her and grabbing the wheel. The truck veered viciously and skidded; Jess screamed. The wheels seemed to lose traction on the muddy road, and Jess was aware only of the trees in the dark looming towards them. Then the truck bumped violently, jarring Jess's spine and limbs, as it met undergrowth and vegetation.

"Brace!" yelled Jim, pushing her head down. With a sickening thud and the crunching of metal, the truck at last came to rest. Jess, eyes tight shut, was aware that the terrifying wild movement had ended and raised her head to see that they seemed to be pitched at an odd angle.

Somehow, Jim was outside in the darkness, wrenching open the door at her side and the ground seemed to be a foot or two lower than it should have been. "God! Are you OK?" He reached in to her, feeling around her head and arms, a doctor examining his patient. "We seem to have landed in a ditch. Well, better than crashing into the trees, I guess."

His voice seemed amazingly calm. He reached around her and lifted her down, out of the truck and onto the bank. As he let go of her, she suddenly felt so dizzy she thought she would fall. She must have stumbled because he grabbed hold of her to steady her.

This time he did not let her go. Instead he enfolded her in his arms, pulling her close to his strong muscular body. Her face was crushed in to his broad chest but she didn't mind; it was where she wanted to be at this moment, comforted, safe, inhaling his masculine scent.

"Sorry, I'm so sorry!" he breathed into her hair. "I was supposed to be helping you with your driving and I was going on and on about my crazy theories. God, I could have killed you!"

Jess felt his hands stroking her back gently. "No, it was me!" she wailed into his shirt. "I wasn't paying attention. I – I don't know what happened!"

He held her a little away from his body, his eyes scouring her face, her torso, her legs, as if checking her over for damage. But, then she realised, no, not really like that at all. Not medically, neutrally. Tenderly. He stroked the hair out of her eyes, and rested his hand on her cheek, cupping her face. His thumb caressed the side of her mouth, travelled lightly over her lips. He leaned in, bending down to her, and Jess smelled his earthy scent and knew that she wanted him to kiss her. His mouth barely touched hers before he pulled firmly away.

"You're OK?" he said. She nodded mutely, confused by her unsummoned feelings.

"Yes, I think so." Gingerly she moved her limbs and stretched her back. Everything seemed fine, still working anyway.

"Right," said Jim decisively, walking round the truck and inspecting it with his palms and feet, while Jess shivered. "Thank goodness we're just at the bottom of the school drive. I'll get you up to the flat and then get the guys to help pull this thing out of the ditch. Don't think the damage is serious. C'mon!"

Jess stumbled up the drive with only a few intermittent lamps to guide their way. Jim seemed perfectly confident in his stride, and he took Jess's hand to support her. As they neared the school buildings, he dropped her hand and wrapped his arm around her back, hugging her gently. "OK?"

"I just feel awful! Will you bill me for the damage?"

Jess felt his smile although she couldn't see it. "Sure. Don't worry. We'll see to it. Got the mechanics! Just leave it to me."

At the door, Jim squeezed her hand. "Get a shower and an early night." Maybe she had been completely mistaken about the kiss and he was just being sweet and avuncular after a frightening incident. "See you soon!" And she heard his footsteps retreat along the hallway and down the stairs.

She let herself in to the flat. At least the doors were shut. Sandra was not there although the lights were on, flickering low as they often did in the unpredictable electricity supply. What on earth had just happened? Had Jim made a pass at her? Yes, maybe so. And – oh god! – she liked it. What was wrong with her? She had Simon!

"So, this Quaker thing?" asked Jim a few days later when he came up to the flat to reassure her that the truck was now fully repaired. He had told the Peace Corps field director that he had crashed it in the dark after drinking a bit too much palm wine and he had, according to Jim, slapped him on the back and laughed. "Tell me about it!"

"Oh, well, I was brought up in a Quaker family and was sent to a Quaker boarding school," she explained, curling her legs up beneath her in the armchair. She felt a little awkward after the other night, but tried to pretend nothing had happened. "I know it's a very strong faith for my parents. They're elders of the church. I'm expected to be the same. Oh, I know we're supposed to be good people and do good in the world – and, well, OK, but ..."

"What? You don't feel good enough for them?" *How did he know?* "Or maybe, not in the way they want you to be?"

"Absolutely right." Jess snuggled further into herself and grimaced at Jim. He was stretched out on the chair opposite, legs akimbo, as Jess had seen him on that first day back in October and she was even more aware of his wide mouth, his lopsided sexy smile, and his chiselled chin. "My mother ... oh, I shouldn't really say this, it feels a bit disloyal ... but she always says that motherhood was the most important thing in her life and how important it is to 'mould' her children in proper Quaker ways ... or how *she* sees them anyway ..."

"Oh, god, Jess, that's awful!" Jess wasn't sure whether she felt bad that she'd criticised her mother, or pleased that Jim thought that it was not right – as she did.

"I just feel I'm in a strait-jacket. You know, expected to be someone I'm not. And it's as though if I don't become that person I'll be somehow damned to all eternity."

"God, that's dramatic!" He shuffled so that one ankle rested on his other knee, thighs wide apart, and he combed his fingers through his hair, frowning. "Hmmm ...so they're basically Puritans? Like the Puritans who sailed to Boston and founded Philadelphia?" Jess nodded. "I guess what I know of them is that they seemed to be thoughtful people, peace-loving. I guess they stand for quietness and purity." He frowned over at Jess. "Yep, I can see why you don't fit the image."

"Hey, you!" Jess reached behind her and lobbed the cushion over at him. He raised his hand languidly and caught it with ease.

"But actually," he smiled at her. "I think you are a bit like that. In a nice way. You have a certain calm stillness about you, an aura of assurance and – oh, English elegance, I guess. I like it."

Jess never knew that could be a compliment! She had only ever been criticised by her parents for being too flighty and by others for being too quiet or studious or "stand-offish". So which was she supposed to be? She couldn't be both. She only succeeded in disappointing everyone. It was all very confusing. But she liked Jim's way of interpreting her so much better. She'd have to keep that in her mind; she could be *that* person: assured, elegant with a calm stillness ... yes.

"And seriously, I can see that you want to be your own person."

"I just want to be like everyone else. I just want to be normal."

"Hmm, 'normal' – I wonder what that is. And what about your parents? Aren't they 'normal'?"

"Oh, they're so different from my friends' parents. They're known as good Quakers – very puritanical, straight-laced. Upright decent citizens. Actually disapproving – puritan hang-ups I think. But maybe ..." she paused, frowning, remembering, "I think that things are not always what they seem."

Jim leaned forward. "Folks can be good at heart, well meaning, but sometimes do things that are denounced by others." Jess knew that he was not following her train of thought but going down another track, one that was close to his own heart. One that was about his own experience. What had he done – or was intending to do – that others might denounce? Jess couldn't imagine that Jim could possibly do anything like that.

The following week brought the Christmas choir concert and the end of the school term, so Jess was too busy to dwell on anything else. Her first year group performed their Hansel and Gretel musical play for the rest of the school, to great excitement and hysterical giggling. She had supervised the girls making masks of flowers out of card, to hold up, the centres of the petal circles cut out for their faces to peer through, and in the costume box they found a black pointed witch's hat and cloak, a little girl's bonnet and a boy's cap. It was all very simple, minimalistic, but effective. Betty and Clara were delighted at the play. The only sour note was from Glenda who made loud comments about each error the girls made.

The day before the Timbuktu trip, Jess sang in the choir Christmas concert. Their voices filled the hall with the most magical sounds of the carols and Christmas music they had been preparing all term: Handel's And the Glory of the Lord, A Maiden Most Gentle, The First Noel set to Pachelbel's Canon, and Silent Night amongst other well-known carols many of which the audience joined in. Jim had persuaded Jess to sing, in a trio, the "solo" parts of O Holy Night. The support of the other soprano and alto calmed Jess's nerves and Jim's accompaniment on the piano gave her confidence. She was amazed at how much she enjoyed it all. She felt high with the success of the evening, her face flushed, eyes bright, and her heart filled with joy; she couldn't stop laughing. She would never forget that night. After the concert ended and the choir retired to the prep room, everyone came up to her and hugged her. She peered over their heads and saw Jim across the room, equally surrounded. He nodded over to her and smiled, mouthing "well done!"

The morning they left for Timbuktu, Jim came over to the flat to wish her safe journey.

"And happy Christmas," he said as he enfolded her in a brotherly bear hug. "I guess I won't see you until well after New Year's. So, have a great time." He told her that he had work to do in the north and that's where he was spending the holidays. She had a sudden flash of memory of what he had said about people getting denounced for their actions, however well-meaning they might be, and remembered his criticisms of Nkrumah's life style. In her mind they merged together and suddenly she shuddered. What if …? No, she daren't even think it …

"Just take care," she hugged him back, frowning, but held on to him perhaps a little too long.

He held her away from him, raked his hand through his thick curly hair and grimaced. "Jess, I can't let you get involved." Then, with a sad apologetic smile, he turned on his heel, waving, and walked out of the flat.

Involved with what? Jess frowned. *Did he mean with his activities in the north? Were they Peace Corps? Or political? Or did he mean … with him?*

Jess sat in the passenger seat of the VW Beetle as Chrissie drove along the rough mud tracks leaving the metalled roads far behind. She had done an hour's stint and now it was Chrissie's shift. She watched the scenery as the car bumped over potholes and debris, drinking in every nuance of the changing landscape as they ventured northwards to the Ashanti region, committing it to memory so that she could describe it all to Simon when she returned home.

The scrubland gave way to rain forest and the thick lush vegetation fringing the road seemed to bend towards the little car. She kept her eye on the Land Rover ahead of them and on Sandra's rather erratic driving. From time to time, she could see Glenda reach over to wrench the steering wheel and breathed a sigh of relief that she was not in that car, but with Chrissie and the gentle sounds of Christmas carols on her cassette player wobbling on the back seat.

They planned to stop that night at the rest-house well short of Bole, but by the time they arrived it was already dark and Jess could see little apart from a concrete building by the side of the muddy track. As she climbed from the car she could hear the scraping noise of the cicadas in the bush, loud in the night air. Inside it was dingy with a bare concrete floor and a naked light bulb hanging precariously from the ceiling, but there was a basic kitchen area with a calor gas camping stove and a bedroom with camp beds and mosquito nets. They had brought supplies so were able to cook a simple meal and when the electricity flickered its last, they went to bed in the sleeping bags they had brought with them. Jess had a cotton liner which provided cool comfort in the sultry night air.

In the morning Jess was awoken by the sun streaming intensely through the curtainless, shutterless window. It was hot and humid, and she wriggled out of her bedding, slipped on her sandals and went outside. The air was surprisingly fresh and she watched the egrets and ibises circling a pond of rainwater, listening to the loud croaking "cuk-cuk-cuk", until Chrissie appeared in her pyjamas with a couple of mugs of Milo.

"There is a certain beauty in the isolation, isn't there?" said Chrissie, gazing across the empty savannah.

"Mmm," murmured Jess as she sipped her steaming coffee. "Do you think you'll stay here in Ghana or are you planning to go home to the UK?"

"I guess I'll go home sometime." Chrissie paused and stared into the distance. "I love it here, but ... nothing lasts, does it?" She sounded so sad that Jess put her arm round her comfortingly. Chrissie glanced sideways at her and said slowly, "I suppose you've guessed my secret. I don't think people generally know. I hope not. So this is confidential, Jess. But ..." Jess stiffened. "It's Angus ..."

Of course! The subterfuge, the mysterious visits to Cape Coast, the awkward exchange when Jess first joined the inter-schools choir. Jess knew that something was up. But Angus?

The science teacher at the school! Who did some part-time lecturing at the university college in Cape Coast. Who had an apartment there as well as the bungalow at the school he shared with ... his wife?

"Angus?" Jess echoed. Chrissie, kind, gentle Chrissie, elegant sophisticated Chrissie, her role-model, almost her idol ... having an affair with a married man? Surely not? How could she?

"Yes, I know you probably think it's awful, with him being married and all that." Chrissie gave Jess a rueful smile. "But I love him. It's as simple as that." She sighed. "His wife – I don't mean to be nasty about her, it's not her fault – but she isn't that interested in him. She's involved with someone else, a business man, rather wealthy, in Accra." Chrissie grimaced. "I think it's the heat out here. The different way of life. It does things to people. Expat marriages often don't survive."

Chrissie. Angus and his wife. Sandra and Hank. Oh god ...what was wrong with people? What could she say?

"I'm sorry."

"Angus has a young son at boarding school back in England. He can't leave her yet."

"Ah." Jess felt inexplicably betrayed. *Surely Chrissie had a choice? If Simon was unfaithful to her, she'd be destroyed. She loved him so much. But maybe Angus's wife didn't love him. Or maybe Angus was deceiving Chrissie? What a tangled web. Why weren't people just simply faithful to each other? Where was trust and devotion?*

"I meant to explain before," said Chrissie. "When you joined the choir I thought we'd be outed. But you never said a thing." She touched Jess's arm. "Thank you."

Jess thought of Chrissie's words, "I love him. It's as simple as that," and she couldn't find it in her heart to condemn her friend. She thought of how difficult it must have been, and still be, for Chrissie. She knew her well enough to be sure that she wouldn't have run headlong into an affair without torturing herself with the implications. *The world was such a complicated place.* Jess grimaced.

"Nothing's straightforward, is it?" she said to Chrissie with a rueful smile.

"No, indeed," Chrissie smiled back gently.

They travelled along increasingly rough dirt roads darkened by the encroaching jungle through the damp bleak region of Bamboi before taking the ferry across the Black Volta, a dark swampy river, rife with swooping insects and brooding creatures half submerged along the steep banks. At Lawra they had slept the night in a dormitory of a boys' school, and Jess was thankful for the real mattressed bed. Then at the isolated village of Hapa, they were welcomed effusively by the Chief who proudly introduced them to his forty children, insisting on having photos taken by the

"English mammies" whilst four of his eighteen wives shyly peeped around the hut doorways with ghostly smiles. They crossed the border at Hamale, under the huge replica of the Ashanti chief's stool, waving a temporary goodbye to Ghana, and drove through the dry Saharan sands of southern Upper Volta to Bobo-Dioulasso and Ougadougou. Muslim mosques with elaborately carved towers built from mud or concrete were busy with white-robed Arab men called to prayer. At every stop, Jess found a postcard and charted her journey for Simon.

Christmas Eve dawned hot and the day was sultry and airless in the car as they drove the Upper Volta road between Ougadougou and the Mali border. Jess could hardly believe it was Christmas, which she always associated with cold wintry weather, often snow, not tropical heat.

They pitched camp that evening, in the middle of a nature reserve and as there was no rest-house within reach they set up their camp beds al fresco. Chrissie had brought four felt Christmas stockings and hung one at the end of each camp bed.

"Oh for god's sake!" grumbled Glenda, but Jess noticed that she didn't refuse the little gifts that were stuffed into her stocking.

Chrissie smiled confidentially at Jess as she popped a couple of neatly wrapped and beribboned boxes into Jess's stocking. "Hope you like it!" she whispered. "And this one's from Jim. He asked me to bring it for you."

Jess felt a pang of guilt; she hadn't given him anything but a card. She'd thought about it but wasn't sure it was appropriate. Now she wished she had.

She had bought a small piece of jewellery for each of the others, snakeskin necklaces for Sandra and Glenda, and a pair of delicate gold earrings for Chrissie. She added her gifts to each stocking, and Sandra did the same, but she couldn't help but notice that Glenda did not.

That night she thought that she would find it difficult to sleep on her camp bed in the open air. She felt exposed and vulnerable, even though Chrissie had tried to convince her that there weren't any dangerous wild animals in the area. In fact she slept soundly and woke on Christmas Day to the strains of carols on Chrissie's cassette player.

They opened their gifts around the camp fire. Jim had given her a gold pendant with a tiny Ghanaian drum on it. She slipped it quietly around her neck and tucked it under her top. She didn't think anyone else saw.

"So, Christmas Day and we're on the road!" laughed Chrissie. "Let's hope we can find somewhere for a nice French Christmas dinner!"

They crossed the Mali border without incident. The southern Saharan roads were desert tracks marked out with oil drums every now and then and they followed truck tyre tracks from one to the next. They travelled on, through Mali to Mopti, the sandy, dry, concrete Muslim town on the banks of the muddy murky river Niger, where they could embark the steamboat to take them upriver to Timbuktu.

"*Non. Pas avant demain.*" Shrugged shoulders. Shaking of the head.

"There's no steamer boat upriver to Timbuktu until tomorrow," Jess explained to the others, translating from the thick French accented Malian voice of the steamer captain who they discovered lounging against the dark doorway of a small hotel on the waterfront, smoke from his cigarette swathing his deeply wrinkled features and tattered uniform. Jess had been designated official translator in the French territories of Upper Volta and Mali, even though she was not sure that her French was up to the mark.

She frowned as she struggled with the translation. She could speak French enough to get by, but the accents were so heavy that she had to strain her ears and concentrate hard to make out the words.

"Oh, typical!" shouted Glenda, whose annoyance at all around her had not abated throughout the whole journey so far. Jess was amazed that Sandra had been able to put up with it. She was constantly glad that she was travelling with the gentle and happy Chrissie and only had to endure Glenda's moods when they stopped for lunch and in the evening. And even then, Chrissie and Jess had managed to find excuses for retaining a certain distance from the other two.

"Well, let's have a comfortable night in the hotel for once," suggested Chrissie, peering at the torn notice pinned to the wall which advertised dinner and bedrooms. "We deserve it!"

"Absolutely," smiled Jess. "Let's risk it. He says that there's a sailing at nine in the morning."

The little dank hotel bedroom that Jess shared with Chrissie was crowded with twin beds almost touching and only room to squeeze round them. Their bags had to be squashed under the beds. But the dinner in the restaurant was freshly cooked chicken and spicy couscous, the red French wine was fruity and dense, and the coffee on the veranda was hot and rich: a Christmas dinner Jess would never forget.

Glenda and Sandra retired early to their shared bedroom, and, after a chat and more coffee, Chrissie said she'd go up first to get ready for bed as there wasn't much room for both of them to get washed and changed in their tiny *chambre*.

"You'll be OK out there on the veranda by yourself?" asked Chrissie kindly.

"Absolutely!" said Jess, "I'm enjoying taking in the river view, even in the darkness. I'll be up in about – what – fifteen minutes?"

"Great, it won't take me any longer than that! And in fact I think I'll be off as soon as my head touches the pillow!"

Jess watched the steamer and the activity of the crew readying the boat for the morning's sail. She felt dozy and relaxed from the wine.

The wind was drifting up from the murky water and moaning softly around the buildings of the harbour. The waves lapped the stone embankment and rumbled the cobbles. The cries of the sailors became low melodic songs as they worked. Then, in the hot darkening night, Jess heard it.

The drumming of kpanlogo djembe and the words of the dondo began to fill her mind and her senses. The rhythmic pounding of the drums seemed to be calling out to her, an ominous warning – what was it? What did she need to be warned against? Her future? Her past? Someone? Who? The drumming reached its crescendo and slowly died away, merging itself into the crying of the spirits on the night air. The sailors had gone and the waters of the river beneath her rippled black in the breeze. Jess shivered, and turned, frowning, to go inside and prepare for a night's sleep she knew would be restless.

She had just written brief cards to Simon and her family since they started on the trek, and Christmas night seemed an appropriate time to scribble a note on a postcard she had bought in Ougadougou, so in the semi-darkness, with a torch, before settling down for the night, she had written:

My dear Simon,

Happy Christmas! The trek to Timbuktu has really begun in earnest now that we're actually on the river Niger, a steamboat ride away from the town that seems to represent the furthest outpost of civilisation! We've crossed the southern Sahara desert! It all seems so strange; it is actually Christmas, but one like no other. I guess I'll remember this for ever.

She wanted to say something about Chrissie and Angus, but decided against it as the postcard was all too open and exposed. So she just added:

I just wish you were here too.
With love, J x

She pondered on what she had written, and knew that she didn't wish he was here; he would hate it. He was safely tucked up at home in his comfortable bed-sitting room his parents had set up for him in their large detached suburban home. But as her eyes grew heavy from the day's travelling, she knew that she would not swap with him for the world. And as she listened to the low murmurs of the river, the gentle noises of the night air, she realised that she would hear no more drumbeats that night.

The next day, the river steamer, the *General A-Soumare*, was crowded and noisy. They had left their cars at the harbour and hired a couple of cabins for the night in Timbuktu as they planned to simply sail upriver to see the famous town then sail right back again to Mopti and resume their journey back south east to Ghana.

As the boat chugged into the harbour at Timbuktu, Jess stood on deck leaning against the railings, her bag between her feet for safety. Chrissie's hair, loose for once, was fanning away from her face in the welcome breeze from the water.

"Make the most of the air on the river, smelly as it may be," said Chrissie, "It's going to be very hot and airless in the town."

And it certainly was. Jess could scarcely breathe as she and Chrissie weaved their way through the crowded noisy streets around the enormous imposing mosque, deafened by the muezzin's shrill *adhan*, the call to noon prayers from the minaret, and jostled by the ubiquitous Arab traders aggressively thrusting their wares under their noses. Jess could feel tension in the air, suspicion in the eyes of the passers-by. She quickened her pace.

The sultry heat radiated from the concrete which most of the town seemed to be built with, the same indistinguishable square buildings as in Ouagadougou, and Jess kept taking a swig from her bottle of Fanta which seemed to have little lasting effect on her dry throat.

"Phew! I feel as though I'm walking in an oven. Let's dive into that café, the one with the ceiling fans."

"I wonder how Glenda and Sandra are getting on, trying to find camera film. I don't know why Glenda refused your offer of help with translation in the shops."

Jess shrugged. "Well, I offered, but if she doesn't want my company…"

"Ah, don't worry about it. Their problem. Oooh, look those people are leaving that table under the fan. Let's sit and try this coffee." Chrissie waved her hand at a huge glass coffee percolator on the counter, oblivious to the stares. "I don't know. Glenda's an odd bird. I wonder what happened in her past."

"Why?"

"Well, I just think that if someone is so grumpy and miserable, something must have happened to make her so."

"Mmmm, maybe, I wonder …Oh, er …" she hesitated as a waiter hovered over them. "Er, *deux tasses de café, s'il vous plaît* … er, *avec du lait?*" The waiter frowned as if milk was not normal, but shrugged and moved to the tiny kitchen at the back. Other customers looked over suspiciously at them, turning back to their companions and speaking low with barely disguised furtive glances in their direction. Jess felt increasingly uneasy. The waiter returned with two small glasses of thick black coffee in metal holders, a doll-sized jug of cold milk and a saucer with two little sticky sugar glazed pastries on it. Jess smiled her thanks and the waiter grunted and turned away. "You know, Timbuktu is nothing like I thought it would be."

"How so?"

"I imagined a little mud village in the middle of nowhere, a bit like Kakomdo stuck in the Sahara desert. The final outpost before the track loses itself in the sandy desert, surrounded by miles of emptiness. And here it is, a thriving busy town. It shouldn't be like this." She laughed. "It's shattered all my dreams!"

"Mmm. Who was it who said, '*Tread softly lest you tread on my dreams*'?" mused Chrissie, sipping her tiny glass of coffee. "Maybe it's better to stick to reality, with all its limitations."

But reality came swiftly as they disembarked off the boat back in Mopti. Pausing at the top of the steep gangplank, behind the crowd of women with huge baskets and clutching children that halted any progress, Jess became aware of a commotion on the dockside. Already uneasy, she kept the corner of her eye on the source of the noise as they were jostled down the gangplank. Passengers around her were talking in agitated bursts and pushing at each other, in a hurry to get off the boat and away. She glanced quickly behind her to check that her companions were with her.

Chrissie was looking wild-eyed, shocked. On the dock ahead of her, the crowd of disembarking passengers thinned and revealed three swarthy soldiers, armed with machine guns, faces red with anger, shouting fast in Arabic. A gaunt-thin man dressed in a long white robe, turned to Jess and her companions as they alighted onto the cobbles, and pointed. The largest of the soldiers raised his gun at Jess's chest, yelling so violently at her that spittle arced towards her. *Oh god!* She felt a stream of sweat run down her body as she struggled to speak.

"*Quel est le probleme? Ce qui se passe?*" she stammered, feeling Glenda's bulk pushing impatiently at her back. For god's sake, don't let her say anything stupid, Jess prayed silently. From the French shouts in the crowd she gathered that there was unrest in the region and that everyone was jumpy. She thought she heard 'Haute Volta' and 'Ouagadougou' called out. The bulky soldier switched from Arabic to French but his tirade was so rapid and abrupt, like the stuttering of a machine gun, that she had little idea of what he was saying.

"I don't understand you!" she panicked. "*Pas comprends. Que dites-vous?*"

"Passa ports! Passa ports!" he yelled, gesturing with his gun. Jess fumbled for her passport in her shoulder bag, showering tissues, Tampax and keys onto the dockside. Her brain didn't seem to be capable of controlling her hands and she gestured helplessly. "Sorry! Sorry! *Je m'excuse!*" The soldier grabbed her passport and glared at it. He glanced up at her, frowning.

"*Pas americaine alors?*"

"*Non, non, pas du tout! Nous sommes tous des dames anglaises ... tous les quatre ...le meme ... moi et mes amies, monsieur.*" She gestured at her companions and then at her passport.

The soldier thrust her passport back at Jess and jerked his machine gun towards the road. "*Passez-par! Allez la-bas! Vite. Vite!*"

"What the hell was all that about?" demanded Glenda as Jess ushered them quickly up to the road and the safety of their cars.

"I've no idea," gasped Jess, her hands still shaking, "But there's a lot of unrest in the region, everyone's nervous. I think – I think, a suspected coup d'état. I'm not sure." Glenda puffed in scorn and looked impatient with her. "And maybe something about Ouagadougou. They're after someone or other, poor soul. Let's just get out of here as quickly as we can."

6

JANUARY 1966

It was on the night of New Year's Eve that Jess heard the drumbeats again, at a small stuffy, grubby hotel in Ouagadougou so near the mosque that Jess could hear every word from the muezzin's calls to prayer from the minaret. They had driven fast and urgently south through Mali and Upper Volta towards the Ghana border. She had barely taken in the rocky outcrop of Sangha, stone cliffs in the midst of sandy desert, cliff huts perched on the steep slopes, the houses of the dead.

She had a splitting headache from the glaring sun and oppressive heat, the staring through the windscreen at the road ahead, and the nervous tension that had dogged her since the episode with the armed soldiers in Mopti. She went to bed early and at first she wasn't sure whether the rhythmic pounding was in her head or in the dark stifling streets outside the hotel.

She could hear Chrissie's gentle regular breathing in the bed the other side of the room, and lay there listening. The swell of the drums beat the familiar pattern, rising to a crescendo and dying away. Jess shivered even in her hot clammy sheets.

The rest of the night she tossed as she desperately sought a more comfortable position that might bring her some sleep but it was a fitful troubled slumber. She counted the muezzin's every *adhan* for every *salat*, at sunset, midnight and dawn and the cries echoed in her dreamless mind as they called the faithful to prayer across the faceless indistinguishable buildings of the concrete town .

It was later the next day, New Year's Day, the first day of the year that was to have taken her home again to Simon that all hell broke loose. Afterwards she could remember only the shouting, the shrieks of terror, the chaos of bodies, the confusion of Arabic and French yelled across the crowd at the Upper Volta border. So nearly "home" in Ghana.

She remembered Chrissie stopping the car at the border checkpoint behind Glenda's Land Rover. Opening the door and getting out, looking around for the border guards to check the four passports she held. Nobody appearing out of the guard hut.

Hearing the loud laughing chatter of the passengers alighting from the bus in front of the Land Rover. Noticing the streets cordoned off. Hearing Glenda shouting in impatience at the hut, storming over to the barrier. To her horror, Glenda yanking at the metal barrier, trying to force it open for them to pass through.

Then the crack of gunfire. Shrieks. Screaming women and children pushing, tumbling over each other in the haste to get clear of the bus. Riot squads in tin helmets pouring out of lorries as they screeched and skidded to a halt in front of the barrier. Armed police. Soldiers shouting, running over to the cars, gesturing them all out of the vehicles, machine guns, pistols, rifles, AK 47s, cocked towards them, fingers twitching on triggers. Very young, terrified fingers. Only boys really. But all the more dangerous.

Scuffling, screams, only a few feet away from her, the glimpse of a man on the ground, boy-soldiers surrounding him, kicking, beating with clubs. Black arms pummelling violently. The man's face, mashed and bloody, white shirt soaked now with red, his arms raised to shield his head.

Oh my god!

Jess backing into someone and tripping, falling to the hard stony ground. Looking up to see a young angry soldier aiming his gun at her face. His hands were shaking. Sweat was running down his face.

"*Se lever!*" More gunfire cracking the air. "*La-bas!*"

"Please. Please. *Prie-dieu*!" She shielded her eyes from the glare of the sun and struggled to her feet, looking wildly around for the others.

"*Ou est mes amies?*" she gasped. "*Les anglaises! Je vous en prie!*" The young soldier, hardly older than the girls she taught, jerked his gun to the side. She could see Glenda, red-faced, protesting loudly and furiously, being frog-marched by two guards over to a larger shed behind the hut, a third soldier beside them, covering her with his machine gun ready cocked. She saw Chrissie and Sandra being directed to follow into the shed. *Thank god, all still alive!*

The young soldier pushed Jess towards the shed, urging her on with the muzzle of his gun in her back. "*Ici! Depechez-vous!*"

It took a few moments for Jess's eyes to become accustomed to the dark inside the shed. Her heart pounding, she saw Glenda forced onto a wooden chair in front of a desk, flanked by the two guards, where a thick-set uniformed and be-medalled officer sat, black shiny face frowning, smoking a cigarette. He stared at Glenda as the two guards spoke, much too loudly and angrily, to the officer. At least it was all conducted in French and Jess grasped at a few of the words: "*troubles civils*", "*emeutes*", "*barriere*", "*sans autorisation*", "*severe punition*": civil unrest, riots, barrier, without permission, and then frighteningly "severe punishment".

The officer shrugged his shoulders and, shaking his head, muttered, "*Les anglaises!*" as though the English were a constant aggravation to him. Jess thought he might have sworn but her French was not that good. He sighed impatiently and looked from one to the other of the four. Glenda swivelled round in her chair and the white-faced look she threw at Jess was of sheer terror. Jess had never seen much emotion in Glenda other than anger, sarcasm and scorn. But this was abject helpless fear; a plea to Jess "help me!" And she knew in that moment that nobody had ever defied Glenda before to her face or threatened her and she had no idea how to cope. Whatever had happened in her past, Glenda had grown to clothe herself in projected unassailability. She had grown a protective shell that repelled all-comers. And now they had all glimpsed beneath the outward show to a vulnerability. Fear and an inability to manage the situation. *Yes, we've all been there*! For a moment Jess fought the urge to say, "Too bad, you brought it on yourself." But she knew, rationally, that all four were in it together. They all turned to her. So she stepped forward. *Oh well, nothing more to lose!*

"What do you want me to say?" she asked. She struggled to keep her fury with Glenda under control.

"Whatever you think," Glenda muttered with a bad-tempered sneer. "Just get us out of here." Jess took a deep breath. The officer looked at Jess with interest. She held out the four passports to him, and he examined them, turning over the pages slowly as though every word needed to be scrutinised. Then he looked up at Jess expectantly.

"*Officier ... commandant ... s'il vous plait!*" Jess struggled, "*Je vous en prie! Elle ... elle ... ne savait pas ce qu'elle faisant. Elle vous supplie ... tres desole ... elle sait qu'elle a comporte avec insouciance et reprehensibles ... elle n'est pas un criminal d'etat.*"

The officer listened intently, pulling on his cigarette, then nodded. He seemed to be explaining something to her, and he looked very serious and grave: "*etat d'urgence decrete ... regionale ... mesures d'urgence civile imposees ... personne de quitter sans permission special du commandant ...*" a state of emergency had been declared ... across the region ... measures to deal with a civil emergency had been imposed ... nobody was allowed to leave without the specific permission of the commander."

Jess nodded. "*Je comprends.* I understand." She breathed in deeply. "*Mais nous voulons pas de mal.* We didn't mean any harm. *Nous voulons juste rentrer a la maison.* We just want to get home." She smiled shakily, hoping that it looked sweet and disingenuous.

The officer tapped his cigarette on the ashtray in front of him and then slowly nodded again. His mouth smirked grimly. "OK, but your French is terrible. But maybe good for an English." He glared at Glenda. "I put you in prison but I have to give to you food, water. No, you are foolish English woman. I do not waste on you. Away! Out of my eyes!" He signalled to the guards to take them away, but then beckoned to Jess to stay. He leaned forwards towards her and said quietly,

"You are good to your friends. Go home. But watch that one, the big one, she is not so good. She behave bad and use you to cover her. She will ... how you say ... bugger you all up!" He suddenly opened his mouth and laughed uproariously as Jess retreated out of the shed and into the sunlight, but even away from that insanity, the tension outside was tangible. People were still shouting and gesticulating wildly in the stifling heat. The blood-soaked man had disappeared, but there was a crowd of men corralled with soldiers training their guns on them. Others were huddled in small groups, women hugging their children close to their skirts. Someone shrieked and a soldier fired a round into the air.

Glenda was still shaking and Sandra tapping her on the shoulder as Jess walked across, but she looked up defiantly at Jess. "OK, OK, don't anyone say anything – now let's just forget it. Bloody little Hitlers."

Jess sighed. Her heart was still thrumming in her chest. She would never know the truth about Glenda. And she would always cover herself, as the commander said. Jess realised how perceptive he was. Jess determined to research the behaviours Glenda displayed. Human behaviour was so interesting and she was going to study psychology as well as English at uni next year.

They got back into their cars and the guards raised the barrier. Did she really see them salute as they drove through?

"*Everything's fine,*" she would write later to Simon, "*We had a great time on the Timbuktu trek. No problems.*" She knew that she was trying to protect him from worrying on her behalf but she also knew that she wanted to put it behind her as one of life's experiences. They had all survived. And nobody at home would ever understand what she had been through. She had breathed a sigh of relief as they drove through the border and back into Ghana. It felt like home.

Jess felt quite shaky and unnerved throughout the rest of the trip until they reached Cape Coast again and the school, even though she knew they were safe now. She was exhausted, wrung dry. The image of the man bruised and beaten a few feet away from her would not release itself from her mind. Her ears still heard the gunshots cracking on the air, making her heart thump with fear. She could still smell the pungent cordite in the sweltering air. Her dreams were haunted for many nights.

She felt like a zombie as she crawled through the following days. Even the discovery that rats had devastated the living room cushions one night while they slept, scattering kapok in their wake, had no power to supersede the ghosts of fear. She simply got to work clearing up and making good again.

The end of the school holidays approached and Jim returned from his mission. Jess was working on lesson preparation for her classes the day before term was due to start. Books and papers littered the table. She was struggling to concentrate when she heard Jim's voice calling her name as he bounded up the stairs.

As he stood in the doorway, she felt a strange sense of relief and safety.

"Oh, Jim, it's good to see you!" Jess put down her pen and leaned back in the wooden chair, running her hands through her hair.

"Wow," he grinned, "that's a great welcome! But you look busy. Shall I make you a coffee? Or would you rather I go and leave you to get on?"

"No, no. Coffee sounds a good plan. I could do with something reviving. Actually I need a break anyway." While she cleared her work into a tidy pile, Jim clattered in the kitchen, making himself at home again, finding the mugs and filling the kettle.

"So," breathed Jess as she slumped into a comfortable chair and, taking the mug from Jim, twisted her legs beneath her. "Sorry about the state of the upholstery. We've had rats but I tried my best to stuff as much of the kapok back into the cushions as I could. But, how are you and what's been happening?"

"OK, but hey," Jim smiled as he stretched out on the other armchair, long legs akimbo. "I heard about your adventures. Causing a riot in Upper Volta? Starting a coup?"

Jess felt herself relax to his soothing voice. Gradually, prompted by his gentle questions, she was able to tell him what had happened in Mopti and at the Upper Volta border. When she had finished, he grimaced, rose from his chair and stood over her. He held his hands out to her and pulled her into a silent hug. For some minutes he stroked her back while she wept. She realised that she hadn't cried, even when she explained to Betty what had happened. She had congratulated herself on how controlled and unemotional she had been. But now she needed to find a release, and Jim was so kind and understanding.

"Cry it out, Jess," he murmured, "it's OK now." He explained to her about the effects of shock and trauma, and made it all sound so normal. "So you mustn't bottle it up. Let it go. I'm here for you now. Buddies, hey?"

"I'm OK," Jess said as she dried her tears with her fingers and stepped away from Jim's safe comforting chest.

It was only after Jim had left the apartment that she realised that he hadn't revealed anything about his Christmas, his work.

School term started again and Jess was busy getting back in to the by now familiar routine of the school day, of teaching and marking, of preparing classes, and of the daily life that was no longer quite so strange. The mail service seemed to have gone awry and Jess received no letters from England for several weeks. She wondered whether her own letters had also been delayed. But she was becoming used to the lack of co-ordination of communications. It no longer mattered quite so much that Simon and her family were clearly detached from her world here. In a way, she was glad that they were cushioned from the horrors she was experiencing in Africa. She knew that they (especially Simon) would be quite unable to cope.

And in some respects that made her feel more confident of herself, that she was able to bear it.

But of course there was also the beauty and excitement of her life in Ghana: Biriwa beach with its swaying palm trees and deep blue sea; watching the fishing boats being dragged down the sand into the sea; listening to the rhythmic music and singing across the bush; sipping coffee on the veranda in the warm evening sunshine; the vibrant colours; the exotic tastes; the joyful laughter. Those things she would have liked to share with Simon. What was he doing now? She didn't even know how his Christmas had gone, what he had done, who he had been with, what he had been thinking. They had shared everything before she had come out to Africa, and now ... now she didn't even know where he was.

Choir started again and Jess looked forward to her evenings of singing every week. Jim made her drive the big truck.

"You may have driven all over the Sahara desert but you should keep practising so that you can get your driver's licence when you get back to the UK," he told her.

"Well, not exactly all over the Sahara!" laughed Jess, climbing into the truck, a little nervously, the first Friday evening rehearsal in January. She remembered the last time she had driven the truck and skidded off the track into a ditch. She shuddered.

"Hey, you'll be fine!" Jim reached over and touched her arm. Jess turned to him and smiled. *How did he know what she was thinking?* And what did she really know about him?

Jess felt her eyes constantly drawn towards the piano that night. She watched Jim as he played so confidently, and pondered. Did he have a new girlfriend – maybe up in the north, that's where he went quite a lot? Now that Sherrie wasn't on the scene any more – he hadn't mentioned anyone else, but - maybe he had found someone? Another American Peace Corps girl, out here in Ghana? She had been thinking that there was some kind of mission, some kind of danger up there in the north. She was sure he'd mentioned work, although nothing specific. And he'd sometimes come back looking exhausted. She'd assumed work. Political stuff. But what if it was some girl instead?

He was certainly attractive enough not to be without a girl for long. Tall, strong, muscular limbs. Crisp curly dark hair, chiselled square chin, wide firm mouth. Tonight the dark shadow of stubble on his cheeks ...

He must have become aware of her looking at him as he played, and he turned towards her, without missing a note, and his smile crinkled the corners of his eyes. Jess sensed the singers around her glance in her direction and she felt herself blush. What on earth was she thinking? She refocused and concentrated on melding her voice to the rest of the choir.

"You were a little distracted tonight?" asked Jim as Jess drove very carefully back to the school compound.

"Oh, no ... well, maybe. It's just that I was thinking, earlier on, that home seems so far away, almost a different planet."

"And Simon?"

"Especially Simon."

Jim shot her an odd look. But they were already at the top of the school drive, the apartment block towering up beside them in the dark. "I'm sure it'll all be fine when you guys meet up again."

"Yes, I hope so." Jess climbed down from the truck as Jim came round to take the driver's seat in the cab. He took her arm to help her down the last step.

"Good night. Sweet dreams," he murmured softly. Jess turned and hurried through the dark portico and into the building, her head a mass of conflicting thoughts.

The following Sunday, Jim had offered to meet her at Ebubonku village for her usual Village Sunday mission. Jess was still anxious for news of Adwa and her little girl Amah. She had not seen them or heard of them since well before the Christmas break and Jess's trek to Timbuktu. They had been missing and despite her appeals to the Chief she had no information about what had happened to them. Each time she had asked after them, the villagers seemed to engage in a long loud argument in Fante that even Agnes was unable to decipher. Jess had been distracted looking after countless other babies and children since, but she still felt guilty that she had not done enough for the child and her sad beautiful mother. She had become so tied up with plans for her Sahara trip that she had forgotten them. She had advised Adwa to take her child to the hospital but she knew that was impossible for her to afford the fare. What had become of them? *Oh god, how selfish she was to forget!* She frowned as she trod the short, now familiar, distance from the school compound to the village, Agnes and two other girls following behind, giggling and chatting together in their own private world.

"*Mekyew*! Good morning!" she called in greeting to the women as she wound her dusty way through the mud-built huts to the thatched open meeting-place at its centre. She had arranged to meet Jim there, as he had to drive most of the way from the opposite direction on his return from some business in Accra.

"*Mekyew*!" Brightly turbaned women pounding fufu called back. "*Wo ho ye*? How are you?"

"*Mo ho yie*!" I'm fine, thanks!

She saw that Jim was already at the meeting-place in the clearing. He was standing, thumbs hooked into the pockets of his beige shorts, talking seriously to the Chief, who was nodding respectfully in compliance. Keeping at a discreet distance, Jess was aware of Jim's air of authority. The girls caught up with her and stopped behind her. Jess swung her large tote bag onto the ground at the entrance and Jim glanced round. He smiled, then turned back to the Chief, who wiped his hands on his kente cloth. Jim spoke a few more words to the Chief, who nodded, bowed his head and then backed a couple of paces. In a moment he was gone, and Jim turned to Jess.

"Hi! There's someone here to see you." Jess heard a scuffling noise behind her and turned to see a group of women straightening up from their sweeping in the dust to stand aside for a woman, tall, slim and elegant, head held high and confident, emerging from the nearest hut, gliding slowly towards her as if her feet barely touched the rough ground. She was still beautiful, wearing a fresh bright traditional cloth with a matching turban wound round her head. Gold jewellery, glinting in the sun, adorned her graceful body and her right hand was clutching the little hand of a child. She kept glancing down to check that the small girl was all right, as she slowly and carefully guided her stumbling footsteps. The child's legs were matchstick-thin but she struggled bravely to walk beside her mother.

"Adwa! Amah," called Jess in disbelief. She felt, rather than saw, Jim's smile beside her. "But – how on earth …?"

Jim led the pair to a bench and helped Adwa to lift the fragile little girl gently onto her lap. Fragile she may be, but she lifted her tiny face to Jess and as if the memory of a lullaby flitted across her face, she smiled the sweetest smile, and her eyes were bright.

The village Chief appeared and stood behind Adwa, placing his hand on her shoulder, and it seemed to Jess that his glance down towards her was covetous. Jess gasped and her brain made quick connections.

"She has the Chief's protection?" she said to Jim, "She's his new wife?" She remembered the downcast ragged woman she had sorrowed for before, who had been raped as she fled her own village with her sick child, and relegated to an isolated hut on the edge of the village compound. She knew that this reversal of fortune would not have happened without a strong reason, without an undeniable incentive, an outside negotiation. Something the Chief, and his village, could not refuse. Money.

"You did this?" she asked Jim. "You paid the Chief a dowry?" she blinked in disbelief. Jim frowned at her tone; she knew it wasn't entirely admiring.

"It was the only way." He shrugged and shifted uncomfortably. "I thought it was what you wanted."

"So she could be bought and sold? A woman? Bought?"

"Jess, we're not talking slavery! She has a position of respect now and that means she has self-respect. She has a central hut on the compound, the Chief's protection. The other women, and the men, have to treat her kindly now she's one of them. They've helped her to start growing vegetables and fruit and she's opened a market stall of her own, so she has some money and independence. It's how it works here."

Yes, that's how it worked here. Her high-fallutin' principles were out of place here, not appropriate. Adwa had gained respect – even if it was bought with money – and little Amah had gained her health – again, even if it had been bought when others didn't have the money. Jim had saved them. And probably many others in his work as a medic. How many had *she* saved? What had *she* done? Taught English to a lot of privileged African girls and administered a bit of first aid in two needy villages? Who was she to get on her high horse? She felt ungrateful. What did Jim think of her now? Her heart twisted.

Jess stared at her feet for a moment, then looked up at Jim and held his eyes for a moment.

"Thank you," she murmured. He gestured and mouthed "I did it for you" and her heart melted. "I know."

Jess was still singing under her breath the lilting song she had been singing with the children at Ebubonku when she returned up the hard concrete steps to the flat.

"Nana aberewa poso poso; waye ne nkwan dekyedekye"

"You sound cheerful!" Sandra looked up from the letter she was writing on the table in the living room. Jess paused and noticed that it was a blue airmail letter. Hmmm, she hadn't seen her flat-mate writing one of those for a while. And come to think of it, she hadn't seen Hank around for a while either.

Jess dropped her tote bag on the floor and picked up the dirty coffee mug from in front of Sandra. "Want another?" she asked as she went into the kitchen to re-fill the kettle.

"Please!"

"So how's Colin?" she asked as she set down the two mugs on the table and settled herself on the wooden chair, pulling up her knees to her chest.

"Good," said Sandra, "Yes, he's very good. Looking forward to July." She paused. "You know we were talking about a little diversion trip on our way home? To Europe?" Jess nodded although she could only barely recall the slightly drunken chat they had had over too many lagers one night on the trek to Timbuktu. "Well, I'm thinking I might just go straight home. OK?"

"Of course!" Hmmm. Definitely sounded like Colin was back on – and Hank out? "I'm not sure what

I'll do yet. I do quite like the idea of a bit of travelling before I go home. Once I get back ..." she trailed off thinking of her impatience to see Simon again, yet her reluctance to return to the family home. Although, of course, it wouldn't be for long; she'd soon be at university and away from the stifling house, in term time at least. And who knows what might happen after Simon had got his degree and was free to live anywhere he chose.

"You know, this is such a different world here," and Jess told Sandra what had happened at Ebubonku.

"What? You mean, Jim paid a load of money out for a dowry and the hospital?" Sandra snorted. "Well, he's certainly trying to impress you!"

"I don't think that's why he did it!" Jess objected. "He's a kind man." Sandra pulled a face and returned to her letter.

※

The month ended with the official opening of the Akasombo dam. Jim somehow acquired tickets for the VIP enclosure but at the last minute he told Jess that he couldn't go after all, so she and Chrissie went along out of interest. The VIP area was crowded with smart Europeans and elegant Ghanaians dripping with gold.

"I feel rather uncomfortable," admitted Jess to Chrissie as they were offered glasses of champagne.

"Well, we don't need to stay." Chrissie sipped her drink from the slim flute. "We turned up, didn't we? I hope Jim won't mind if we slip out early. But I guess he'll never know. A bit strange him having these tickets, though, given his well-known antipathy to Nkrumah. Not his kind of thing, I wouldn't have imagined."

"Yes. I did ask him but he was a bit vague. Woow, this is going to my head rather quickly. I feel quite woozy." What on earth would her tee-total parents have said about that? She didn't care to think. So many Rules broken …

Jess was feeling quite light-headed as the bubbles rose. She caught odd snatches of conversations and laughter around her and they seemed to jangle in her brain.

"… brilliant ambassador for his country …"

"ha ha … and he went to the African Presidents' congress with his girlfriend …"

"… pretty little girl … Sixteen? Seventeen? … well, younger body than the wife …"

"… so good for him, I say!"

She heard a commotion some way over to her left and turned to see what was happening. The crowd was blocking her view and she craned her neck to try to see beyond the bright kente cloth and elegant European women in their large inappropriate hats. Jess drew in her breath. A brief glimpse only. A tall, imposing figure almost hidden behind the moving crowd. Hands raking through crinkly dark hair.

No! It couldn't be! It didn't make sense. But it looked very much like Jim.

"Chrissie! Over there, look!" she pointed but the crowd had closed in again and the figure had disappeared. "I'm sure it was Jim!"

"And why would he be here when he said he couldn't make it and gave us the tickets, Jess," Chrissie reasoned. "You must have been mistaken. There are so many people here." She smiled. "Maybe you're seeing him everywhere," she teased.

Dear Simon, she wrote later that night.

A strange day hobnobbing at Akasombo with the great and good of Ghana! Chrissie and I went but we escaped early straight after the main event. I don't know whether you would have liked it. But you would have looked very in keeping and wonderfully handsome in that dress suit you wore for the university ball. Goodness that seems a long time ago now. What a night! In so many ways!

She wrote a little more about what she had been doing, but it seemed odd: everything at home was drifting into a mist. The reality was here, now, in a place that Simon didn't share.

Jess thought about her vision of Jim in the VIP enclosure at Akasombo. She had been so sure it was him. But it couldn't have been. Could it? In many ways he was so lovely and kind, he looked after her and cared.

And she had to admit, he stirred her heart. She was thinking about Jim as she switched off the torch under the mosquito net and settled herself under the sheet. The drums had started again in the villages and she listened to the rhythmic pounding on the muggy night air, rising and falling with her breathing as she drifted into sleep.

7

FEBRUARY 1966

The Harmattan had been blowing in from the Sahara for two months now, bringing with it the dry sandy winds. This was the hottest and, apart from the occasional torrential downpour, the driest season. It would blow itself out by March and then the rainy season would start. Jess was sitting on one of the two wicker chairs on the veranda one Saturday morning, reading "Arrow of God" by the Nigerian writer Chinua Achebe, watching the palms swaying and trying to catch the breeze to relieve the intense heat of the season. She could hear the strains of the Rolling Stones' "Under the Boardwalk" drifting up from the school hall where the sixth form girls were dancing to their Dancette record player, and she hummed along with the music. As always, the western songs brought back memories of home. And of Simon.

She kept his photo as a bookmark in whatever she was currently reading, because she was so afraid of forgetting what he looked like. And if she forgot, she felt she would lose him. And if she lost him, what would she do? Her life, her dreams would be shattered forever. She lifted the photo now out of the back of her book.

She stroked her hand over the well-worn picture as if by doing that she could run her hands over his face. She embraced into her memory the fresh faced, soft full pink-lipped, blue-eyed young man she loved. Yes, she could see him now, leaning against the doorway of the college house, slim, sensitive, gentle. She gazed at his high cheekbones and rounded chin, his fair hair that curled round his ears and the nape of his neck, brushed aside longer on his brow, and she wanted to hug him, look after him, reassure him and say, "It's all going to be OK."

They had so much in common: their families were friends, they shared a religion, they liked the same things, books, films, music, and loved discussing them. They loved just being together, sharing, understanding each other. Their lives were intertwined. Forever.

She would go home in a few months' time and they would just pick up where they had left off last summer. She would go to university and they would see each other at weekends. Simon had assured her that he would drive up to her as often as he could; he loved driving, it was a lovely cross-country drive through the English countryside. He insisted. He was so full of life, so enthusiastic about things. So unlike her slow silent father. So much freer than her family. Life was an adventure for him. And it would be for her too when they shared their lives. "I'll do whatever I need to, just to see you …" he had said, stroking her hair and holding her tight.

Jess smiled to herself, just thinking about the beautiful things he said to her, before she came away and now in his letters to her. How she longed to be in his arms again.

And yet a little voice in her head whispered that she had changed this year, experienced things she would never be able to explain, never be able to share. Was their love strong enough to move on from that distancing? Yes, of course, she told herself, she would tell him all about it when they were together again and he would understand. He was a very sensitive and understanding person. But still she shivered.

A sudden strong gust of wind tore the photo from her grasp, and whipped it against the concrete supports of the veranda wall. Oh god, if she lost it she wouldn't be able to keep him close! She dived after it and grabbed the corner before it was blown away. But it was torn and dirty. Tarnished.

She straightened out the photograph and slipped it back into her book, reached for her glass of cold lager and lime straight from the fridge and started to read the next chapter.

"As you keep telling me, your mother would have a fit!" said Sandra, flopping down into the wicker chair next to Jess. She gestured at Jess's lager, and then at her own.

"Yes, probably!" smiled Jess. She was seeing more of her flat-mate lately, and since her break-up with Hank, she seemed to have become more sympathetic and open. It appeared that Sandra was becoming disillusioned with Glenda too, who, she confided, was trying to get her to do all the work at Guides, while she remained the figurehead, taking the glory. On several occasions Jess had provided a shoulder for Sandra to cry on when Glenda had an outburst of rage at some small misdemeanour.

"Glenda still cross with you for not agreeing to take the Guides session instead of her this week?" asked Jess.

"Yeah. God, that woman. She's so lazy." Sandra leaned back and fanned her out-stretched legs. "So hot out here! D'you know, I used to think you were a bit off with her, but maybe you just saw through her before me."

"Oh, I don't know. She's quite convincing! But she's so up and down. Very tense and easily enraged if something doesn't go her way. Then very enthusiastic at other times. Look how she was when we were planning the Timbuktu trek. Totally high with organising it!"

"Wasn't she just!"

"I was looking up some stuff about psychology recently. I don't know much about it, but it seems really interesting. You know, I applied to uni to do it along with English."

"Woooh! Sounds like hard work to me. I'm just doing straight Maths."

"I just thought I'd like to do something a bit different. And I was talking to Jim about how fascinating psychology is. It's not his subject – obviously that's medicine, but he got some books from the Peace Corps library about it. So, anyway, I looked up Glenda's quirks and the thing is – I think that maybe she has some kind of 'condition'."

"Like what?"

"Well, at first I thought maybe there was something in her past that makes her like she is. But then I found out that there's something called 'manic depression'. The symptoms seemed to fit. Extreme highs and lows for no apparent reason. Taking it out on whoever's around. Going crazy for very little cause."

"That sounds like Glenda!"

"It's apparently also linked with finding it difficult to relate to other people and sustain relationships. Mainly, I think, because they tend to be very bound up with themselves and blame other people if things don't go their way."

"Sounds even more like her. But what's to do?"

"Oh I don't know that there's anything unless the person themself recognises the symptoms and wants to do something about it."

"Well, *I* wouldn't like to say anything!"

"God, no! Nor me. But maybe it helps to put a label on the behaviour, understand why she behaves the way she does?"

"Oh, I don't know. What's the point of just knowing a label when you also know there's nothing you can do to make it better?"

"Hmmm. True." Jess wrinkled up her nose. "I guess it just means you can say to yourself that it's OK, it isn't your fault when she goes crazy."

"Why would you think it's your fault?"

That's the difference between us, thought Jess. She sat sipping her lager, now somewhat warmer, in companiable silence with Sandra who had closed her eyes and was dozing in the sunshine. Jess read and listened to the sounds of the bush: the shrill calls of the parakeets, the "cow-cow-cow" of the plantain-eaters, the rustle of the palm trees, the slow soft footsteps of the villagers making their way along the dry dusty paths, the distant pounding of fufu and the djembe.

The month of February moved on slowly and certainly, and Jess found her days filled with teaching and marking, preparing lessons, reading the set books for her classes. There was a comforting routine about the mundane tasks of living and working that helped her settle back to a kind of normality. She looked forward to choir with Jim on Friday evenings that signalled the start of the weekend, and on Saturdays driving to the town with Chrissie, reading and catching up with chores, walking under the palms on Biriwa beach in the afternoon with Sandra or Jim if he was around, or Chrissie if Angus was at work. Sometimes they drove to the beach after nightfall, and lay on the warm sand side by side under the swaying palms, looking up at the tropical night sky and watching the stars. And always Jess would murmur "the same moon shines …"

On Sundays visiting the villages, still striving to persuade them to use the nets she cadged from Jim, still patching up the tropical sores and sadly soothing the fevers when the inescapable mosquitos had done their worst.

But towards the end of February something happened that changed everything.

Jess had staggered under the weight of exercise books ready for marking, back up to flat 4. She had just dropped the pile onto the table when a familiar deep voice called out from the yard below.

"Any of you guys at home?"

Jess leaned over the veranda wall and smiled, "Yes, Jim! Me! Come on up." She was filling the kettle as he strode in through the doorway. "Coffee?"

"Please. Listen up – I've come to see if you want to come up to Accra with me? I'm staying over until tomorrow – bit of business to do at HQ."

"What? Now?" Jess thought quickly. She had nothing else on for the rest of the day and no lessons tomorrow as her classes were off on a day's geography field trip. Why not? Marking could wait till the weekend for once.

She sipped her coffee and chatted to Jim as she packed her essential items into her overnight bag.

"So where do we stay?" she asked.

"Peace Corps HQ hostel, not terribly glamorous." Then he glanced at her and grinned. "Oh, OK, there's two separate rooms!"

"Of course!" laughed Jess, scribbling a note for Sandra and propping it up against her pile of marking on the table.

It was good to break the routine sometimes, she thought, as Jim carried her bag downstairs and lifted it into the back of the truck, alongside his own. As they drove the rough road to Accra, Jess suddenly remembered the overheard conversations at Akasombo, and asked Jim about Nkrumah and the conflicts surrounding his presidency.

"He seems to be either adored or hated," she puzzled, "What great passions he arouses in his people!"

"Yeah, sure," replied Jim, glancing at her sideways as he swerved the truck expertly avoiding the potholes. "But a lot of folks have no choice but to love him. Publically, anyway."

Jess frowned. "You mean giving an outward show of loyalty? But what makes you think it's not genuine?"

"You've had your classes ordered to line the road to Cape Coast?"

Jess remembered two occasions when this had happened. The school bell had rung unexpectedly at the wrong time; it was still ten minutes to go before the end of the lesson. In confusion and amidst anxious chattering, the girls trouped outside to the compound quad where Betty and Clara were standing rigidly at the front. In solemn firm tones, Clara informed the assembled pupils and staff that the President's aides had requested that they line the route of his cavalcade and respond to the prompts of the cheerleaders. She told them, through gritted teeth, to collect a national flag from the box held by the senior prefect and follow Miss Booth down the school drive to position themselves at the roadside while the President's car passed.

How silly it had all seemed to Jess. They had waited standing in the full hot sunshine for an hour before the cars approached. The girls had ceased their resentful grumblings and fallen grimly silent when they were given the signal to wave their CPP flags, cheer, and call out "Hail Nkrumah! Long live our great Nkrumah!" They had to practise it three times before the aide was satisfied that it sounded enthusiastic enough. As soon as the cavalcade had passed by on the road into town, the girls had dropped their flags on the dusty ground and run back up the drive to the classrooms, leaving the prefects to gather up the trampled green and black cloth. "Teenagers!" thought Jess, forgetting that she was still one. Clara said not another word about the event, and no word of reprimand ever passed her lips.

"He's away right now, apparently," said Jim, breaking in to her thoughts. "Gone to visit his buddy Zhou Enlai in China." There was something strained that Jess detected in his voice and she thought she saw his hands grip the steering wheel a little more tightly. "Interesting that he spent some formative years in London and Washington. But then came back to Ghana, and campaigned for independence. Apparently he had links with the Soviet Union and with Marxism when he was Prime Minister in the 50s. Then when he was made President in 60 everything changed. He'd organised strikes before but suddenly he opposed them, instituted the Preventative Detention Act, imprisoned people without trial for 'treason' if they spoke against him. Well, I guess that's dictatorship for you ... So, no, folks don't speak out."

"I heard," began Jess hesitantly, "that there are people who 'disappear'?"

"Ah ... yes. You've heard that, have you?"

"At Legon. University lecturers I think." She struggled to recall what she had overheard at Harriet's party. "What's all that about?"

Jim grimaced. "I don't think you want to know," was all he said, and changed the subject to the next choir concert.

They arrived at the Peace Corps HQ hostel in the centre of Accra and Jim handed Jess down from the cab. The city was hot, dusty and suffocating, but the street was oddly quiet. The hostel seemed strangely silent, echoing and deserted. The man at the reception desk fumbled with his papers and dropped his pen as they walked through the door. He glanced nervously at Jim and handed him a note. He scanned it quickly and his face paled. He glanced at Jess, frowning. "Sir? You've heard?"

"Yes," replied Jim curtly, ushering Jess quickly through to the rooms. His face shut tightly. Tension stretched at the air. He dropped Jess's bag on her bed and said, "Look, something's come up. I'm so sorry, Jess, but I need to deliver something to the American embassy. Please stay here till I get back. Promise me you'll stay in here." He patted her arm as though she was a child. "I'll get a drink and a snack sent up. I'll be back soon."

Jess heard him in the room next door and then footsteps retreating down the hall. Obediently, she retrieved her book from her overnight bag and lay on the bed reading, although she found it difficult to concentrate. There was a knock on the door and she jumped. The reception officer brought in a jug of coffee and a plate of cookies. He did not say a word and left quickly, closing the door behind him with a quiet click.

Half an hour later she felt she couldn't bear it any longer. What was going on? She slipped out of her room and noticed that there was nobody at the reception desk, so she slipped out on to the street. Independence Street was oddly empty; there were none of the usual beggars sprawled on the filthy pavements, none of the usual noise and bustle, the crowds, the traffic. The office buildings looked deserted. Where was everyone? A sudden screech of tyres as a car swerved and skidded round the corner and sped past her. A loud crack. A car backfiring? Then screams, shouting, rent the air. All at once she knew what she was hearing, because she had heard it before, in Upper Volta: the sound of gunfire. Again and again. Over and over. Another car, bucking to a halt, skewed across the road. Someone leapt out and ran down the street.

Jess dived into an office doorway, heart pounding in her breast, deafening her with its terror. She crouched on the dusty grimy step along with the rubbish, cans, wrappers lobbed aside, and pressed her hand to her chest. For one long weird moment there was stillness. A shocked hesitation in the world.

Then the shooting started again. As far as Jess could tell the noise was coming from a couple of streets away. Which was where the government buildings were. Which was close to the American embassy.

The shooting was closer. She quickly calculated whether she had time to run back to the hostel. Dare she emerge on to the street and run? Gingerly, she peered round the wall of the office doorway. What she saw stilled her heartbeat. Uniformed men – they looked like soldiers, but their uniform was not quite right – were running down the street, some crouched and shooting haphazardly, some shooting in to the air.

They were shouting: instructions, warnings, orders. There were battle fatigues, camouflage outfits, green and brown helmets, rifles held aloft or clutched menacingly. Jess cowered back into the hollow of the doorway and scrunched herself up as small as she could, gripping her knees to her body, muscles taut.

Bullets must have hit the wall beside her because she felt the impact and saw the concrete dust spurt out. Four, five soldiers crept, crouching, across the opening to her refuge, backs towards her, staring across the street. Stopped, fear exuding from them along with the stink of their sweat. Rifles raised. Jess shrank further back into the cave of her doorway. If they started shooting from there, return fire would surely get her.

She heard long, long bouts of shooting, scuffling, the screams and muffled noises of someone falling, scraping the wall, moaning. Someone had been shot, very close by. It would be her next.

They say that in the last moments, your life streams past you like a dream in fast forward. Or that you see everything before you in slow motion. Neither is true, thought Jess. You think only of that moment in time. You do not think of the past, or of the future. You just hold on to 'being'. She'd survived what happened in Mopti and in Upper Volta, but now in Ghana, in Accra, she could not imagine how she was going to be able to survive this.

But the soldiers did not fire in front of the doorway where she cowered, trembling. They moved on down the street. Jess took several minutes to summon up the courage to look out again. Soldiers were tightly clustered on the far side of the road, poised but staring intently the other way. Near the corner of the street, a bulky uniform lay motionless, felled at an odd angle. Dare she run? Dare she run past him? She was shaking violently. It was her only chance.

She ran, her legs fuzzy beneath her, hardly able to support her weight. She had just reached the body of the felled soldier when she heard a shout and her legs gave way. She stumbled and sprawled on the pavement. Her hands felt blood, sticky on the concrete.

More shots rang out. She saw the dust rise angrily, smelled the acrid cordite, felt her leg jerk and a sharp pain that made her yelp. She heard the scream and realised it was hers. She could feel the coldness of the hard ground and knew that at least that meant she was still alive. But she felt as though she was dying, her life ebbing away on the streets of Accra. She could just about move her head and she saw the thick tyres of an army truck rumble past her, inches away. Another crack of fire. She thought of Simon. She'd never see him again. They would never have that future together that she had dreamed of for so long. Would he cry? Would he grieve for her? Never to love another. And her family: would they always think grimly of her wilful determination to go to Africa, to catastrophe?

The sounds of the street echoed in her head and faded. As they blurred, she heard, instead the haunting drumbeats again, pounding louder, softer, louder, softer. And now and then, the pain in her leg grew louder than the noise in her head.

So this was it. Alone in the street. On a filthy pavement ...

She must have blacked out. Then, in a mist, bodies leaning over her. Faces above her, bending towards her. Hands on her leg. Strangely numb. Voices urgent. Then footsteps retreating and quiet again.

"Get up! Get up!" someone shrieked. She could hear. She was alive. She looked up. The blood on her hands wasn't her blood; it was pumping from the soldier beside her. She saw the huge gash in his chest, raw and shining, the tatters of his shirt ragged around the wound. A great enormous gaping wide hole. The whiteness of his eyes, his contorted face. And she knew then that even if she were allowed to live, it would haunt her dreams forever.

"Get up!"

"How?" she squawked. "For god's sake! I'm shot!"

She struggled to raise herself up on to legs that couldn't hold her, and looked into the barrel of a machine gun.

"Please," she begged, "I don't know what's happening."

"*Miss?*"

Jess looked up at the face behind the machine gun. A flash of memory: a young man helping her at the school when the flat was flooded after New Year, scuttling around scooping water with buckets and pans. A young man who looked about fourteen. "Kobina?"

"Quick! The others will be back soon!"

He grabbed her arm and pulled her to her feet. Seering pain in her left leg. Her head exploding. She fell against him.

Somehow, he ran, dragging her with him. She could feel something hot and wet running down her leg and filling her sandal. Oh god, she was bleeding. Badly. She must get to safety. With a strength she didn't know she possessed, Jess stumbled alongside Kobina to the hostel entrance, where he left her and disappeared down the street. Two American officers were standing guard at the door. She heaved and, bent double, struggled to regain her breath. When the officers rushed to hold her up and her breathing became regular again, she looked back down the street. She was never to see Kobina again.

She was helped into the Peace Corps building and set down on a sofa in the reception hall. A sheet was slipped carefully and efficiently under her leg. She was aware of latex-gloved hands feeling around her calf, gently pressing. Slowly and jerkily she told what had happened.

"Oh, my god!" Footsteps through the reception hall and a familiar voice. Her eyes focused through the pain: Jim. The others (there seemed to be three) quickly provided him with a resume. "Right: strong co-codamol, and a shot. Antibiotic, tetanus. We need to get her to hospital." He leaned over Jess and gently brushed her hair away from her face. He smiled down at her. "Jess – a bit of a mess, but it's better than it looks, a flesh wound only on the left leg, we think, the bullet passed straight through, no bones touched and not deep." He smiled, "You were lucky – a graze, really!"

"Then why hospital?"

"For a more thorough check and to keep an eye on you. You're suffering from shock, obviously. And I think you've damaged your left foot too, probably when you fell on the pavement. We'll get you cleaned up, but I think it's a fractured metatarsal and maybe ankle chip, and a flesh wound on the side of the foot."

She smiled weakly but as they gave her the shots and the painkillers, she felt the searing pain overwhelm her and she passed out.

8

MARCH 1966

So it was from her hospital bed that she learned what had happened that day. President Nkrumah and his government had been ousted in a coup d'état. So secret had the plot been that few people knew what was to occur that day in February. As Jim had told her Nkrumah was away in China, well away from the events in Accra, but he knew that returning to Ghana now was not an option. He had diverted to Conakry in Guinea and was currently under the protection of the president there. The army had turned on him and were now set to establish a new interim military government.

"And did *you* know about it?" asked Jess a few days later, propped up comfortably against soft pillows in the European part of the hospital at Cape Coast where they had transferred her. Jim was sitting perched at the end of her bed, reading her medical notes. The school had insisted on special treatment and she guessed that Jim had pulled strings with his medical colleagues to provide her with a very pleasant room to herself. "Hey, no problem!" he had said, "I just feel it was my fault. I shouldn't have risked taking you to Accra that day." But Jess knew that it was her own fault; Jim had told her to stay in and clearly something had happened; she was just too curious for her own good. She blamed nobody else but herself.

"I think that it was a question of grabbing the moment. The President was away. They thought it could be achieved with as little bloodshed as possible." It was only afterwards that Jess realised he had not actually answered her question.

"I gather they are saying that the CIA had something to do with it?" Jim looked at her sharply.

"Where on earth do you hear these things?" he said, as he excused himself to grab the attention of the surgeon who was walking past the open doorway. She had, in fact, overheard quite a lot over the past few days; the talk had been of nothing else. She also knew that they were claiming that there had been no casualties, "a quiet bloodless coup" they said.

But Jess remembered the fallen soldier on the pavement on Independence Street and the gash on his chest. Maybe he had been alive and so they were counting him as a "no casualty". She hoped he was OK. But when she had asked nobody seemed to know what she was talking about. And she was so bleary and drugged that she was no longer clear what had actually happened and what she had seen. It was all like a blurred, half-waking dream.

Jim came to visit her every day at first, but often seemed distracted. Then he told her that he would make it up to see her as much as possible, but all the Peace Corps had been told to return to, and not leave, their "stations" until further notice, so he would have to return to Cape Coast. All foreign volunteers had been advised to remain vigilant and to keep clear of probable danger areas.

The nurse came to dress her left leg each day and her foot was bound where it was gashed but the broken metatarsal was left to heal itself. She was treated with great care and attention and she was aware that guilt pervaded the air like the Harmattan winds that blew around the building and that lulled her into drug-calmed sleep. She did not hear the drumming from her hospital bed in the town. The villages and their djembe rhythms seemed far away.

Chrissie, Sandra and Betty all came to visit her as soon as they heard the news of the events in Accra. Betty assured her that she must forget her classes until she was well again; they had found a temporary replacement teacher, so she was on no account to worry herself about anything. She had brought a pile of letters and cards from her pupils which she read and laughed and cried over, and which insisted that the replacement teacher was nowhere near as good a teacher as she was.

Sandra told her that communication with the outside world was not yet restored and so their families would not yet know they were alive and safe. "But they'll have heard something of the coup through the BBC world news reports so they'll be worried," she added, flapping a piece of paper at Jess. "Betty's been briefed to get in touch with them as soon as it's possible to get messages through ... oh, and – what does it say here?" she peered at the paper, "to let the, er, 'Methodist Missionary Society know immediately if there is any worsening of the emergency situation, so that foreign nationals could be rescued, especially from remote postings' God, rather exciting, actually!" Jess had visions in her bleary brain of hefty camouflage-clad paras being dropped from helicopters in the middle of the bush to lift her up to safety. Somehow it seemed in her mind to look like Faye Wray being lifted up by King Kong from the Empire State Building in central New York.

"Oh, and do you want me to contact your family about your injury?"

"No, thanks, it's OK, Betty and the service organisers have got it all in hand," Jess assured her, although she knew that the letter to her parents, sent but not yet delivered to the UK, had simply said that there had been a peaceful transition to a new government in Ghana and that everyone was safe. Jess had decided not to elaborate on that basic information. It was better that everyone back home in England believed that she had not been involved in any way. She knew that she needed to keep Simon in blissful ignorance too; he would worry too much if he knew the truth.

Chrissie sat with Jess in the first few days holding her hand as she drifted in and out of drug-induced sleep. Jess heard her soft voice telling her about what was happening at school and at choir, but only fragments lodged in her brain. She would have to ask for an update later. She just felt so weepy and emotional; the slightest kind word made tears course unchecked down her cheeks.

Her mind drifted a great deal to Simon, now that she had time to do little but think of him, as she lay lightly covered by cool cotton sheets.

"I do hope he's OK," she admitted to Jim shakily on his last visit before she was due to be discharged. He had apparently slipped out and driven unannounced from Cape Coast to Accra, without any mishap. "It was his birthday a couple of weeks ago, before we went to Accra that day, and I sent him a present – well, it was only a little book of Ashanti stories, it's difficult to send much from here – but I haven't heard anything from him." She bit her lip to stop the tears.

"I'm sure everything is fine," Jim smiled. He reached over, refilled her glass with water, handed it to her, and then made a rather ham-fisted job of plumping up her hospital pillows. Jess giggled painfully, recalling that she had often told him he would never make a great nurse – doctors never did! Jim feigned an offended pout. "But you never told me - how did you meet him, then?"

... He was her brother's friend and she wasn't sure she even liked him at that time. But he had phoned and asked her, and, at thirteen, she had never been out alone with a boy before. All her friends had, or said they had, and she felt proud of herself that she was joining their world. He had taken her to the cinema. But it had not been a success; he had been really awful.

The heart-sinking heat of humiliation flooded back to her.

It was amazing to think of that now, her wonderful romantic Simon, how he had changed.

But in those days he was a grotty hormone-ridden teenager, not gorgeous at all; it was almost impossible to think that it was the same person. She had difficulty linking the two images into one. She had hated every minute of the evening, his arrogant roaming hands, his demanding flick of the head to indicate that he wanted her to move over to him. Who did he think he was? God, she hated being treated like that.

He had phoned her a couple of days later for a second date (god only knows why; hadn't he felt her discomfort? Was he so self-absorbed that he imagined any girl would be falling over her feet to be with him?). But she had told him thank you but no, thanks. She supposed that she had sounded arrogant too as she had said that he needed to behave more respectfully to girls. She smiled grimly at herself as she thought of that now; what a little madam she must have been.

But yet really in her heart she knew she was right. She had wanted to be treated like a lady, with care and consideration and courtesy. As though she was cherished. Not as though she was the local tart.

He had gasped "oh" and abruptly slammed down the phone on her. Well, tough. Her heart had rapped beats in her chest and the handset had trembled in her shaking hand, but she knew she had done the right thing.

Afterwards his mother had phoned her mother and told her that she was very disappointed in Jess; how dare she not want to go on another date with her beloved wonderful son? Dear Simon was so upset.

Yeah, Jess had thought, more like angry at her not complying with him. Talk about spoilt only child! Oh, little did his mother know him, thought Jess at the time, or how he treated girls. Or maybe she did know, Jess had pondered, and thought it was OK.

Her own mother had been upset too: "why, Jess? I can't understand you! He's a nice, well-connected chap, from the right family, Quaker friends of ours. Why?"

"Because he was arrogant and patronising, and he made me feel awful!" Jess had shrieked, "I hate him! I don't care about who his family is – I'm not going out with him again!" and she had run off up to her bedroom to cry bitterly. Why didn't her mother understand?

And then, later, at neighbouring single-sex boarding schools, he had ignored her, except for one horrible occasion at the joint Strawberry Dance at the end of one summer term when he had, clearly encouraged by his friends, asked her to dance with him.

"Well...OK," she had agreed, hesitantly, full of foreboding, and he had danced stiffly with her in a silence punctuated only by the odd coldly formal comment.

"Right", he had said when the song ended. "Duty dance over."

He had walked abruptly off, leaving her stranded on the dance floor, rudely not even taking her back to her seat as the boys were supposed to do, and she had been obliged to walk the walk of shame alone, weaving her way through the other dancers, slinking back to a solitary chair whilst her friends had enjoyed the next dance with their partners.

She had looked across the dance floor and had seen him and his friends laughing and high-fiving each other. Then she had remembered a saying about dealing with threatening mad dogs: avoid the eyes or they'll make you flinch, hold your head up high and never show fear. So she had tossed her head and walked as proudly as she could to the table of soft drinks and nibbles, hoping she transmitted a "couldn't care less" attitude to anyone who might have been watching her. As she stood there taking an inordinate interest in canapés and cheese sticks, inside she had seethed.

And so she had kept her distance from him, as much as she could with one of her brother's friends.

For four or five years she had detached herself from their history. She had seen other boys.

And to her, for all that long time, he had become, as he had started, just one of her brother's friends who came to the house for their frequent vacation parties. That, she convinced herself, was all. She had grown a protective shell around her as far as Simon had been concerned.

She seemed to spend a lot of energy trying to fight off Maurie, whom her mother, annoyingly and inexplicably, increasingly encouraged in the absence of Simon: both Quakers and her mother's Rulebook clearly stated that only Quakers could be trusted.

What a difficult time it had been, she thought now. Teenage years, growing up. She wouldn't want to go through all that again! Simon, as he was then ... Maurie ... ugh ... But of course there was also Andrew, she recalled, funny, lovely Andrew, a friend of Simon's who had come to their vacation parties with him. How could she have forgotten Andrew?

She looked forward to spending time with Andrew; they shared a quirky sense of humour and he was sweetly affectionate towards her.

They often spent hours sitting side by side on her mother's sofa laughing about – well, goodness knows what, she couldn't even remember now. He always seemed to sense if she was "down" and he cheered her up so much.

"Hey, come on, Jess, let's see that gorgeous smile!" he would say and hug her. She felt as though she had known

him for centuries. His smile, in his eyes as well as his mouth, was heart-melting. When he looked at her, in that way, she felt good, and good about herself. He made her feel attractive, appealing, interesting.

They began to go around together with a crowd of mutual friends, to the cinema, bowling, to parties and coffee bars. Always with a group of others. Yet he always talked with her, sat by her, laughed with her, saw her home, looked after her: her and not any of the other girls in their group of friends.

A lot like Jim, actually.

So, how strange it all was, she thought, as she remembered what had happened to her next.

She thought back to the Day that Changed Everything, as she now considered it. During her last year at school, Jess gradually became aware that Simon seemed, at a number of their parties, to place himself between Andrew and herself, to join them in their joking, kindly teasing sessions. At first it had annoyed her that he butted in, but then she realised that she felt flattered that Simon, as well as Andrew, seemed to want her attention after all, to spend time with her, to talk alone with her.

Gradually she saw that Andrew had started to slip quietly away when Simon approached her, making some excuse to leave them together. Gradually she had forgotten the juvenile insults of five years ago, and her mind had pushed the events of her thirteenth summer into its deepest recesses.

And in the end, Simon had absolutely bowled her over. She couldn't even recall, now, what he had said or done. But somehow she came to know that he was "the one", he was clever, talked vivaciously about so many things, politics, philosophy, jazz (all of which she was quite in awe of). He seemed to be so knowledgeable, worldly-wise. He liked driving fast and playing wild jazz piano. He was exciting, opening up a whole new world for her. And sweet, kind, gentle Andrew disappeared.

And suddenly it was inevitable that Simon should ask her to go driving with him in the Cotswolds the following weekend. It happened at her eighteenth birthday party. It had been arranged for the Easter holidays when she was home from boarding school in her final year, with A levels coming up in a couple of months. She was due to go out as a volunteer to Africa that summer.

And then all the past hurts retreated, disappeared into a fog of memories barely recalled. A new life, two new people had emerged, with different hopes and dreams. They had both changed. They had both grown up. He had stroked her hand and said he loved her. His mother had welcomed her with open arms into their family as if none of the past had happened. Her son was happy now with Jess, and that was all that mattered to her. That Simon should have what he wanted. And that of course was what she wanted too, wasn't it?

Her own mother was in a state of blissful contentment that Jess had got together, at last, with an acceptable (more than acceptable!) chap: "from a good Quaker family!" she had said with satisfaction, "and well known to us – one of us". The seal of approval from her mother, happy now that Jess was being dutiful, acquiescent. But it didn't really matter to Jess what Simon's background was; she just knew that she loved him, whoever he was, wherever he came from, whoever his parents were, whatever his religion or politics.

Simon never referred to what had happened when she was thirteen. And neither did she. It was past. Erased. Of course, it no longer mattered. Life had moved on. She had never thought of it again ...

Until this moment. Telling Jim she had voiced her thoughts and memories aloud. Leaning back against the pillows of her hospital bed she had hardly been aware of what she was saying: drifting in and out of memory as she had drifted in and out of consciousness in the first days after the shooting. Jim had simply listened, uncritically, without any judgement of her. That was what she liked about him.

"I wish I'd met you before, when you were sweet sixteen," he teased gently, "before you got all worldly-wise and experienced!"

"I'm not sure that I'm that now!" she smiled back weakly, sinking further into her pillow. "Maybe that's more a description of you."

He ruffled her arm affectionately, then sat back and looked at her seriously. "Well, I'm glad it was a fairy tale ending. But I know I wouldn't have treated you like that – "duty dance" indeed! Then messing you around. Pushing his way in again when he saw there was someone else interested in you!"

"Oh, I don't think it was quite like that," Jess retorted defensively.

"Sorry, I shouldn't say such things about your guy. It's just that ... well, I wouldn't have done that to you. You deserve better. You're a lovely girl, Jess."

"Goodness!" she snorted and turned away.

"Ah, you're not used to compliments. You should be." He paused for a moment then said softly, "You are your own person, remember that, Jess. You have to do things your own way, however people try to push you on the path they've laid out for you. Sometimes you have to pull away from your parents, your upbringing, however difficult it is, and know that the world won't end if you do."

Jess watched Jim's narrowed eyes as he spoke, the furrow on his forehead, and she knew that he was talking as much about himself as about her.

She remembered Jim's words long after she had left the hospital and returned to her flat. And even some time after that, too, when those awful events happened, the events that she could never have predicted.

⁂

She was installed back in flat 4 but only on the condition that she rested with only gentle exercise, and that she did not return to work for another few weeks. She had a pair of ungainly wooden crutches with which she could hobble about the flat, to the bathroom, and onto the veranda where Sandra carried an armchair for her to sit and read in the sunshine. She was also able to write letters now that the communication system was restored. She had received a glut of airmails from home but it was difficult trying to organise them all into chronological order whilst bearing in mind that it would only make sense to respond properly to the latest, with brief references to the previous ones that had been superceded.

Jess had gained some fame – or notoriety – amongst staff and pupils alike, and they came hesitantly to visit, shyly bearing gifts as though the shooting during the dramatic coup d'état had made her a heroine and they were bringing offerings: a book, a bunch of wild flowers form the bush path, pawpaw and pineapples, paper and pens.

Sandra was brilliant, looking after her like a mother with her sick child whilst she struggled with the crutches. In between classes she ran up to the flat to bring her a drink or a snack. Chrissie sat with her in the evenings and at weekends whenever she could. Betty and Clara, clearly anxious guardians *in loco parentis* (despite Jess's protestations that she was really too old for that), brought her meals and sent Joseph to wait on her fulltime, like a combination housekeeper/cook/nurse. He would carry her out onto the veranda at first until she could make it on her own, and later down the stairs and across the compound to Betty's bungalow for a change of scene. Only once did he refer to Kobina. "Gone" was all he said, shaking his head.

But it was Jim's visits that she really looked forward to. He spoke very little about the coup, only that the National Liberation Council was now in charge and that General Ankrah was the new Head of State. He seemed to know that she didn't want to be reminded of the events in Accra and he took pains to keep any difficult news from her. She was aware of that and didn't ask any more. But he borrowed the Peace Corps record player again for her and she loved to see him slip the large black vinyl discs from their sleeves and ask her to guess what he had brought for her this time. Familiar Mozart or Vivaldi or something new, classical or jazz.

He would talk her through the music or the song and tell her stories about how the piece came to be composed or about the musician's life. Then she would lie back on her cushions and close her eyes, letting the music drift through her mind, filling her senses and her soul. It was a time of peace and contentment. And so she held on tightly to this time, to the here and now, and knew that she would never, *could never*, tell anyone back home what had happened to her, they would be so worried, and so instead she wrote:

Dear Simon,

I think the mail has gone crazy! It's even worse since the change of government – nothing for weeks, then suddenly they all catch up together. I do know that communications have been "down" for a while now and I don't know whether you have received anything from me in the meantime. You seemed anxious in your last letter, about the coup and everything. I guess you read about it in the UK press, too, but no, don't worry; we're all fine here. It was, as they say "a quiet bloodless coup". Everything is calm. We have a National Liberation Council now which has announced that it intends to reorganise the country's economic policies. They say that they want to reverse the previous policy of giving priority to prestige over "the concerns of the common man" and to provide food that will be available to all at low prices. Yes, I thought you'd like that! Well, we'll see …Anyway, I'm glad that you're going to the college ball with Leslie (?), of course I'm fine with it – oh, no, working it out I see that it was last week – or the week before? I hope you haven't succumbed to the cold and the 'flu epidemic we keep hearing about – or maybe that's all blown over by now? Soon, we'll have the monsoon that will bring the Great Rains (I feel I have to put that in capitals!). Is it true that there's to be a general 70mph speed limit in England? We keep hearing all sorts of rumours on the bush telegraph, half of them you simply can't believe, like the Queen's about to abdicate!!! Oh, a couple of ghekkos have just run over my foot! Sorry this is rambling again. Anyway, I do look forward to getting back home. I have wonderful thoughts of England in the spring and summer. How I long to be back with you …

It was only when she was able to return to her work, to her classes and her village work that she began to hear the drumbeats once more. It was as though the talking drums were reminding her that it was not over yet.

9

APRIL 1966

The dry heat of the Harmattan was giving way to monsoon skies, heralding the rainy season, but it was still hot and exhaustingly heavy, although not quite so oppressive as before. Jess welcomed the rain as a respite from the heat, and secretly she sympathised with the girls when they ran out of the classroom into the square in the middle of a lesson, lifting their faces to the cool shower, whooping and laughing.

"Come on in at once!" she would call, trying to maintain a stern expression. "Or you will all have detention!"

"Oh, miss," they shouted as they returned to their desks, dripping but knowing that their cotton dresses would soon dry off, "It is so good to have you back!"

And Jess could only turn away to hide her delighted smile. Yes, even with her slight limp and occasional pain in her leg and foot she was happy to be back to the routine again.

The first time she walked along the bush path again, now a little more muddy than before, on her way to Kakomdo on the Sunday morning after her return to work, she felt a relief and contentment as though she had been brought back home. Betty had urged her not to walk the uneven path yet, until her leg was stronger, to wait a while, but she would not wait, and hobbled – only one crutch now, almost back to normal – knowing that she must get back to reality again. The sun was on her back, and the trees in sharp relief in the bright clean light. She felt as though she could see every leaf, every insect in the crowded vegetation each side of her, so clear and luminous was her vision. It was as though she had awoken from a deep sleep and could see everything anew. The rain showers had washed away the dust from the bush and cleansed it afresh. Jess could smell the rain and the sweet perfume of the flowers, bougainvillea, flaming flamboyant, sweet hibiscus, and in the background the top notes of the village wood fires and spicy cooking. She could hear the birds cawing high up in the trees towering above her: plantain eaters and forest flycatchers.

And as she walked she sang softly to herself: "*nana berawa posso posso, wah ne kwan detche detche....nana aberewa poso poso, waye ne nkwan dekyedekye*", savouring the rich sounds on her lips and in her throat.

The village children came running out to meet her, bare foot and wearing the same torn cloths, dancing and jumping, clutching at her free hand: "Come, come!" The chief was waiting for her under the thatch of the meeting place in the centre of the village. His grin was broad. "Hello, missy." His English had not progressed over the months, but then neither had Jess's Fante. He helped her to sit down on the bench and rest her crutch on the earth beside her. Then to her surprise a group of children filed into the clearing and started singing for her a beautiful song in vernacular, with the most wonderful harmonies she had ever heard. *Goodness, it would take her choir months to get those parts right and the rhythm fluent.* It was good to be back.

The women shyly approached bearing food on leaf platters, rice and fufu and chicken. They offered them to her like gifts in church. Small children brought her flowers and laid them at her feet. By the time she left to head back to the school compound, Jess was in tears.

How kind people were, even when they had so little for themselves. This touched her even more than the reception she had received at choir on Friday two days before. As she entered the hall with Jim steadying her arm, everyone had stopped their chattering, stood up and clapped her. She had turned to Jim with a querying look.

"I guess they think you're a bit of a hero!" he whispered. "Totally over the top!" But when she sat down in her usual place, resting her crutch on the seat in front of her, Jim had settled himself at the piano and begun the intro to her favourite song of the moment, *Cantique de Jean Racine*. And they had all risen to their feet and sung it to her. Of course she'd cried and Jim had had to pass her his handkerchief to wipe her eyes. A new girl sat next to her and helped her to reorganise the music scores; she introduced herself as "Leslie" (*"Leslie"? Surely that was a guy's name? There had been a Leslie at school – or was it spelled differently: Lesley?*) She frowned but the moment passed as the rehearsal was very busy preparing for the forthcoming concert and Jess had a lot of catching up to do.

To Simon, she kept everything neutral; she realised that she couldn't tell him things that would beg the question of what had actually happened in Accra that day. She couldn't tell him about the lovely welcome back she'd had to classes, to the villages, to choir, without explaining why. She realised that the lie – or rather, as she saw it, avoiding the whole truth – reverberated into a whole mess of other "secrets" she must keep, whatever her good intentions to protect Simon and her family from anxiety had been in the first place. So she wrote:

Dear Simon,
    Here, we're all wondering about this Sekou-Toure business; the army have said that they're ready if Nkrumah wants to come. Help!! I don't really think he'd be mad enough to invade us though. I was

intrigued to see reports of the mock trials in the villages throughout the country, even the burning of the hut in Nkroful in which he was said to have been born (a shrine during his regime). Word is that Fatia and the children are in Cairo living in luxury, apparently in a house that Nkrumah had built from Ghanaian State funds! There's lots of propaganda both ways; who knows what's the truth. I had to smile at the purple prose the other day in the paper, something like (in a nutshell) the bottom has fallen out of our economic bucket and we are left floundering against the tide in a fast stream of disaster! Love it! Oh and we hear that another "subversion camp" was found in the north ... We're all very interested here in what's going on and talk about it all the time, but Harriet and Sarah who were here again this weekend are quite dismissive. All they seem to be interested in is partying and men. They were taking a group of their pupils round historical sites (castles and forts) here on the coast. They stayed overnight and until lunchtime – god, they are boring and depressing! And Harriet managed to clog up our loo with vomit – probably from drinking too much! Anyway, you asked me about happiest moments here: well, being independent, living without parents or mentors or school teachers, doing stuff for myself, making decisions for myself. I've almost forgotten what films are and theatre and television, coffee bars and restaurants, parties with records playing ... I just like the simple things we have here, like singing in choir and talking to folks from all over the world about their countries, seeing the kids I teach improving, reading in the blazing afternoon sunshine, going down to Biriwa beach to watch the fishermen hauling their boats up the sand to bring in their catch, and the waves, and the swaying palms, sitting on the veranda drinking coffee and chatting to friends, watching the sunset and thinking ... Sometimes I wonder how I'll manage when I get home – but, yes, I know that you'll be there with me ...

It was Sandra who first began to talk about plans for going home, still a couple of months away.

"What are you planning to do?"

"Goodness, I hadn't really thought about it!" Jess looked up from the examination papers she was attempting to compose. She took a swig from her coffee mug amidst the chaos of books and old sample exam papers around her on the table. She put her pen down and stretched her aching spine into the chair back. "Oh maybe travel a bit in Europe before heading home to the UK?"

"Well," Sandra picked up Jess's crutch from the floor where it had fallen and replaced it against the chair. Jess rarely used it now; her leg was much stronger, and she only relied on her crutch when she was tired or walking on rough uneven ground. "I know I said I'd go straight home, but I'm rethinking. Colin says he's fine with it if I break my journey. Wants me to be able to make the most of the trip, before I get tied up with uni, bless him. So I was thinking of making a detour over to Italy. Florence, Rome, Naples. That sort of thing. What about travelling together?"

"Oh, yes, that'd be great!" Jess thought of how much Sandra had changed over their time in Ghana; she was so much more kind and friendly than she had been at first, less sharp and caustic, much more helpful. Jess knew that she had fallen out with Glenda and no longer saw Hank. While Jess was incapacitated Sandra had gone around with Chrissie more often. Maybe that was it. *The people you spend time with and your shared experiences have so much influence on how you are. Jess wondered how she herself had changed over the year in Ghana.* "And maybe a stop-over in France too to see my old penfriend, Genevieve – she lives in Pontarlier, Doubs, near the Swiss border." Jess paused thinking of other possible hosts. It would be like doing the Grand Tour in Europe! They might as well, while they were out here. "Actually, I have a penfriend in Bulgaria, too, in the capital Sofia. We've caught up with each other recently, when I had little to do but lie in bed writing letters! We might see if we could pop over there too." Jess smiled at herself. *"Pop over there"*? How the world seemed so much smaller now.

"Where's Bulgaria?"

Jess's mother had the same bewildered response when Jess told her family about her travel-home plans. *"I think not, Jessamy,"* she wrote, *"why would you want to do that? Foreign countries, unhygienic sanitation, dirty food, nasty diseases! You need to come straight back home safely after your service, back to civilisation. You cannot go gallivanting all over Europe by yourself. In addition you have been invited to the wedding of our dear Friends John and Ann at the Meeting House at the end of July."* Who on earth were John and Ann? Jess decided not to argue but she continued to make plans with Sandra for their next adventure. Her mother didn't know the situations Jess had found herself in here in Africa – and never would, if Jess had anything to do with it! She had survived, hadn't she?

༆

It was Easter, and Jim, now officially allowed away from his "station" in Cape Coast to go to Accra, to the Peace Corps hostel, was adamant that Jess should go with him so that he could assuage his guilt, make it up to her and give her a "real vacation", albeit only a weekend, after the fiasco in February and the long recuperation.

"I'm not sure," said Jess, frowning, "I haven't been back to the Peace Corps hostel since IT happened."

"It's all fine there now," said Jim gently, "I'll be with you every moment. I won't leave you for a second – promise! I guess you really need to go there again, to confront the memory and shake your fist at it!"

"I like that!" Jess laughed. Jim smiled, then his face became serious again.

"I do understand, you know. I know what you're feeling. You don't want to relive it. And absolutely right and understandable. I've been there too, it's a scary place, psychologically. But ... I think you have to. You need to. I'll do all I can to make it good this time."

True to his word, he took her to Achimota to see a production of *Pirates of Penzance*, outdoors on a dry early evening, under the stars. Jess watched the fiery orange-streaked sky and indigo clouds as she listened to the music, before the sudden fall of night and darkness. How Simon would have loved this.

The officers at the Peace Corps HQ hostel were different from those back at the end of February and Jess felt a strange comfort and relief that they would have no recollection of seeing her then. It helped her to distance herself from those events, as though it was someone else, not her. In fact, apart from bullet holes and mortar damage evident in the walls of structures around the government buildings, there was little to remind her of that day.

She wandered around Accra streets, busy and chaotic once again, with Jim at her side. She couldn't help but notice that he glanced over at her from time to time to check she was OK, attentive and vigilant, while all the time distracting her with news and amusing stories. They took coffee in little bars on the streets behind the embassy, savouring the music, sometimes live highlife bands, sometimes Accra's latest favourites of European pop on the speakers: dramatic rhythmic *'Keep on Running'* and the high-pitched desperation of Roy Orbison's *'In Dreams'*.

They ate at the crowded restaurant in the Ambassador Hotel, with its noisy cosmopolitan clientele. She had changed in to a cream linen shift dress and scooped her hair up into a chignon on the top of her head which she hoped looked a bit like Audrey Hepburn in *Breakfast at Tiffany's*, but doubted it was as glamorous. She felt so much better now, after all that recuperating, sitting in the warm reviving sunshine. At least the sun had blessed her hair to a deep auburn, and even without her make-up (which she had long since used up and which was irreplaceable here in Ghana, even in Accra), her skin was clear, smooth, and lightly tanned to a golden sheen, healthy and peachy. She really did feel truly sun-kissed.

Jim ushered her to an outside table in the quietest corner of the veranda. "The usual," he nodded to the waiter, and Jess wondered how often he came here. And who with? She couldn't find an acceptable way of asking and Jim just smiled. He looked very handsome and suave in his fresh white short-sleeved shirt that did not hide his muscular chest, and his slim cream trousers that hugged his athletic body. Jess wondered what kind of girl he brought here: attractive, glamorous, sophisticated, worldly, experienced? All that she was not? Was that what he was doing when he disappeared for long stretches of time, saying he was called to the northern territory? He was her good friend but there were lots of things she didn't know about him.

"Sir?" the waiter hovered again. "The wine list."

"Any preference?" Jim raised his eyebrows at her. Jess shook her head and waved her hand to indicate that she wanted him to choose. He ordered a Sancerre on ice.

Jim's "usual" turned out to be a variety of dishes to pick from: fish, chicken, little steaks, rice, fufu, yam and fried plantain, fresh tomatoes in herby oily dressing. Jess was spoiled for choice. "What a lovely idea," she murmured to Jim as she spooned a little from each platter. "Like a buffet, but all at your own table."

"Yeah," he agreed, "Quite like home."

She told him about her plans for the trip home and her university place. She talked about her return to the UK and the more she spoke the more it all seemed strange and remote, just as coming out to Ghana had seemed strange and remote last year. She no longer knew which was her reality. She looked at Jim and tried to remember Simon's face. It was Simon who felt like a dream now, drifting in and out of her consciousness. It was Simon who didn't understand – didn't even know – her experiences this year. His face, their hugs, their kisses, drifted into another world, the world of half-remembered dreams.

By the time she had savoured the delicious mango pudding and finished her third glass of wine, and was sipping a smooth Tia Maria with her coffee, Jess felt hazy, relaxed and soothed. Jim was telling her about the new Ghanaian government but she was barely listening, lulled by his deep voice and smiling eyes.

God, he was so good-looking. And the way he was smiling his lovely lopsided smile now across the table at her as he spoke softly, his eyes on her alone ...

"I know I'm not supposed to say this, Jess ..." God, what was he going to say? That their friendship was over? That he had a new serious girlfriend? That he couldn't manage to see her any more? Even as a friend, because his new girlfriend would be upset? Her heart skipped. She drew in her breath, steeling herself ready to receive something unwelcome. But he was smiling softly at her. And his eyes dived in to the depths of hers. "In case anything happens, I want you to know ..." He raked his hand through his thick dark hair. "That we've shared a lot this year. That we've laughed together and cried together." He snorted. "Or rather, you've done the crying and I've held you. That I was so desperate when you were injured. And that I love you."

Did she hear right? What was that he said?

He reached across the table and rested his hand on hers. She could feel the warmth of his body. Hers shivered in response and she gasped. Oh god. Her whole body was crying out to him. "Let's go back." Numbly she nodded. He didn't seem to mind that she didn't say anything in response to him.

Jim's arm was around her shoulders as they strolled back down Independence Street to the Peace Corps building. She didn't shake it off. But she didn't speak either; she didn't know what to say, or what she felt. He didn't seem to expect her to.

They walked through the Peace Corps drawing room. It was much like the one in Cape Coast, grand, reminiscent of colonial days, with a piano in the corner. Jim sat down on the stool and raised the lid. "Just for you," he said quietly. "I want you to remember this night."

He played her favourite, the Mozart, which was the first thing she had heard him play. She settled herself on the soft armchair beside the piano and leaned her head back on the deep cushions, and closed her eyes. It was beautiful. How was it that he loved her – is that really what he had said? – when all the girls fancied him, when he could have had anyone? He was handsome, clever, caring, and strong, so why *her*?

When the music finished on a drift of soft notes, she opened her eyes again, drawn from her dream and met Jim's eyes as he looked up from the piano keyboard at her. The moonlight falling through the large window caught his hair. He looked so gorgeous. He reached across and touched her hand. He frowned.

"What you were saying at dinner about the trip home. Going to Europe. Going back home. Going to university for three, four years ... Do you ... I shouldn't ask, but ... do you have to go back?" he asked so quietly that she could hardly hear his words and had to lean in to him.

He moved from the piano and crouched down in front of her. He reached out and gently brushed a stray hair from her face, tucking it behind her ear. Jess shivered. He smiled at her and whispered, "Oh, Jess, you're so beautiful. You don't even know how lovely you are."

She felt her heart beating with the rhythm of the village drums across the bush. All those times he had been the one to sit with her, comfort her, soothe her. All those times he had talked to her about Ghana, teaching her the culture and ways of this new country of hers, theirs. All those times he had driven with her, played piano for her, sung with her. All those fears she had held in her heart when he was called away to some emergency in the northern territory. All those times they had shared.

But she heard her mother's voice cutting through the drumbeats: *Jess he's not a Quaker, he's not one of us, how can you trust him, you don't know his family, you don't even know him …* It was true, she didn't know *everything* about him, not all his story, yes there were gaps, blank pages. Yet a part of her was whispering: sometimes you have to take a chance … *don't you?*

Her heart stirred at what might happen but she was afraid too. She saw her mother's pursed lips: *what do you think you're doing, Jess? You don't behave like that … impure thoughts … a girl who even thinks that, she's sullied, nobody will want her… marked down as a strumpet … we don't have such things in this house …* She had to tell him.

And so she did. She told him of the times since she was little, in the bathroom, in her bedroom where her silent father had crept in the darkness, doing things – not to her, but to himself – making her watch. Trying to tell her mother. But her mother, so strict, so censorious, so clearly unable to believe her daughter. She had given up, no longer tried to speak the unspeakable. As her father had demanded, she kept silent. Who would believe her anyway? She had felt alone for a long time, different from others. Simon had made her feel better but in the depths of her soul she still felt somehow sullied. She could never tell Simon; he was too close to her family. Would he even believe her, knowing the righteousness of her religious background, which mirrored his own? Even with Simon she suppressed her feelings, wondering with a wicked confusion of excitement and fear about what would happen when he finally wanted more.

Would Jim reject her now, think she was the one who was disgusting, like her mother did? She forced herself to look up at him.

His eyes were sad and pained.

He reached out and enfolded her in his arms. "Oh my lovely girl," he whispered. But she pulled away, awkwardly, fearfully. She could hold it in no longer, her tears and sobs wracking her body.

"Oh god, what has it done to you?" Jim murmured gently as he reached round and stroked her back until her crying was stilled. "Listen, Jess, you are the most kind, clever, thoughtful woman I know. Make a groundhog day. Live it over, but differently – start again. It's not that what happened didn't happen, you can't pretend that. But start over. That was then, this is now. Don't allow what your father did to destroy you. He was selfish and cruel and it wasn't about you at all. You're brave, courageous. You're glamorous, exciting." He looked into her face and smiled, "And hey, don't be afraid of this. I know it's all confusing for you, but you are exciting and sexy – and that's a good thing, a nice thing to be. It's what everyone else wants to be. And you are IT!"

He stood and pulled her to her feet. He took her in his arms, strong determined arms that held her tight and safe. She didn't pull back this time. She felt his hands, his long fingers, sweep through her hair and catch the band which held her up her chignon. She felt a slight tug and her hair fell over her shoulders. He caught it almost too hard and, bending down to her, buried his face in her hair, breathing in deeply as if to hold on forever to her scent. She felt his hands caress her face, sweep over her cheekbones as if she were fragile.

For a moment he held her away from him, still gripping her arms, but looking at her with wonder. His eyes were dark and deep and her heart became as feint as air. She felt only the warmth in the depth of her body and the trembling of her breath. His eyes questioned her and she responded by cupping his face and trailing her fingers down his face. She smiled through the remains of her tears. He brushed them away. "You OK?" She nodded, afraid of her own voice, and kissed his cheek softly.

His lips searched for hers and as he found them he groaned between deepening kisses. "Oh, Jess, my beautiful, good, sweet Jess," he murmured. "I want to show you how I feel."

She knew what would happen but she couldn't resist. She saw and felt and held his strong hard body, and her heart, her legs, her soul melted under his touch. And all she knew was that it was beautiful and wonderful. Somehow he led her into his room, and gently laid her on the bed. He was gentle and slow and tentative, giving her time and space to draw back, but she found that she didn't want to.

And much later, as the light streamed in to the room and Jess began to wake to the chill of the morning air, she shuddered, her body cold. Where was she? What had happened? Had anything happened? What had she done?

She became aware that Jim was standing in the doorway to the room, strong, muscular, a white towel wrapped around his middle.

"Jess," he said with a frown. "I've given it a lot of thought. I want you to come back with me to the States. I want my family to meet you. I … I want us to have a future."

A future? America? Suddenly, a searing light flashed in her head: but what would she do in America? Who did she know – apart from Jim? She didn't even know anywhere in the States: Washington, New York – they were backdrops, sets in movies. What if people were more like Hank than Jim? And what would she do about university, a career? She'd have to start all over again. But back at home she had Simon, who she'd known for years, who she was confident of knowing, who was waiting for her, longing for her to return to him. She had a university place ready for her. She would have a career, maybe as a teacher, in the sort of schools she was familiar with.

She felt the cool cotton sheets around her, felt her body, different. She stared at Jim. But it was Simon's familiar face that looked back at her. Jim was gorgeous and she should be thrilled but somehow she wasn't. What did she know – really know – about him? *What was she doing, for god's sake?*

Oh god, how could she? What had she been thinking of? If only she could turn back the clock. What was it that Jim had called it – make a groundhog day. Have the time back again – but make a different decision. She loved Simon. He was the love of her life, of course she knew that. He was part of her family. Her family knew him, approved of him. They were all a part of the whole. He was safe. He was "one of us" as her mother had said.

OK, go back, go into fast reverse ...

"Do you have to go back?" he asked so quietly that she could hardly hear his words and had to lean in to him. But then she would have pulled back.

"Yes," she would have replied. "You are the nicest, kindest, loveliest guy. But I have Simon. And he is the love of my life. I know that I will spend the rest of my life with him. Marry him. Love him, look after him for the rest of my days."

That's what should have happened. And in her conscious mind, that IS what happened that night.

※

Jess wrote to Simon as soon as she returned to the school. What should she say? In the end she just wrote:

Dear Simon,

Just heard the details about the General Election – I know it was the end of March but it takes a while for news to get through. I expect you're pleased about Harold Wilson's majority. But I do feel sorry for Ted Heath. He looks so bewildered and sad. Talking of politicians, Dr Busia (very well-known politician here) was at school this morning. He is the uncle of one of our girls and came in with her father who has just been released from prison, detained as an opponent of Nkrumah. He hadn't seen his daughter for many years. Dr Busia was in England for a long time, exiled I believe, so we had a good chat. But three of the girls I teach have fathers in prison now; they'd been MPs in Nkrumah's regime. They're allowed by the NLC to hold Press Conferences and their prepared defence speeches are televised. All quite odd! It's getting really confusing. Fathers out of prison, fathers thrown in prison – men claiming to be uncles and fathers turn up at school wanting to see girls, and we haven't a clue who they are! There's also talk of Nkrumah's opponents still "disappearing" or being taken hostage by gangs still loyal to Nkrumah, so nobody knows what's going on! It's all a mess. A good thing to come out of it all is that we're now getting a government grant for books and each school can buy their own rather than having the Ministry decide for us. "Animal Farm" is allowed again. I'm putting in my requests asap! But I expect you are more excited about World Cup fever ahead of June than my lil' ol' remote concerns here in Africa! BTW, I hear that The Beatles are "more popular than Jesus" now, according to John Lennon!!! Anyway, must go – we've had school exams and I'm inundated with marking papers and writing reports …

Jim had been taken aback but circumspect about Jess's explanation. He had shrugged and said he understood, but she knew that she had hurt him. He had stayed in Accra for some business matters and had gently but firmly put her into a taxi for the journey back to Cape Coast, saying that he'd see her to talk properly as soon as he got back the next day. He'd kissed her full on the mouth and smiled as if to say, maybe you'll change your mind. "I've not given up hope," he whispered into her hair before he swung the taxi door shut and waved goodbye. The last thing she saw was his sexy lopsided smile, his curly dark hair and his raised muscular arm in its crisp white shirt.

The following day, her mind was still in turmoil and she tried to focus on marking the examination papers, to concentrate on anything, *anything*, but Jim or Simon. Sandra was out for the day with Chrissie, up and out before Jess had awoken from her disturbed sleep, and she had come in late the night before so Jess had not had to say anything about the weekend with Jim.

Jess plunged herself into assessing her pupils' answers to the questions on the term's texts and refused to let herself think. But she kept glancing at her watch and as the day drew on she became increasingly concerned. Jim had told her that he would be over by midday and it was now five thirty. It would soon be dark.

She knew that something was very wrong. Despite what had happened in Accra, Jim would never let her down. He would never just not turn up and leave her worried. Something must have happened to him. But who could she contact? She had no way of communicating with him.

When their houseboy John returned with a pile of laundry at six o'clock, much later than usual, she asked him what had kept him. He stood leaning against the door jamb in his arrogant way, and smirked.

"Late late in Accra, miss."

"Accra? You've been in Accra?" Jess couldn't think why this disturbed her. "Have there been any accidents or anything on the road? Only I was expecting Jim – you know, the American …"

"Oh yes, I know, miss. Not good man. Bad man. I heard he was taken."

"Taken? What on earth do you mean?" John threw her a sly look.

"On the street by the President's palace." *No president now, no palace*, thought Jess, her heart sinking. "By the President's guard." *No president now, no president's guard. Or not officially.* There was something in John's expression. Triumph? "No more work in the northern territory now!"

She remembered John's looks of hatred towards Jim, his insolence to him. A gnawing suspicion chewed at her heart. John has betrayed him. Betrayed her by default. How dare he?

She stared at John and his expression did not waver. His mouth was contorted in a sneer. This was someone who knew that he was protected. What the hell was happening here?

She remembered odd things Jim had said, his trips to the north which were never properly explained, his evasiveness, his criticisms of Nkrumah and his government, that glimpse of him at Akasombo when he had said that he couldn't be there. She could hear him now: *"Just between us, I guess I know quite a lot. But keep that quiet, hey?" "I can't let you get involved."* When she'd asked anything he'd either avoided answering directly or he'd said firmly *"you don't want to know."* He'd said, *"Things are not always what they seem."*

She thought of her own doubts and musings when they were friends and nothing more. Now it was different. Now she was involved, like it or not. Now there was a closeness which couldn't be denied even in her determined loyalty to Simon. Everything had changed that night.

The next day Jess went to the Peace Corps HQ in Cape Coast. Jim still hadn't been in contact with her.

"Jim? Jim Kennedy?" she asked at the desk. The unfamiliar US officer stared at her blankly. He must be new. How many times had she been there with Jim – for goodness sake! "Look, I'm worried. He hasn't been in touch."

The officer shrugged but not before Jess caught a flicker of unease. "Sorry, ma'am. I don't know and I can't give out any information even if I did." His face closed and he turned away to answer the telephone. He glanced over at her as he spoke in low undertones into the receiver. *He thinks I'm some groupie, some flighty hanger-on.* The man covered the receiver with his hand as he turned back to her. "Sorry, ma'am." It was clear to Jess that he wanted her out of there. He watched her all the way out of the door.

Where was he? What had happened to him? Jess considered the talk of people "disappearing". Before the coup, when Nkrumah was in the presidential palace there was talk that it was rife, apparently, or so they had been saying at Legon, but there were still rumours even now of loyal "Kwame gangs" capturing people opposed to the deposed president. Is that what had happened?

It was all quite nightmarish, the way nobody knew anything, or nobody was saying. Gossip was rife. Sandra was horrified. Chrissie was astounded. Everyone was astounded. But none of it helped Jess find the truth. It was as if Jim had disappeared off the face of the earth and nobody could help.

Jess didn't even know his family's address or how she could get in touch. She slept badly, often not falling into slumber until nearly morning when she would dream of haunted visions, cold, despairing ghosts, and then wake abruptly when the alarm startled her and she would crawl out of bed in a daze to force herself into the day's duties.

It was on one such morning that a rat scuttled across the stairway and she stumbled on the stairs as she hurried, late, to her class. She was still a little unsteady on her feet, even after all this time since her injury, and she fell badly. It would not normally have been disastrous, except that she twisted her injured foot beneath her and heard an ominous crack again. She sat in a crumpled heap on the dirty stairs shouting for help and felt the blood from the wound opening up again. This time she did not cry; she felt oddly numb.

It was the following week that she awoke to a searing pain in her foot. She staggered in to the bathroom to pull off the bandage the school nurse had fixed. The pain was unbearable, as bad as when she was shot. Desperately she tore at the dressing.

Her wound was a mess of tiny writhing yellow maggots.

Horrified, she wrenched on the tap and thrust her foot under the flow of water that gushed and burped intermittently. And now she wept.

Sandra, awoken by the noise, immediately boiled a kettle of water and made Jess bear it as hot as possible as she poured it over the wound.

"Hopefully, it'll sterilise it," she grimaced. "Keep doing that and I'll raise the alarm with Betty." Jess sat perched on the edge of the stool in despair.

"Well, actually," said the elderly European doctor at the hospital where Jess was rushed at dawn. "Maggots clean out the dead and decaying tissue, you know." He calmly inspected the wound and declared it "as good as could be expected" which didn't fill Jess with confidence. He put foul-smelling antiseptic liquid on it and ordered the nurse to dress it and give Jess an injection and a course of antibiotics. She was told to keep her foot raised in a fracture shoe as it seemed that she had split the fracture again. Then he asked Jess how long she had planned to stay in Ghana. "I really think you should go back to the UK. We do our best here, but to be frank with you, it'll heal a lot better in the English climate." He washed his hands under the tap and the water gushed and burped as it did in the apartment. "If you were my daughter, I'd say that to you."

She packed her trunk and her suitcase with a heavy heart. She slipped a photo of Jim into her cabin bag. Where *was* he? In an odd kind of way, she couldn't have envisaged staying without Jim around. It would never have been the same. She insisted that her precious kpanlogo drum be kept with her in the cabin too, the one that Joe had given her when Jim took her to the drummer's village that day back in November – *it seemed a lifetime ago!*

Crying girls came to see her off, vowing to write to her to improve their English and to tell her all the news. She was to be their English sister.

Chrissie and Sandra hugged her tightly with sad faces and wished her a safe journey, ordering her to keep in touch.

"I'll let you know," whispered Chrissie, "if there's ever a wedding for you to come to!"

"Forgot to tell you," grinned Sandra, "You're not the only one going home early. Harriet flew back last week. You'll never guess – she's only got herself pregnant!" Jess wanted to say, she'd not done it all by herself, but she couldn't help a malicious glimmer of hubris. How hard she had become. She guessed that the wealthy parents would pay for a private operation in a London clinic and a recuperative "vacation" in Switzerland.

Betty took her to the airport. "I think you'd like to know, dear," she said wonderingly, "that two Peace Corps officers arrived this morning with a lorry load of mosquito nets. They said they were taking them to Kakomdo and Ebubonku and fixing them up securely over the children's beds. They also said they were arranging for supplies of quinine tablets to be administered daily to them."

"Oh that's wonderful!"

"It was strange ... they said they had special instructions. And that we were to tell you. They said your name most particularly. Very odd."

As the plane taxied down the runway, Jess stared out of the window, distraught, committing to memory the land she had come to love, her African home.

10

MAY 1966, ENGLAND

The BOAC VC 10 touched down at London Heathrow under grey overcast skies. Jess had never felt so confused. Her foot ached. Her heart was in turmoil. She loved Simon, of course she did, and she couldn't wait to be back with him again. He was her steadfast love, the one who was always there for her. But he wasn't going to be at the airport. He had said that it would be embarrassing in front of her parents who were meeting her off the plane. So he would see her the next day when she was home. She could hardly wait. She wanted him to hold her tight. To feel safe again.

Her parents had arranged that they should stay overnight at a small hotel in London before driving back to Birmingham as the drive would be too much for Jess after the long flight. Or for her father who had only just passed his driving test and acquired an old second hand car. Her mother fussed over her with the grimness of a Victorian ward sister, sighing loudly as though the whole episode was a great inconvenience to her personally.

In the morning, they found that her father, immersed in his own silent distracted world as always, had left the kpanlogo and flight bag on the back seat of the car overnight on the road and forgotten to lock the doors, so that thieves had simply removed them in the night, without even having to break in. The drum that Joe the drum-maker in the village had told her signified the love, and the loss, that he saw in her eyes. So she had no djembe and no photo of Jim. Her father had not apologised but just grinned as though it was of no consequence. "It's only a drum," he mumbled. "You can get another one."

※

She sat on the sofa with her leg propped up on an upholstered stool, broken foot encased in its ugly black fracture shoe. She was alone in the house, her family all out today. She still held in her hand the photo she'd had at her bedside in Ghana, the one of Simon leaning casually against a doorway in the college quad, smiling. She had been committing it to memory, as she had done all year, remembering him, reviving their closeness. After all that had happened to her, she longed to see him again and only wished that she could jump up and throw her arms round his neck, holding him to her at last, pressing herself against him, feeling his warmth and his love again. Her hand trembled and she kept looking at her watch, longing for eleven o'clock when he had said he would be there with her.

All the drama and the extremes of Africa were fading from her heart. Memories, to be regretted or savoured, but all to be hidden in her heart with relief now that she was home, safe, her adventures over, and her calmer life with Simon resuming. Or maybe more like a new secure life beginning. Peace, joy, tranquillity: that's what she needed now, and Simon would know that, would respond to that need, and enfold her in safety and security.

She heard the front door open. Her mother had left it on the latch so that she wouldn't have to get up to open the door.

"Hello, are you there?" The familiar voice she loved and had missed for so long. Her heart really did, as they say in romantic novels, skip a beat. She felt strangely nervous, a fluttering in her chest. She hadn't been able to move to brush her hair, powder her nose. She hoped she looked OK for him: her skin was clear and healthily smooth from the African sun, and had been proud of her golden tan, but she was aware that her face now was pale and pained from the injury and the long journey home.

"Yes, in the sitting room." For a moment she almost dreaded him walking in. She felt a heavy sick sinking in her stomach. She was shaking with anticipation, the moment she had waited for over a year. She had dreamed of it, especially lately as the time approached. Their reunion.

"Hello." He stood there, in the doorway, looking at her. His fair hair was ruffled and rakishly flopping over his forehead. A tweed jacket hung nonchalantly over his left shoulder, his thumb hooked through the label tab. She hadn't seen him do that before; it seemed a quite uncharacteristically fashionable and suave posture. But she liked it. He looked very sexy. She smiled at him. At last! She waited for him to cross the room, perch on the sofa beside her, and enfold her in his arms with the words of love he had written all year on those blue airmail letters.

But he didn't move, just looked at her. There was an odd expression in his eyes. She felt disoriented. She patted the sofa beside her, unable to stand up and hug him. Odd that he needed that gesture. Was he so insecure at the reunion?

He looked uncomfortable, shifting from one foot to the other. His lovely, beloved face, the face she had longed to see again, was frowning, his brow deeply creased with anxiety.

"I can't stay," he mumbled, looking away from her. *What? Surely he didn't have somewhere else to go? Not today, of all days?* Her hand went to press her heart. She could feel the thumping deafening to her own ears, noise drowning out all sensible thought.

Then, with resolve, he said, a little too loudly and too rushed, "Listen, I have to say this. Jess, things have changed. We're not as we were."

She gasped. *My god! What was he saying?*

"Not as we were?" she whispered, shaking her head a little in puzzlement.

"Neither of us." He shifted his weight again to the other foot and puffed a hard sigh through rigid lips. "You're different as well … I expect … well, I'm sure … you must be …"

She shook herself, trying to retain some control over her body and her mind. What on earth was going on?

"But … but how can you say that?" she stammered. "You've only just come in, we've not even talked yet." She felt herself glance wildly round the room as though searching for something that would make sense. Why? Why? Was he just fearful that she might be different after all her experiences that were different from his own? Was he worried that she might not want him any more? Did he just need reassurance? She wanted to hug him and say: everything will be OK, we just need time. "It's bound to be difficult. We have to – well, to find each other again." She stuttered, unable to grasp what was happening. She heard the pleading whine in her voice, and hated it. She'd never been like this in Ghana. Oh god … breathe … please stop this shaking ... breathe ... lower your voice ... stop it squeaking ... slow ... slow ...

"I've been thinking about it a lot," he said, now calm, as if he had managed the difficult part and now he had regained his usual confidence and composure. "We have to have time out ..."

"Time out ...?" she echoed blankly again. She didn't understand this new situation. She felt disorientated. Her world shuddered.

"Well, actually ... we have to break up." His face was hard and unyielding. His eyes cold blue.

Then suddenly, she realised what was happening. *He'd already decided. It was nothing to do with her, them, her return, his fears, insecurities.* He had clearly been thinking carefully about this meeting today, maybe for some time, and he had prepared himself for it. Prepared himself to dump her today. Suddenly she thought, oh god, maybe even while he was writing those loving letters to her in Ghana, he was actually composing the dumping words. And she had no idea. Why would she? Oh god ... For her, it was a total shock, completely unexpected. Now, *he* was calm, in command, looking at her with an unfamiliar slight, sympathetic smile, such as you would smile kindly at a friend in trouble. She was trembling.

"Break up?" she whispered. As she said those irrevocable, disastrous words, her heart was confirming them. That was it, then. All finished. All the heartache and concern for nothing. All the love for nothing. It was over.

"Yes." That one word shattered her with its finality, and its shocking brutality. "Well, that's all. I'm off now. I have … another engagement." He turned to go.

Then she understood. Abruptly she was hit straight in the body with a terrible certainty. A moment reliving the bullet in Accra. That sinking feeling of recognition of her fate. It took away her breath. There was no turning back for him. It mattered nothing that she had come back to him. It mattered nothing that she loved him. Because he was now in a different world; one which did not contain her any more. Irrevocably.

"You've met someone else?"

He stopped, his hand on the doorknob, and turned to her, but this time his face contorted. His eyes were not looking at her kindly any more. "Why do you jump to that conclusion? *For Christ's sake!*" He was looking at her with undisguised contempt. "*Jess!*" he almost spat out her name, as if it left an unpleasant taste in his mouth. And she remembered the way that Jim used to speak her name, often and with tenderness, as though even the sound of it was melodious and tasted sweet on his lips. "You just can't accept that someone doesn't love you."

She was speechless. She remembered the loving words he had sent to her across the months. *Why, if he didn't mean them? Why would he do that?* And what on earth had caused this change in him? Then she remembered her mother's constant criticisms of her, the little nagging voice of insecurity that had lodged in her heart and, she realised, was still buried there. Her feelings of not being *enough*, needing somehow to be more, so that she would be everything he wanted. But she had loved him so much. She had loved him with all her being. Unconditionally. Enough to leave Ghana. To turn away from the possibility of finding Jim. To come back to the certainty of Simon and their future together. Why didn't he know this? Why would he want to throw away a love like that? A love that would be there for him forever.

What an idiot she was. An utter idiot. *Of course* he had found someone else. Someone better. Someone more attractive. More sexy. More engaging. More fun. More intelligent. More skilled socially. A nicer person than she was. Someone from a better family. Well, that was what he deserved, after all, wasn't it?

She watched his hand turning the door knob. Just go, Jess, thought, for god's sake, just go! Her foot was hurting badly. She knew she was going to cry, but she couldn't – *wouldn't* – break down in front of him. Not now. Not any more.

Not ever again.

He turned one last time to her. His words were calm but stilted, considered, thought about over a long time … and much more dangerous. He had rationalised his feelings about her and probably about the "someone else" as well, justifying his actions and his decisions.

"You see, I want someone I can be *proud* of, proud that she's mine, someone all the other blokes want – but that I know *I've* got," he paused and Jess wondered what on earth was coming next, "I don't want to be nasty, Jess, but over this year I've been thinking about you a lot – you're a good friend but you're also a good little Quaker girl, and I've realised that I don't want some pure, virgin nun, all innocent and buttoned-up, conventional and unexciting ... I don't know, it's just that ... It's not you ... it's me – I want more than this, more than, well, more than *you*."

She wanted to say: *that's not true, I'm not that person, you've got it all wrong! Maybe that was then – but this is now!* But Simon had already turned away from her, pulled open the door and walked out of the room.

Stunned, Jess heard the front door shut firmly behind him.

She realised that she was still clutching his photo to her body. She held it away from her and stared, an involuntary gasp emitting from her heart. *Oh my god.* He was not smiling knowingly at her. He was grinning seductively at someone out of the range of the photo, away to the right. She felt sick. She had held on to that photo all year, almost as a talisman, keeping it by her as she had tried to keep Simon by her, loving him, and longing for them to be together again. And all the time it had been an illusion. The words in his letters had been fake. Had he just been keeping her going until he made up his mind?

What on earth would she do now? All her plans were devastated, bombed out. She was looking at the ruins of her life, her dreams.

She realised that tears were coursing unchecked and silently down her cheeks. She looked at her broken foot, her damaged leg. *God, what a mess.* In so many ways. Then her body racked in a loud violent sob, and she sobbed until she was spent.

※

She cried herself out over those next few days. She told her parents and her brother that it was all over between her and Simon. Her mother actually hugged her but then became unusually silent and Jess felt her disappointment oozing from her with every glance. Her father grimaced. Her brother glowered. Little else was said, apart from her mother muttering under her breath about missed opportunities. She felt so alone.

Gradually Jess pulled herself out from the fog of shock and despair. She struggled to pick up with old friends again, and to keep her devastation under the covers of her bed at night. By the time a package arrived from her chosen university, enclosing details of the pre-course reading, "freshers" week and the arrangements for accommodation on campus, she was ready to take a deep breath and look life in the face again, albeit shakily. She took Simon's blue airmail letters out of her bag and placed them, still untouched, in a box that she locked and slipped at the bottom of her wardrobe. She couldn't bring herself to destroy them, not just yet – but she would, in time.

And she began to see more clearly now; the rain of her tears had stopped shrouding the view of her way ahead. She remembered what Jim had said about her: "*Jess, you are the most kind, clever, thoughtful woman I know. You're brave, courageous. You're glamorous, exciting.*" He'd said, "*You're a lovely person*", "*You're beautiful, Jess*", and she actually began to believe it. He'd said, "*You are your own person, remember that, Jess. You have to do things your own way, however people try to push you on the path they've laid out for you. Sometimes you have to pull away from your parents, your upbringing, however difficult it is, and know that the world won't end if you do.*" Yes, he was right. And she found comfort in remembering his words.

Because Simon was wrong: what he had said, that's not what she was like, who she was. She never *had* been like that. She thought too that she must have been so wrong about Simon and what he represented. She must have been swept along by the excitement of this love, the prospect of escape from her stifling home, yet knowing that her family's approval meant security and stability. "One of us" her mother had said, "from a good Quaker family." All along she had trusted in him and tried to be caring for him, putting him first. And maybe going along with her family's ideas and visions.

Perhaps now she needed to do things her own way, whatever that may be.

Hadn't Jim known all along and tried to warn her? Hadn't the drumbeats been warning her? What if they weren't drumbeats warning her of Ghana's dangers but of dangers back at home, in her life, in her emotions, in her relationship with Simon? What if Joe the drum-maker had seen what she herself had been incapable of seeing at the time? "Love and loss. And the fear that binds them …"

And what about if Jim was the drumbeat – the drumbeat of her life? Was that what Joe was saying? Jim had seen her at her worst, when she was so ill with malaria and still fancied her. She had revealed so much of her true self to him. Jim knew the worst about her and still loved her, wanted her. He wouldn't have judged her. It wouldn't have mattered to Jim whether she was a "good Quaker" or not – or any other image. He would have just wanted her to be *her*. She thought of him saying "make your own destiny. Sometimes you have to follow your heart not what someone else wants for you." After all, why was she afraid of insecurity? She had travelled to Africa, the other side of the world, for goodness sake. She had coped with new experiences, a new life, with tragedy and pain and joy. She could cope again. She had her university place; she would not forego that. She would learn all about psychology and English. She would get her degree, so that she would be more useful.

But then she would return to Ghana and search for Jim. She would find him. She knew that now.

It was all there, her future, in the drumbeats.

AUTHOR'S NOTE

I have tried to represent the momentous political events which happened in Ghana in 1966, as accurately as feasible, bearing in mind that these are written here as they are perceived by the character of Jess and in the light of a writer's license to create drama and consistency of plot.

President Nkrumah was deposed as president of Ghana on 24th February and at 7 o' clock the announcement was made that "the armed forces, in cooperation with the police, have felt it necessary to take over the reins of power and dismiss the former President, Kwame Nkrumah, the Presidential Commission and all Ministers and to suspend the Constitution and to dissolve Parliament. This act has been necessitated by the political and economic situation in the country." The report continued to declare that "the country is on the brink of national bankruptcy." Only three days before, Nkrumah had passed through parliament his "socialist budget" which the announcement claimed "increases the economic burdens and hardships of the population."

K.A.Bediako (in *The Downfall of Kwame Nkrumah*) says: "it is hard to believe that such a take-over could happen in Ghana at a time when any whisper of complaint on the policies of the government was risky and could mean imprisonment without trial in a country in which security men and women maintained a band of secrecy around their identity ..." (1966).

Nkrumah had led Ghana to independence from British colonial rule nearly ten years before, in 1957, and became the country's first prime minister and president. He established many huge projects in Ghana, including Akasombo Dam on the Volta River which was opened in January 1966.

He was on a state visit to China in February 1966 when his government was overthrown in a military coup d'état led by General Kotoka and the National Liberation Council. He later hinted at a possible American complicity in 'Dark Days in Ghana' (1969). Some argue that this suspicion was based on false evidence originating from the KGB; others claimed that CIA documents provided evidence of the involvement of the US President in the overthrow.

I have tried to reflect many of these events in my novel, *Drumbeats*.

Whatever is the truth, Nkrumah never returned to Ghana and was exiled in Conakry, Guinea, where he died of prostate cancer in 1972. He was buried at the village of Nkroful, where he had been born, but his remains were subsequently re-interred in a national memorial tomb in the capital, Accra.

In 2000, he was named "Africa's man of the millennium" by listeners of the BBC World Service and the "hero of independence".

In 2009, President John Atta Mills of Ghana declared 21st September to be Founder's Day, an annual holiday celebrating the legacy of Kwame Nkrumah and glorifying his presidency.

If you enjoyed this book, *Drumbeats*, and want to know what happens next to Jess, why not try the second novel in the trilogy, *Walking in the Rain*, and the final novel, *Before I Die*, due to be published in early 2016.

REVIEWS on any of Julia's books are very welcome on Amazon at http://www.amazon.co.uk/Julia-Ibbotson/e/B0095XG11U/ref=ntt_athr_dp_pel_1

and Goodreads at https://www.goodreads.com/author/show/6017965.Julia_Ibbotson

To find out more about Julia, go to her WEBSITE, and you are welcome to leave a comment, at www.juliaibbotsonauthor.com

ABOUT THE AUTHOR

Julia Ibbotson is an author and academic, and lives in the middle of the English countryside in a renovated Victorian rectory with her husband, an orchard, a kitchen garden and far too many moles. Their four children are now grown up and they have four grandchildren. She was a school teacher for many years before becoming a senior university lecturer, researcher and writer. She loves travelling, choral singing, walking, sailing and swimming, as well as, of course, gardening and cooking for family and friends.

Her books include the Drumbeats trilogy:
Drumbeats,
Walking in the Rain, and the forthcoming
Before I Die

Memoir/recipe book:
The Old Rectory: Escape to a Country Kitchen

For children:
S.C.A.R.S, the children's fantasy story of dragons, knights and a boy who slips through the fabric of the universe into a parallel medieval world threatened by the evil Myrthor, the heart of darkness.

Academic books include (among many academic papers):
Talking the Walk
International Research in Teacher Education: current perspectives

Printed in Great Britain
by Amazon